HE HAD SEEN THEM often in her
nightmares—their eyes fiery
with passion, their grins ravenous, their coming like the trampling of soldiers. Only this time the dream
was real, as real as the smell of her flesh
burning under their grip.

mary magdalene

ELLEN GUNDERSON TRAYLOR

LIVING BOOKS
Tyndale House Publishers, Inc.
Wheaton, Illinois

Living Books is a registered trademark of Tyndale
House Publishers, Inc.

Library of Congress Catalog Card Number 84-52667
ISBN 0-8423-4176-5
Printed in the United States of America

95   94   93   92   91   90   89
12   11   10   9   8   7   6   5

TO DENNIS
A Friend of
My Restoration

And I will restore to you the years
that the locust hath eaten (Joel 2:25).

CONTENTS

If the Son therefore shall make you free,
ye shall be free indeed (John 8:36).

Note to the Reader

For twenty centuries, Mary the Magdalene has fascinated all who are familiar with the story of Jesus. Interpretations of her character and relationship with the Lord have spanned the gamut of fantasy and rational deduction.

The Talmudists may have referred to her when they spoke of "Miriam with the braided locks"; but to Origen, for whom she was Mary "Gadal," her name was prophetic of godly strength; to Jerome, she was Mary "Migdol," and he connects her with the watchtower (Migdal) of her town, implying the steadfastness of her faith. For Webber and Rice, creators of the twentieth-century rock opera *Jesus Christ, Superstar,* she was a troubled woman, seeking love, and finding it in a man who baffled and frightened her, yet turned her life around.

From the strictly spiritual approach of the early church fathers, to the more human analysis of a skeptical generation, Mary's portrait has never been satisfactorily hung in the gallery of history. But neither have the mystique and intrigue of her story diminished.

For this author, a twentieth-century woman, Mary Magdalene began to demand attention when I entered an arena of life experiences which would identify me as never before with the conscious struggle of humanity, and with the world of lonely womankind to which I had once been blind. Though my "years of the locust" cannot compare with the Magdalene's suffering and torment, I have —due to the breakup of my marriage—tasted the cup of bitterness, isolation, and fear which is common to many. I have had to find my way through a "wilderness" by faith. My sympathies have been broadened to include all lonely hearts and searching souls, as I have walked through my own valleys.

You may ask, "How much of this story is fact and how much is fiction? How realistic is it?" I answer, "Yes, indeed, there was a women's movement in ancient Rome; yes, streetwalkers do take on pseudonyms; yes, incest is interracial and crosscultural." But beyond this level of reality, Mary Magdalene is, for me, a symbol of suffering humanity. While her story was apparently one of degradation such as most will never have to endure, we all have our "demons," our "locusts," our individual "flasks of sin." And what Jesus did for Mary, he can do for any wounded being.

After all, are we not all "drugged" by the world from time to time? Do we not all possess an alter ego? Have we not all been betrayed and then abducted from the spiritual? And when we find our Liberator, are we not awkward lovers, inexperienced servants?

I am grateful to my parents for helping me through my valley; and I thank Jana Hunting, lifesaver and confidante, for her helpful suggestions toward this book's development. My first two works, *Song of Abraham* and *John, Son of Thunder,* afforded much personal satisfaction as I walked with these great men through their times of growth. But *Mary Magdalene* has allowed me to revel in the sisterhood of history, and it is to womankind and all her sons that I devote its pages.

Ellen Traylor
Spokane, Washington

Prologue

The stony wall of the chamber was cold against the creature's back, but the poor being did not take notice. A trickle of sewer water found its way through a narrow aperture near the chamber floor, which was lower than the street outside, but the creature did not recoil at the odor. Sounds of bawdy laughter coming down the corridor from the warm dining hall of the nearby inn did not attract the figure's attention. Only as the dark of evening was closing in through the high window of the cell did the creature begin to stir.

It was as if evening, or the threat of darkness—a darkness more complete than the gloom of the cell—were causing a swell of fear to run madly at the pitiful one enveloped in the shadows.

A low groan issued animal-like from the humped form, though no one was near to discern it. With effort, the being raised itself up on its haunches. It thrust its head warily toward the departing win-

dow-light, as if fearing the approach of some un-
named terror, and braced itself with a crabbed hand
against the slimy moss of the street wall. With each
sound of feet or traffic above, the pathetic form
trembled and drew back, but then peered toward
the dim light again, waiting.

Presently its fearful expectancy was rewarded.
A storm of running feet was heard outside, rushing
down the street toward the window. The creature
lurched violently back into its corner and let out
a whimper. The feet slid and shuffled to a halt right
before the opening and jostled for positions as close
to it as possible. There were so many of them—
more tonight than ever before. And the voices that
accompanied them were haughtier than ever.

"Quiet, now!" one of the voices commanded, its
youthful masculinity strangely shaking the being
in the cell. "One at a time—a half-shekel apiece!
But quietly—or my father will hear and send you
all away!"

The hilarity tempered to a low *huzzah,* as boy
after boy paid his drachma and got to his knees to
peer in at the object of curiosity.

As each did so, his eyes were assisted by the light
of a bright torch borne by the leader and thrust
ruthlessly between the grates of the window. At
the first flare of light, the poor one hid its head in
the corner and shook terribly, its claws buried in
its hair and its voice raised in a howl.

"Ha-ha!" roared the boy who knelt now at the
hole. "Are you certain it's a woman, Josiah? It hardly
looks human!" The young fellows behind him
laughed uproariously and kicked at him to move

on and let someone else peek in. Josiah, the leader of the rowdies, did not reply, but only snickered and nodded his head. "Be patient," the kneeling boy snarled at his cohorts. "She has yet to show me anything. I can see only her back and hair! I have paid for more than this!"

"You have paid for nothing, if you cannot make her respond!" Josiah replied, his lip curled in a bitter sneer. "Have you nothing to win her over?"

The kneeling one fumbled in his cloak for a moment, then drew out a small package. "Indeed I have! I hear you do not feed the creature much, so she should appreciate this succulent morsel!" As he unwrapped the prize, the other boys drew back, choking and laughing. "Horrible, Machem, horrible and wonderful!" Josiah praised him. "Toss it in!"

With a splattering thump, the piece of rotten, worm-infested fruit hit the floor, and the creature jerked involuntarily toward the wall. "See this!" Machem insisted. "Josiah, let them all have a look, won't you?"

Josiah shrugged and took all their payments in advance, while as many as could manage to squeeze together held their faces to the bars. The boys were quiet as the creature shook in silence and at last turned in curiosity to examine the source of the foul odor. They waited breathlessly for it to crawl into the light for a better look. Only a shimmer of whispers passed between them as they did their best not to frighten the figure into hiding again.

The creature did not look up at its enemies, but only stared through a tangle of long, oily hair at the little mound of garbage on its floor. A profusion of disgusting rags covered the hunched body, parting here and there only where the seams had ripped or the pieces did not meet. A spastic finger pushed its way out from the being's ragged huddle and slid along the floor toward the fruit, pausing as the arm drew it back now and then. The boys stifled their delight and continued to watch as the finger at last dipped into the fleshy fruit and flicked its long, curving nail at one of the white parasites imbedded there.

Barely could they control themselves when the finger foraged back through the dark mass of hair and found the creature's mouth. The smack of satisfied lips was more than they could contain, and they fell over one another in guffaws of unleashed delight.

Josiah poked at them and ordered them out of the way so the other boys could have their turn. "But we did not see what we paid for!" Machem complained.

"You paid to look in!" Josiah reminded him. "If you cannot make her respond beyond that, then you are the loser!"

"A real man can make her respond," another boyish voice interjected.

"You, Caleb? Indeed!" Josiah laughed. "You are less a man than anyone here!"

The others roared in agreement, their toothy grins mocking the slight, underdeveloped fellow who had accompanied them unbidden tonight.

"I may be the smallest of you all, but I am more man than any of you!" he insisted, his pubescent voice cracking awkwardly as he strained for courage in confronting them.

Josiah looked at his comrades, then nudged Machem in the ribs. "How confident the little weasel is!" he sneered, and Machem laughed disdainfully. "Well, Caleb, what can you do to save the evening?" Josiah condescended.

Caleb glanced at the gang of adolescents who had always spurned his attempts at equality. Though they looked down at both his stature and status, he worked past them like a little wedge, toward the window.

"I, too, have a package for the thing in there," he leered, kneeling carefully, dramatically, before the grate. The small satchel in which he had brought his admission money was pulled from under his belt and he released the drawstring slowly, heightening the suspense.

The creature in the cell had returned to its corner, its back once more to the intruders above. The rotten fruit was missing from the floor, having left only a wet splotch where it had rested. The creature suckled it ravenously in the shadow.

"Here, animal!" Caleb taunted, hoping to impress his heroes with his daring. But they were not much impressed until he pulled forth the content of the bag, a crude phallic device made of cheap metal and covered with goat's hide.

"Where did you get that?" Machem stammered, his eyes wide and his admiration suddenly stirred. Josiah leaned forward and glimpsed the object, grunting enthusiastic approval, as the other boys shook their heads in amazed wonder. Questions buzzed around Caleb's head. "Where? How? Did your father give it to you?"

"The here and how are not important," Caleb gloated, certain that this move of his had won him a slot in their fraternity. "The response is what matters!"

At this the boys all howled their agreement and pushed him to toss the artifact into the cell. "The response, indeed!" Josiah cried ecstatically. "We will have it now, for sure!"

With a soft jangle the device hit the stone floor and lay still in the torchlight. The creature, stirred again by curiosity, turned slowly about.

Once more the boys above waited breathlessly as the figure slowly crawled to the center of the stone-cold stage. This time its dark hair parted for an instant as it bent over the object, and the spectators almost caught a glimpse of its face; but just as quickly the sight was lost and they restrained groans of disappointment. For a long while the creature stooped over the device, turning its head from side to side as if studying the intruder with caution.

Then, suddenly, an eerie cry rang forth from the being and it snatched the object up in its ragged hand, holding it high overhead and shrieking demoniacally. As it did so, its face came into full view, and a gasp arose from the spectators. Through thick, tacky strings of ropelike hair, the light revealed a face unlike any they had ever seen—apparently human, but grotesquely distorted, not by any physical abuse but by years of misery and indescribable anguish. Beneath encrusted grime could be discerned what must, at one time, have been a face of some distinction—even, perhaps, of beauty. The dark, tormented eyes were sunken in pockets black with despair, but the high cheekbones and finely chiseled nose were nearly aristocratic in outline. And the bluish lips, though hideously contorted, were full and ripe.

The young men above fell back, speechless, at the revelation. "Josiah!" Machem whispered. "We will never doubt your word again! The creature *is* a woman—an animal woman!"

"Did I not tell you she was beautiful!" Josiah laughed. "Why does your voice quake? Don't you recognize her? She is the woman we found on the street over three years ago. My father's beautiful 'day lady'!"

Machem answered nothing, but tremblingly peered into the cell once more over the shoulders of his companions.

The pathetic figure beneath continued to wave the object overhead, but was now spitting out profanities and snapping doglike with her teeth.

"You have gotten her to respond, at least, Caleb!" one boy called out. "Too bad you had to use a device to arouse her!" At this a chorus of laughter rose and another fellow added, "Maybe next time she'll ask for you, yourself!"

Caleb took the jibes good-naturedly, despite the mocking tone. There was no time to contemplate his status, however, as all attention was on the woman.

"The response!" Josiah cried. "We are about to have it!"

"The response!" they chanted, "Come, lady! Come!"

The devil-hounded soul beneath was rising to her feet, and the boys went mad with anticipation. But to their dismay, she seemed to be fighting off the object which, though under the control of her own hand, appeared to have a mind of its own as it dove down at her again and again. The boys watched incredulously as she stared wildly at them and then at the device. Suddenly her arm managed a hideous strength, and her spasmed fingers flung the artifact defiantly from her. As it careened into the sewer, slamming against the floor and coming to a slippery halt, the leather came off, revealing the metallic shaft, and she laughed with insane triumph. Then, before the young men realized it, she was dashing at them, laughing and leering. As she howled up at them, taunting, defying, she tore off the rags that concealed her ravaged body and shook herself wildly before them.

The boys had come for just such a show, but they were unprepared for its impact. There was more here than erotic display. It was as if the essence of evil, capable of terrorizing any man, were pushing forth through that window grate. The youngsters scrambled over one another in dread and ran madly down the street. Only little Caleb remained, but not out of courage. He was paralyzed with fear, his fingers molded like small iron bands to the bars.

The woman howled blindly at him and then lunged, her crooked nails tearing at the tender flesh of his young hands. Reflexively he shrank back, falling against the torch, which nearly set his clothes on fire. He tumbled into the gutter and clutched his wounded fingers to his chest.

As he tore away into the night, the devil woman hung from the bars, jumping like an Ethiopian ape against the wall.

At last, in utter exhaustion she fell to the floor, where she lay prostrate, weeping heavily and moaning in torment, or staring stupefied, her eyes glazed and fitful.

After a long hour, she seemed to calm and rose painfully to a sitting position. She looked dazedly about the cell, as if suddenly awaking from a nightmare and finding herself in an alien place. With a nearly normal posture she turned herself this way and that, peering incredulously at her hands and covering her exposed body in humiliation. She raised her face and stroked it with her fingers, as if wondering at its condition. Then as she felt her tangled, matted hair, she wept again—but this time with some understanding.

Her eyes fell at last on the lewd phallic device which had enraged her, and she shook with despair. Slumping to the floor, she refused to look at it again until the moonlight caught it, amid the swimming sewage, in a gleam.

Something in her stirred—a memory perhaps, she could not tell—of a different time, many years before, when she had slumped before another moonstruck and silvery sacrifice. . . .

PART I
The
Abduction

But whoso shall offend one of these
little ones which believe in me,
it were better for him that a millstone
were hanged about his neck, and
that he were drowned in the depth of
the sea (Matthew 18:6).

CHAPTER ONE

Three pairs of feet, small and bare, kicked up the tawny Galilee sand. In childish contest they raced beside the marbled blue of the great lake that mirrored their slopeside home.

The owner of the feet that led the contest, while the largest of the children, ran with defined femininity, and her laugh, high and jubilant, bore a teasing quality. "Magdala is not far, little ones," she sang. "Hurry, and you may win yet!"

A girl and boy, barely more than toddlers, panted up behind her, their eyes wide as their mouths, and their arms eager to catch her. As she feigned exhaustion and collapsed upon the warm bed of the beach, they attacked her with hugs, kisses, and squeals of abandon. Though this was the way these contests always ended, with big sister losing by willful default and the babies scrambling over her like tiny Greek wrestlers, none of them seemed to tire of the game. It was a good way to end these late afternoons when Papa sent them scavenging down the shore.

"My children will never be beggars," Papa had always sworn. No matter how hard the times might be, or how low their rations, they must always find some way of avoiding the loathsome station of the alms-seeker.

Magdala, their little town, spread itself up the beach a way and back toward the provincial hills of their native terrain. Mary, the eldest, pretended to scold the two who had pinned her to the earth with chubby, dimpled hands. "See, there is home. It will be dark soon, and you know Papa will be sitting in the door waiting for us," she chided. "We must not strain his patience."

Tamara and Tobias stared sadly at Mary, who winked at their crestfallen faces. "Where are your satchels?" she asked. "Be quick, now! Papa will be very proud of his twins when he sees the riches you have gathered."

The two youngsters scrambled off to get their sacks, which had been rudely cast aside at the outset of the wrestling match. Tobias' dark eyes sparkled when he returned. "Found three fishes!" he boasted, holding wide the mouth of the burlap bag.

"And I found a good rope!" added Tamara. "Why did the fishermen throw it away, Mary?"

"They only left it because it was too badly snarled with seaweed," Mary replied. "Don't forget how we had to work to undo it."

"But my fishes are all ready to be cooked," Tobias

bragged. "We don't even have to cut them open!"

"You mean clean them," Mary corrected, and at this she mused tentatively. Three good, cleaned barbels were never left behind by fishing fleets accidentally. She knew all too well that some kind sailor had seen the children scouring the beach for whatever of value might be found and had purposely left the prize where they would easily spy it. Mary had hesitated to take the fish, wondering if Papa would receive the gift of charity.

The little ones hurried up the beach ahead of her now, their stout legs spurred by enthusiasm. Mama had taught Mary to think often of Jehovah, who gives all good things, and as she watched her brother and sister, gratitude welled up in her. Though the twins wore homespun, their little bodies were well formed, energetic. They had never gone without food, not even when Mama had died giving them birth. Kind neighbors had brought plenty of milk to see them through the first days of their lives.

At this memory, Mary held her head high. Papa would not scold them for taking the "charity fish."

The little house of the Bar Michael family sat not far from the busiest intersection of Magdala, the point where the road from the lake, and another road leading into the western mountains behind the village, formed a junction. Since Mary had been old enough to take notice, she had been glad they lived here. There had always been so much grown-up activity right outside her door, that for most of her life she had thought her little seaport town must be the largest and most important city in the whole world. She knew of Herod's Tiberias, only three miles south, down the shore, and of the fishing ports of Capernaum and Bethsaida, not far north. She knew that Jerusalem, in the southern province of Judea, must be utterly magnificent; and Rome, the earth's grandest achievement. But for Mary, these were fantasies, not touching her limited reality, and her hometown was everything.

There could be no more active or colorful marketplace than Magdala's, she was certain. Strategically located at the junction of the two roads, it caught both north-south and east-west traffic. And today, as the three children carried their treasures through this quarter, they found themselves thrust squarely into the boisterous, hawking, body-jolting bustle of the adult economic system. Mary's two charges stayed close at her heels, and the three, forming a little train, wove their way through the plaza with the grace of experience. "If you cannot hold my hand, grab onto my braid," she had often told them, and today Tobias did just that, clinging to the heavy weaving of mahogany hair that hung shining beneath her veil.

Past row upon row of little shops, stalls, and simple pads laid out on the stone pavement, through heaps of textile from Phoenicia, tables of wood carvings from Lebanon, racks of glass beadwork from Egypt, fruits and vegetables from local farmers, and dripping, honey-laden pastries from neighborhood bakers, the children made their course. Scattered everywhere were the stands of the fish picklers, whose wares were desired throughout the Roman world, from Syria to Spain. Mary wished that someday her father might provide her with fish again to sell to the pickling industry, for this brought the revenue which had, at one time, made her family prosper—just as Magdala itself prospered on the wealth produced by the salted delicacy.

But their father was not well and had not gone out with the evening fleets to pursue his old fishing profession for three years. He had not cast a net nor mended one since his wife had passed away—when his own spirit and love of life had passed with her.

As Mary had predicted, Michael Bar Andreas sat in the door of the little house the children called home. To his right, upon the doorpost, hung a tattered strip of black cloth, a piece of mourning. He had placed it there the day his wife died, and had never allowed it to be taken down. Mary was still not used to seeing it there, though she came and went through this entrance every day. It was a painful reminder of the sad time, and she tried even now not to look at it.

"Nine years old, and already a great beauty!" Papa greeted her. Mary smiled shyly and lowered her eyes. One thing she had never doubted, with all her papa's reminding, was her personal comeliness. She may have wondered whether food would last the day and whether firewood would stretch through the coldest Galilean nights, but she did not doubt that she was the crown of her father's heart.

"We found some wonderful things, Papa," she

responded. "Show him, children." She made sure Tamara's rope was the first prize to be displayed. As Michael marveled and Tamara jumped about, clapping her hands with small-girl pride, Mary turned quietly to Tobias, hoping that the find of fish would meet with approval.

Toby reached into his sack and pulled forth one heavy barbel at a time, laying them neatly in the lap of Michael's robe. Strangely, Mary's attention was drawn to the thinning black hair on top of Papa's head as he bent over the prize. She had never thought of her father as old. He had always been the most handsome man in Galilee to her adoring mind. But a little stir of pity rose in her as she watched his dark eyes widen and the full, beard-framed lips part in surprise at the magnificent find. There were hints of gray in the eyebrows, the mustache. And it struck her now how hopeless was this man's station, to be so smitten by a meager pile of dead fish.

For a fleeting moment pride replaced pity as she thought Papa was about to praise their success. But suddenly the man's expression of amazement was clouded. "Where did you find these?" he demanded.

Toby jumped back and hid behind Mary's skirt. She instinctively shielded the little boy, though Father had seldom struck any of them. Her voice quivered. "They were lying upon a stone, Papa."

Michael relaxed a little as he contemplated his older daughter, and his eyes softened. "Upon a stone, child? But then, they were left there on purpose." His voice was controlled, his patience under careful guard.

"Sir, they were. We . . . I only thought. . . ."

"You thought amiss!" The words hammered sharply.

Mary and the twins drew back a bit, cautious of the big man's mood. How quickly their warm and receptive father, the center of their small universe, had altered everything, coloring it gray and overcast. The sturdy figure rose from the stoop, his big hands grasping the scaly offering by the tails. Like a thundercloud, Michael Bar Andreas moved into the little house. The children hesitated, then followed the one who represented provision for their needs, though he had not performed that office since the birth of the twins.

Mary's stomach tightened, and she held the little ones close behind her. She had seen Father angry, but this time he seemed almost alien to her.

Michael moved through the courtyard, which was framed by the small but comfortable rooms of the house, until he came to the splashing fountain at the center. He then turned to the children and held up the catch. "If these fish were still alive, we might use them as pets in this fountain! As it is, they are of no use to us." His tempestuous eyes flashed and he wheeled about, storming toward the little oven-pit, which still smoldered from the morning flames.

"If these fish had been captured by our own nets, they would be of use to us as food for our bodies. As it is, they are not fit for our little fire!" Here

Michael stopped his ranting and studied his children, who watched him in shuddering silence.

"We will not eat the offering of charity," he asserted. He then handed one fish to each child, laying the moist mounds of rejection like refuse upon their open palms.

With a flick of his head he sent them out the back door of the court. Mary knew what he expected, and she led the two toddlers to the alley gate.

In the narrow lane that separated their home from a neighbor's was kept the dung and garbage wagon. Silently the twins watched as she hesitated before it, tears flowing down her smooth, olive face. With shaking fingers she placed her fish on the dung heap and then turned to Tamara. The small girl followed in kind, but Tobias hung back.

"They were already cut open and everything," he lisped.

"Cleaned, you mean," Mary corrected, bending over him. The little boy's lower lip quivered as he fought to hold back his great disappointment.

"Do you want big sister to do it for you?" Mary offered, running her hand through his black hair.

Nodding, he handed her his trophy, and when she put it on the heap he began to cry.

Mary knelt with her twins, and the three children Bar Michael leaned together for a long time like penitents before an altar until their little sacrifice of Galilee silver caught only moonfire in the dark Magdalene alley.

CHAPTER TWO

bove the western hills behind Magdala, only a melon-wedge of sun was still visible. In a moment the sky and the sea would be dark as pewter. Already the bluffs that hemmed the dappled waters far across the lake were losing the scarlet glow of evening.

Mary had never come down to the beach at this hour alone. Many an after-supper evening had been spent here walking with her father and the children as they watched the fishing fleets pull out from shore, etching long wakes across the surface of the night sea. The lake of Galilee was so pure, its waters so clear, that fishermen were obliged to toil after dark, when their boats and nets would be less visible to the wary fish below. And Mary could still remember when, before the twins were born, she and her mother had stood upon this shore, watching until Papa's boat was just one white-sailed speck among many upon the moonlit waters.

But Papa had not raised a sail or pushed away from shore for so long that those times were a hazy memory. The fact that Mary had come down here tonight, hoping weakly that she might find him with the other fishermen, was evidence of her desperation. Papa had left the house and had not returned since last night's incident with the three "charity" fish.

A cold wind blew down from the hills, stirring the sea far out from land. Mary shivered and held her worn cloak tight over her head and shoulders. She had loosened her long red-black hair earlier, letting it serve as warming insulation beneath her hood, but only as the sky had darkened. It was best not to do so in broad daylight, when strange men might witness the event. A Jewish female with scruples would not tempt a masculine heart with her beauty, and a woman's hair was one of her greatest attractions. Mary could remember Mama's instructions to this effect. And though she was yet too young to fully comprehend, she obeyed.

Tonight such proper behavior was second nature, not conscious, because Mary's mind was on one thing only: finding Papa. She could not stay out long. She had left Tamara and Tobias in the house unattended, as soon as she had been certain they were asleep for the night. Should they happen to awake and find her gone, Mary knew what fear would fill their hearts.

But the possibility that Papa was here grew less plausible with the fading of the sun. Hardly a man was left on shore as Mary scanned the beach one last time. Tears stung along her lashes, and as she cast a final glance seaward, the night air brought them forth in small trickles down her cheeks.

She turned her face toward town, and at that moment the brilliant light of the Migdal-Nunayah, "tower of fishermen," leaped to life. As long as Mary could remember, that beacon, the great landmark of Magdala, had been a source of wonder. Rising like a giant above the flat housetops of the village, it had been built by pious men and represented God's protection. The fortress was symbolic of safety by day and guidance by night. On those evenings when she and her mother had come down to shore, they had never failed to turn homeward by the time its light shone, for it heralded the closing of the city gates, the exit of the last ship, and the end of Mama's day.

Just as the light was a marker by which fishermen could keep their bearings in relation to the shore and town, so it served as a point of comfort for the little girl who, spurred by its flare, ran back toward town. She would feel better once inside the walls.

Pleasant as Magdala was, however, Mary was grateful that she did not have to travel far through its streets before reaching her door. The market square was frightening in the dark. No booths crowded or confined her way, no hawkers' voices, rowdy and demanding, filled her ears. She wished they did. The liveliness of day would have been preferable to the hollow fear that snapped at her heels as she raced across the empty pavement.

Her steps would skirt the central fountain of the

square unless she paused there for breath. Only reverence for propriety persuaded her to do so. The cool waters would refresh her from the run, and she would enter her house more peacefully. "A lady never charges through a door," her mother had taught her. "She enters with grace and harmony."

"Yes, Mother," Mary whispered, and she sat down upon the stone steps of the cascading pool. Her heart drummed as she smoothed back the hair that clung to her perspiring forehead. The waters of the spring were sweet. Dalmanutha, "cool fountain," it was called; its fame as an oasis for weary travelers passing through had earned it equal status as a landmark with the great tower of the town, for Magdala was often called "the region of Dalmanutha."

Mary reached into the refreshing liquid and brought a splash of it to her hot face. A deep breath calmed her somewhat, and she rose to be going. But just as her foot reached the pavement, an unsettling sound echoed across the square. The brawling laughter of a group of Magdalene rowdies spilled out from the dimly lit doorway of a nearby tavern.

Mary was frozen momentarily, afraid that to move would attract attention. She had often heard the carousing din of the street people—had even, on occasion, risen from her bed at night to peer out her narrow window into the marketplace beneath her gallery room. Once or twice, when she was younger, she had called for Mama in nightmarish fear. The gentle woman had quieted her, answering her innocent questions regarding the strange sounds and the peculiar folk barely discernible through the haze of interrupted sleep.

"Daughter, they are people who do not know Jehovah well. They are not happy, though they seek to be. Pray for them, and thank God for our strong walls and for your strong papa who guards us."

Mary had almost grown used to the babbling, the lusty cries, the profanities she did not understand. When Mama had died, however, her fears had risen afresh, and though her father had tried to comfort her, his patience was not like Mama's. "Papa who guards us" was unable to feel the depth of the little girl's apprehensions, and so Mary had resigned herself to fending off the alien sounds in silence.

A pillow over her head, or an attempt at "pleasant thoughts," as her mother called them, usually helped, and she found that the sounds would fade if ignored. Sleep would return, and morning would wipe away the mystery of the dark hours.

Still the haunting effects of the night sounds were buried deep within her. And this evening she felt their impact very keenly, for she had no strong walls about her; and Papa, insufficient though his comfort was, had exposed her to even more trauma by his absence.

But yes. Papa might be home now! If she ran quickly enough, perhaps the noisemakers would not catch a glimpse of her. She would fall into her father's arms and be safe.

She tried not to breathe hard as she fled the marketplace. A lady did not pant, she was certain.

But just as home drew into view, that which she feared came upon her.

"See—a pretty fawn!" one rough voice rang out. "She flees the archers!"

A ricochet of bawdy laughter followed this, as a half-dozen male pursuers shouted from the shadows.

She glanced once behind her, just long enough to make out the nature of the hounds. Young and strong, they ran well, despite their drunken condition. The little girl was terrified, her feet seemingly leaden, though the door was now within reach. Her fingers tingled with the palsy of fear, but the latch at last moved upward and she managed to force the great barrier open just as the stench of alcohol filled the portice. She scrambled into the house and threw all her weight against the door. How she wished this were just another nightmare she might wake from! But the shock of lock against jamb was absorbed by the crush of human flesh and bone, and the rugged, masculine fingers caught between the door and the portal were real enough.

A weak cry escaped her lips as the bloodied hand extricated itself, but as she sunk to the floor of the entryway, head spinning, two strong arms lifted her up.

"My pretty Mary," Papa's voice was warm and reassuring. "How you have frightened me! Where have you been?"

Mary looked into the handsome face of the one she feared and loved above all others. "Oh, Papa! I was looking for you!"

The big man carried her into the courtyard,

where he sat with her a long time, cradling her in his arms. He offered no explanation of his whereabouts, and Mary did not press him.

"Papa, men chased me. Did you hear them? Papa, they nearly came through the door!" She studied his face plaintively, but he only stared into the vacant yard, his silent preoccupation compounding her trauma.

"My beauty, my dark-haired beauty," he responded at last. But this was all he would say. And as he confirmed her worth to him, she sank into sleep with the only confidence she knew: she was precious to him; she was worthy, for she was beautiful.

The awareness that his breath reeked with the same stench that had marked the drunken pursuers reached her only subconsciously.

CHAPTER THREE

The next few weeks saw a growing tension develop within the household. The twins were too young to be aware of the change, but their open joy for life was instinctively being replaced by inhibition of laughter and play. To Mary the shift in mood was more obvious. Papa's temperament was becoming less controlled, his management of schedules and routines more erratic. His absence from home repeated itself over and over, while Mary's loneliness and fear grew more intense with each disappearance.

Concerned neighbors came to call, suspecting that all was not well with the children Bar Michael. But loyalty to Papa constrained Mary to fabricate stories to cover his negligence. Since the girls and young women of Israel received no formal schooling, Mary was not observed outside the home, and so her neglected condition went unnoted by any authorities. Left in charge of her brother and sister sometimes for two or three days in a row, she came to know despair as her closest companion.

The little ones had gone to bed hungry this evening. Mary and the twins had scavenged what they could off the streets, but though there was kindling sufficient for a small blaze in the courtyard, there was nothing to cook.

A twist of gray smoke curled through Mary's hair and her eyes smarted as she bent over the low flames to prod the embers. Sometimes she missed Mama so. The familiar ache of grief rose from wounds which had healed only superficially. She could still remember the domestic lessons received at Mama's knee beside this very fire pit. From the time Mary was old enough to grasp a few words, Mama had taken advantage of every opportunity to give her housewifely instruction. This chain of learning was expected of mothers and daughters in Israel. While the young boys spent their days in school and in apprenticeship to their fathers' trades, girls learned the economics and efficient management of the home.

Mary's mother, though, was not acting only in obedience to tradition. It was her chief joy to prepare her daughter for the domestic vocation. To keep a husband happy was a woman's primary aim in life, Mama had counseled. And daughters were expected to cater to their fathers and brothers as preparation for their later role as wives.

Mary suppressed the tinge of bitterness that disturbed her tonight at the thought of her own father. Despite his failure as a provider and rock of confi-

dence, she had always respected him, and the growing anger within her these past weeks must not be
allowed to surface.

Still it was increasingly difficult to contain her
bitterness and insecurity. She sat gazing into the
flames and hesitated to turn for bed, knowing the
dread which darkness and the appeal to sleep
would stir within her.

Her face glistened in the firelight, as tears once
more marred it. She remembered the night she had
fled the pursuers down the marketplace and the
comfort she had found in Papa's arms once she
reached home. But her body shivered now at the
memory of his placating touch. She attempted to
recapture pleasant thoughts of him, but growing
disgust was consuming the place where love had
always managed to thrive.

She shook her head and set her shoulders
squarely. "Never shall I run to you again, Papa," she
whispered. "Never shall I let you hold me again!"

Mary had bundled herself in an old afghan and
fallen asleep beside the dying fire, but it was not
the descending cold that woke her. The sounds of
the street people which had so often jolted her
from slumber seemed unusually loud this evening.

As she roused herself from the stone bench
which she had unwittingly made her bed, she perceived that the door to the entryway was open,
allowing a chorus of raucous babble to flood the
courtyard. And she also saw that Papa stood in the
doorway, speaking angrily with a stranger. She
could not make out the man who confronted her

father, except that he was very large, his silhouette nearly filling the portal. Nor could she make out the exact nature of the conversation, except that Father shook his head violently, his voice rising.

At last a satisfactory conclusion seemed to be reached by the two men, and Father, taking a satchel which was grudgingly handed him by the stranger, slammed the door. The people outside did not stay long after that. As their footsteps reverberated down the empty street, Papa slumped against the courtyard wall. For a moment he studied the satchel grasped in his hand, and a tremor went through him. It was only after Papa had stepped into the moonlit court that he noticed his little girl sitting upon the bench, her eyes wide as she studied his peculiar behavior. At the sight of her, shame filled him. For a long while he stood silent, as if searching for an explanation to give her, or awaiting some inquisition. But Mary only eyed him cautiously, noting the way his body weaved uncertainly under the influence of strong drink. She knew him less at this moment than she ever had.

At last, Papa managed a posture of defiance, throwing his shoulders back and jutting his chin forward, mocking the girl's bewildered gaze. "Have you never seen a drunken man?" he snarled, taking a staggered step in her direction. "Mark me well, girl, for you shall see such things from time to time!" A derisive laugh belched forth, and he pointed to his face with a crooked finger. "Are the eyes a bit too red? Eh? The nose a bit too red? 'Tis only the face of your father, little Mary! Why do you start so?"

At this, Papa reeled toward the bench. Mary quickly avoided him, jumping up just as he collapsed forward. She stood back, horrified, as Papa lay draped over the stone seat. For a long while he did not move, only repeated thickly, "You shall see more of this. Mark me well. You shall see more!"

A night wind was blowing down from the hills, pushing small clouds across the sky. Mary watched her father silently until he began to snore in his stupor, and she felt safe enough to draw near. Pulling off the old afghan in which she had bundled herself, she placed it gently over Papa's cold back.

It was only then that she again noticed the mysterious satchel the big man had handed Papa at the door. It had been flung carelessly on the courtyard floor when he fell across the bench, and now lay with its mouth gaping invitingly. Very quietly she approached it, bending down and keeping an eye on Papa as she fingered the opening. She lifted the bag and held it open to the moonlight. Within lay a small pile of fresh fish, much like those the children had found upon the beach weeks before. Their glistening silver sheen sent a chill to Mary's heart.

The next morning Mary rose to the sounds of firewood being cut and to the smells of roast fish and baked bread. The toddlers, apparently awakened by the same sensations, were scrambling down the gallery stairs. "Come, Mary," they called. "Papa has a big breakfast for us!"

Mary sat up on her pallet. For her the horrors of the previous evening would not yield to the

warm liveliness of a seemingly normal household.
She dressed slowly and then, coming out, watched
for a moment from the gallery as Papa, hampered
by two clinging children, prepared the savory feast.
She could see from his red eyes and blotchy complexion that he had not yet overcome the effects
of last night's drinking. But he put up a merry front.
His old laugh rose through the little building as
the twins, who had not eaten the previous day,
giggled and whined for the meal to begin.

"Soon enough, my babies. It is coming, soon
enough," he assured them. "Where is your sister?
Go and fetch her."

But Mary was on her way, and as the children
ran to meet her, she could only eye the food upon
the fire with widening suspicion. "Where did you
get the fish, Papa?" she inquired forthrightly.

"Mary! Such a sleepyhead you have been! Since
when do you leave your poor papa to struggle
alone over the fire?"

Mary only rephrased the question, her eyes nar-
rowing. "The fish, Papa. Were they given to us?"

Papa continued to busy himself with the cooking
and did not answer, but his smile faded momentarily and a little twitch worked at the corner of his
mouth. "Given to us? Child, you know your papa
better than that!"

Mary sensed the awkward avoidance of her question but was determined not to be put off by good-
natured manipulations. She crossed her arms and
studied him firmly. "You don't expect us to believe
that you were out fishing yesterday!"

Still Papa continued with his work, but at last he looked at her and a bit of warning anger flashed in his swollen eyes. "This breakfast is earned, rest assured."

Mary knew she dare not push the matter further, so she saw down quietly. However the food had come, she must be grateful for it. She suppressed her curiosity for the moment. But when she caught Papa watching her during the meal, she saw, between his strains of anger, flashes of silent sorrow. Her mounting suspicion warned her that all was not well.

Papa did not eat much, and he rose to leave before the children were finished. As he headed, again without explanation, for the street door, Mary noticed his wistful glance in her direction. And though he turned quickly away, his unvoiced burden had not escaped her.

A curl of fragrant smoke rose gently from the drippings of the broiling fish. As Mary studied it, a spiral of fear wound its way through her soul.

CHAPTER FOUR

S ince the twins had eaten well this morning, they were exceptionally energetic and eager to play. Mary had not taken them out, except for their daily scavenging hunts, during these weeks of Papa's absences. The great watchtower of Magdala was one of her favorite spots, and they were all headed now in that direction.

The tower sat on the highest plot of ground within the town walls. But though it was centrally located and surrounded by something of a city park, only the narrow, twisting lanes, typical of Magdala, led up to it. As the three children made their way through the streets, they were spotted by other youngsters who had wondered where they had been all these days. Several boys, too young for school, and girls of various ages darted from the open doors of houses and ran happily toward them.

Suzanna, a perky little blonde, was most enthusiastic. The same age as Mary, she was her closest friend. Mary often referred to her as "Lily," for that was the meaning of her name in Hebrew, and it captured the essence of her pastel beauty perfectly.

Though she was the daughter of Simon, a wealthy Pharisee and leader of the synagogue, Suzanna did not consider social position in the choice of her playmates. She was the envy of the local girls for her rare blue eyes and fair coloring. But her spontaneity and insightful, mature qualities had not been easily come by. It was through suffering in her young life that Suzanna had gained depth of soul, for she had been born with a crippled leg, an infirmity which could just as easily have embittered her.

"Oh, Mary!" she cried, clapping her hands and laughing gaily. "I have come to your door so many times. Why do you never answer? Have you been away? But no," she corrected herself, "someone said you were walking home from the beach only yesterday, with your satchels and everything, as you always do. You haven't been away. Mary, where *have* you been?" This was all said in such haste and excitement that Suzanna was positively breathless, and Mary giggled in response.

"Not away . . . just. . . ." Mary paused, not knowing how to explain, and ashamed to tell her friend the exact reasons for her recent seclusion. "Things are well," she asserted at last, attempting a weak smile. But Suzanna was not convinced. Her bubbly nature was put in check as she studied her friend's withdrawn attitude; and when Mary lifted her gaze again, she found Suzanna somber and reflective.

"Mama is very concerned for the twins," Suzanna said, watching them as they ran ahead now, up the lane which led to the tower.

Mary remembered that Suzanna's mother had been one of the neighbors who came to provide for little Tamara and Tobias in their first weeks of life. But she squared her shoulders, feigning confidence. "She needn't worry," she insisted.

Suzanna did not pursue the issue further but was silent the rest of the way up the hill. As they walked, the weeks of Mary's ordeal began to descend on her with such a weight she felt her head would burst. It was as if being back in touch, however temporarily, with her effervescent friends was bringing the horrors of her situation into focus, rather than alleviating the pain. She wished desperately to cry out her entire story, to tell of Papa's strange alteration, of her home's dark pallor, and of the fear that had become her daily companion.

But honor for her father, however she felt toward him, must not be violated. She watched the dirt road pass beneath her feet and bit her lower lip to rein in her emotions.

At last the tower was in sight above the closest rooftops. The children rounded the last corner and stood before a grassy knoll blossoming with well-trimmed flower plots. Stands of ancient olive and fig trees provided shade where the tower did not cast its shadow, and from these, Mary's eyes were led up and up to the top of the grand old lighthouse.

A sense of strength was what it had always imparted to her, and today it ministered once more to the girl's needs.

Mary felt the warmth of Suzanna's hand as it was slipped into her own, and soon her friend was tugging on her arm. "Come, Mary," she laughed. "The hill is steep. Help me run to the tower!"

Mary supported her in a hobbly run, and soon their feet picked up pace and their hearts were pounding with excitement. At last they collapsed with laughter at the foot of the lighthouse. The release of childish joy had helped unburden Mary's spirit and she rolled in the green grass jubilantly.

The two girls sat, stifling their giggles and holding their sides as the keeper of the tower passed by, eying their escapade with adult disdain.

"Oh, Mary," Suzanna declared, "you are my very dearest friend in the whole world. Let's swear that we will be best friends forever!"

Mary sat upright and looked at Suzanna with all the sincerity of childhood innocence. "I swear it," she promised.

Mary did not find sleep easy to come by this evening. She and the twins had spent the entire afternoon in the park and at the homes of friends, where they had been catered to with food and motherly attention by a variety of concerned and doting women. Suzanna had managed to make the way smooth for Mary, as she intercepted the anticipated questions: "Where have you been, Mary? Is your father well? Do you lack for anything?" Suzanna, with sensitivity beyond her years, answered for her friend—something to the effect that everything was coming along well with the children Bar Michael.

A smile had imprinted itself on Mary's face today. And a plan was forming in her mind. She lay on her cot in the quiet of her gallery room, with her covers thrown back. Her wakefulness and the warmth of the evening made her blanket unnecessary and too confining for her tossing and turning.

She had been praying for days that Jehovah would help her to provide for herself and for her brother and sister. Any hope that Papa would come to his senses was long gone. The Bar Michael children, for all practical purposes, were on their own.

But today her prayers had been answered, she was certain. The visits she had made to her friends' homes had sparked her thinking. Every one of their mothers was overtaxed with domestic work. Few of them were wealthy enough to afford servants. Boarders carried some of the burden, and here and there a hired woman came in for a few hours a week. But most of Mary's neighbors were not affluent, as were some Magdalene folk. And the wives and mothers were assigned the drudgery of just too many chores.

Mary had a strong back and had been trained well in household work. She would not ask for pay; she wanted only to be supplied with leftover food, clothing—whatever the families could spare as fair exchange for her labors.

She plotted her course for the next day, planning whom she would go to first and just what she would say. Her enthusiasm for the project kept her awake, her heart pounding and refusing to let her sleep.

Oh, Jehovah was good! She marveled. She lay on her stomach, resting her head on her folded arms and musing about the kindness of God. A phrase from some Psalm of King David which Mama had taught her nudged at her memory:

> *When I remember thee upon my bed,*
> *I meditate on thee in the night watches,*
> *For thou hast been my help,*
> *And in the shadow of thy wings I sing for joy.*

As she repeated the phrases again and again, they became a soft rhythm in her head. The smile she had worn all day stayed with her as at last she drifted into a pleasant slumber.

But just as total rest was about to envelop her, she was jolted awake by a scuffle outside her door. Raising herself on one elbow, she heard rough voices beyond the curtain that covered the entrance.

"Papa?" she stammered, certain that she discerned his voice among them.

No one answered before the curtain was thrown back and several black silhouettes confronted her in the gallery light.

"Papa!" she cried in a strangled tone. Panic gripped her as the figures approached. She recognized them now: one was the big stranger who had given the sack of bread and fish to her father just last night. The others were the young men who had chased her through the streets weeks before—

and now Papa had brought them home—to her room!

Her father only watched silently from the shadows as one by one the young men, six in all—and then the burly stranger—approached her bed, used her, and used her.

CHAPTER FIVE

Sunlight attempted vainly to work through the curtain at Mary's door. It pelted the fabric with warm, entreating fingers, but the curtain did not move. The occupant of the room, who was usually awake at the first hint of daylight, did not stir, did not rise with childlike anticipation to face the new day.

There was no child quartered here this morning, and no hope felt with the summons of the sun. There was a nine-year-old peering out from beneath her blanket toward the golden glow that caressed the drape—but she was no longer a child, and she did not want to move.

Her young face was haggard today, the lines of her mouth bearing a tension and the furtive eyes a strain which should not have marked anyone so young.

She was afraid to lift her bed-cover, afraid to

move her legs. It was as if her body were foreign to her—someone else's body, someone else's arms and legs. She was afraid it would not respond to her demands, that it would never be her own again. And so she lay rigid, terrified of finding that her fear was true.

The beauty of yesterday was gone. All she could remember was the night. She lay as though paralyzed, unaware—staring intently at the curtain but not seeing the light. Only the recurring drama of the dark, approaching men was real to her.

It was not until the morning sounds of the twins reached her from their little corner of the gallery that she was jolted into the present.

She did not know where Papa was. She hoped he had left with the others and not returned. She hoped she was alone with her brother and sister. But the twins would be descending on her soon, and she must not let them see her like this.

She managed to raise herself up and to swing her legs out from under the covers, but as she did so, she found that she hurt desperately, that parts of her she had not known existed now throbbed with pain. Stifling the urge to cry out, she lay down again and waited, wiping away the tears that had forced their way to her eyes.

No sooner had she gained this composure than Tamara and Tobias were upon her, laughing and crawling over her bed.

"No, children!" she pleaded. "Sister is not well today. Let's not play."

The little ones looked at her sadly and wondered if she was sick. But she assured them she was only very tired, and concealed her pain as she rose to dress. Pulling her outer garment over her tunic, she stepped cautiously to the gallery and looked out into the courtyard.

There was no sign of Papa. "Come, children," she called. "We will see what there is to eat."

The twins bounded happily down the stairs. "Will we see the tower again today, Mary?" Toby asked.

"And the mothers?" Tamara's eyes were bright as she remembered the kind women who had pampered her yesterday.

Mary did not answer. Her mind was preoccupied with seeing that no one else was in the house. She hushed the children and told them to wait at the foot of the stairs as she stealthily moved to peer around the banister and then venture into the yard.

"Why must we stay here?" Tamara whispered. "What's the matter, Mary?"

The older girl continued her cautious entrance and did not reply. As she came in view of the entryway to the street, however, a chill of horror gripped her. Seated on the low stone bench, which had been blocked from her sight by the fountain, was the big, bearded stranger who had accompanied the six young men last night.

She glanced in terror around the court and stepped, catlike, back toward the stairway, warning the children to keep quiet. Papa was not here, and she hoped the man had not seen her. Her knees grew weak and she placed a cold hand on the railing, holding herself erect.

For a long moment nothing happened. The twins read her fear and did not move. She motioned to them to hasten back up the stairs, hushing them with a gesture as she followed.

But as she looked toward the gallery, her heart stopped.

"Come, little ones," Papa called to the twins as he looked down upon his eldest daughter with expressionless eyes. And then, speaking to her, he said, "You will be happy to do what you can to help your family, Mary. It will be well with you. Remember that it was the only way."

Mary stared incredulously at him. Somehow she knew what he was asking. "No, Papa!" she cried. "I cannot do this." Her eyes were wide with unspeakable terror, and she turned to run.

But the stranger waited, now, at the fountain, and when she nearly collided with him in her haste, he reached for her. The hideous memory of his body and breath overwhelmed her, and she staggered beneath his grip. His viselike hand completely encircled her slender upper arm, and he lifted her nearly off the pavement, jerking her toward his bosom.

"You will learn to like it with me, little woman," he laughed, leering as through a carnival mask.

She struggled but still he grasped her to him, filling her reeling consciousness with garlic breath and yellow teeth.

The last thing she would remember, before the blackness of oblivion overtook her, was the cry of the children on the gallery.

CHAPTER SIX

The days following Mary's abduction would be a blur of gruesome memories, each blending into the other like the swirls of a rancid pool. She would remember being taken outside her home and rudely thrust into the back of a waiting wagon. She would remember the wagon racing down the back streets of Magdala, around vacant corners where no one would hear her screams. And she would remember her first introduction to the Magdala Inn where she was to spend the greatest part of her days for many years to come.

The inn was a very large establishment, and though Mary was led into it through the back door, she soon made out that the premises fronted on one of the main thoroughfares of town. It would be a few days before she entered the main dining hall of the building, but she had glimpsed it sufficiently in passing to be impressed with its opulence. The quick look she was afforded as she was ushered down a back corridor provided a multitude of sensory messages. The predominant one was of darkness, a darkness which the dim lights of candles and small wall torches served more to emphasize than to dispel. But revealed by the smoky glow was a long stretch of bare floor bordered by piles of colorful pillows, all large enough for sleeping upon, and haphazardly strewn along the walls. The remainder of the hall was filled with long tables, their dark wood oiled and gleaming gorgeously beneath the wall flares.

Much more met her eyes in this quick scanning: brass and copper, purples and reds, velvets and silks. But she could not interpret it all.

The room was quiet this moment. In fact, she saw no one in it, but there was a distinct aroma of heavy perfumes and incense spilling forth through the door. She had often smelled the oils and ointments of the herb and spice merchants who traded in the market square. These crafty peddlers lured their customers by fanning the essences of their wares into the open air. But Mary had never experienced so intense and variegated an aroma as she did today. Jasmine, myrrh, aloe, cinnamon—all blended into the most delicious and pungent of sensations.

But these impressions were afforded for only a moment, as the terrified girl was pushed past the dining hall and farther down the dusky corridor toward a low, curtained arch at the far end. At this point, all but one of her captors unhanded her, and she was left staring up at the big stranger who had first taken her from Papa's home.

He studied her briefly, his eyes dark and penetrating, and Mary tensed, poised for flight. There was no room to run, however—no place to which a small girl might escape. The forbidding face drew closer now, and the hulking figure bent over her. "We are skittery, aren't we?" he said, his leek-heavy breath wafting over her in warm heaves.

Mary could not reply, but only leaned into the wall, as if hoping it would give under pressure and provide space for retreat. But her keeper was persistent. "It will do no good for you to shy away," he laughed. "You are rightfully mine. There is no place for you to run."

She trembled, but found her voice. "No! I am not yours!" she cried, shaking her head violently and slithering from the heavy hand that reached for her arm. Slumping to the floor, she wept convulsively, and the man stooped down beside her. For a long moment he let her cry, and when she tired there was silence between them. She could not bring herself to look into his face again. But at last he spoke: "Mary."

The word hung like sackcloth in the narrow space between them. This was the first time she had heard her name spoken by her captor, and the tone with which he pronounced it was demeaning, humiliating.

The nightmare of indignities perpetrated upon her the evening before returned in an instant, the memory sweeping over her like nausea. Her vision blurred and her head reeled. But from somewhere deep within, rebellion rose up. She would not escape into unconsciousness.

Behind her, the curtained arch opened and a buxom woman in scarlet entered the corridor. Stepping around the little humped figure on the floor, the woman scrutinized her.

"Is this the new one, Ezra?" she asked, addressing Mary's captor.

He gave a complacent chuckle and winked up at the woman. "Indeed! A beauty, isn't she?"

CHAPTER SEVEN

The room beyond the curtained arch would eventually be as familiar to Mary as any room in the Bar Michael house. In fact, soon she would come to forget the little home on the Magdalene corner, the now-unfamiliar inn would increasingly define her world.

But the first time she set foot inside this apartment, it was as foreign as the tent of a Babylonian harem. The woman who had inquired about her in the hall ushered her quietly into this sanctum at Ezra's departure. She warned Mary to be silent, though she need not have bothered, for the young girl was too frightened to speak. The room was nearly dark, its high windows covered by heavy shades. Again a rich blend of aromas, mostly of perfumes, pervaded the atmosphere. But this time sounds mingled with scent. Though hushed, the tones indicated the presence of several other beings in the room. They seemed to be all about her, and a tingle crept up her neck as she translated the sound of heavy, even breathing to be . . . she was not certain.

But now her eyes began to aid the translation. She discerned that the room was full of women, all reclined on mats and low cots around the edge of the chamber. And the women were sleeping. It was almost noon, and they were asleep!

The buxom female who had charge of her led Mary straight through the center of the room to a far corner where a small mound of blankets awaited her. "Rest here," the woman directed. There was no hospitality in her tone. Her words were a command, and Mary obeyed instantly, sitting upon the pile and asking no questions.

"You will keep quiet for Hannah, now, won't you, missy?" she warned, shaking her a little by the shoulder.

Mary realized that the woman referred to herself, and quickly nodded compliance.

"Well, good." Hannah smiled, standing erect and placing a hand on her broad hip. "It would not be wise for you to waken my ladies. There's a good girl." Then, directing a chubby finger toward Mary's fear-filled face, the woman insisted, "This is your place. Stay in it until I return."

Mary nodded again and watched bleakly as the woman made her way back through the chamber and passed beyond the arch. The girl drew her knees up under her chin and wrapped her arms about her slender legs. Though she was surrounded by a roomful of sister human beings, she had never felt more alone. Bewildered, she peered around

the dark chamber at the strange slumbering bodies
... and she waited.

Mary had no idea how many hours passed before
there was any hint of stirring in the room. Because
all light was shut out of the chamber, she could
not discern the time of day by any movement of
the sun. And because she was too fearful to close
her eyes, she did not nap all afternoon. This,
coupled with her emotional state and with the fact
that no one came to give her food or drink during
her lonely vigil, was bringing her to the point of
utter exhaustion.

It was only when a manservant entered the quarters and lit a wall torch that Mary realized it must
be evening, and the sleeping women only then
began to rouse. As they did so Mary was more
fearful and perplexed than ever. She had seen such
females from time to time, hanging about the street
corners and the market square. She had never understood much about them, except that they were
"bad." She did not really know in what sense they
were "bad." She had occasionally watched them in
curiosity when they passed down her street, but
"nice" people did not have dealings with them and
never discussed them or their business. All of this
Mary had come to realize through implication
rather than through direct instruction. Because of
the silence regarding them, she knew they were
outcasts; because of the disdain shown by reputable
folk toward their appearance in public, or even
their mention in passing, she knew they must be
"wicked."

Mary could not be certain that she had ever seen any particular one of these women before, though likely she had. They were not such that decent people noted individually, but only in type. As she sat observing their behavior at close range now, however, and within their own domain, she found herself studying them as people. Here they related freely to each other, and Mary saw them differently. Within these four walls, they were not on display; they were not competing for an audience or a clientele, as they did on the street. They were family—strange family perhaps, as compared with those Mary had known—but family nonetheless.

The first woman to draw Mary's attention was the first to rise. While many were stretching and yawning and groaning and lolling on their mats, this one was very quiet and sat up almost as soon as the torch was lit. For a moment she paused silently upon her bed, the cover drawn up close to her chin. Her wide, dark eyes scanned the room as would those of a cautious doe entering an open space. When at last she carefully thrust one leg from beneath her blanket, and then the other, her movements were so graceful, so fluid, that she went unnoticed by her companions. And upon rising she turned her back modestly to the room, draping her naked frame as quickly and privately as possible. This last gesture alone would have set her apart from the general gathering, as the others, upon rising, seemed to have as little concern for modesty as any woman Mary could imagine. Nor did silence characterize anyone but this quiet lady.

As soon as the light was lit, and "Doe-eyes" was

dressing, the room was full of commotion. Accompanying the yawns and groans, and the lolling dalliance, were raucous rebukes and jesting with the manservant. He was simultaneously and alternately commanded to extinguish the light, exit the room, come this way or go that, climb into so-and-so's bed, hang himself, help so-and-so dress, disappear forever, show them his "wares," and otherwise amuse them. Mary did not grasp the significance of these instructions, but she marveled at the man's composure as he went neatly about his business, filling wash basins, hanging clothes, and ignoring their taunts. When at last he turned to leave, it was with a self-satisfied smirk. "Take a good look at me, ladies, before I go," he called over his shoulder. "I'm the last real man you'll see tonight!"

With this he slipped through the arch, drawing the curtain just before a volley of hairbrushes and other feminine paraphernalia pelted the drape. Instantly, a chorus of epithets, half-angry and half-hilarious, flew after him, and the women were ready for their "day" to begin.

As Mary studied the proceedings from her quiet corner, she began to perceive something of a hierarchy within this little society. While a number of the women were more boisterous than the others, one in particular seemed to command the most respect. Isobel was her name, Mary quickly learned, for she was frequently addressed to answer some question or other, or to settle this dispute or that. And there were numerous disputes. In this corner two women grappled for a turn at a wash basin;

in another three vied for a coveted piece of glass
jewelry; and over there someone was offended that
her order for a particular perfume had not yet been
filled. Isobel was repeatedly called upon to inter-
cede, and this she did with much facility. She was
an amply endowed woman—bosomy, muscular,
and tall—and her penetrating eyes and resonant
voice went directly to the core of each problem.
She seemed to have a way with words and a ready
wit. She was able to discern who was most to blame
for each flare-up and how it might best be solved.
But she was no diplomat. When her patience was
strained, she simply made a unilateral decision
which all knew could be backed by physical force
alone.

There must have been twenty women in the
room. Many were extraordinarily beautiful; others
appeared to have been so at one time, but were
prematurely aging and bore lines of hardness and
bitterness about their mouths and eyes. Despite
the bombarding theatrics of the chamber and the
intriguing variety of its characters, Mary's attention
was increasingly fixed upon Isobel. The woman
with the great shock of auburn hair and the torso
like a river barge seemed to dominate the entire
room, her very demeanor and person earning her
center stage whether she spoke or not.

Mary blended silently into her obscure, shadowy
corner while she watched Isobel in fascination. No
one noticed her, and for this she was glad. But
Doe-eyes, who had also maintained privacy to this
point, suddenly became the focus of yet another

quarrel. It seemed that the jeweled girdle she fastened about her midriff was a disputed item. One of the more volatile characters, Debra, whose sharp, angular face had once distinguished her with a kind of haughty beauty, was sparring with the meeker woman. "You know it's mine," Doe-eyes insisted. "Judah Bar David gave it to me a week ago." "Liar!" Debra shrieked, her face now displaying only hardness and hawkish will. "Judah meant it for me!"

As Doe-eyes turned impatiently to her mat and continued to fasten the wide band about her waist, Debra lunged at her, ripping at the fragile accessory with pointed nails. "Give it to me, Rachel!" she cried, designating Doe-eyes by her proper name. Rachel grappled with Debra valiantly, but was no match for the stronger woman.

Suddenly the fine girdle burst assunder, the beadwork of glistening gems tumbling to the floor, scattering in all directions, skittering beneath the furniture and into cracks of the floor tile.

At this, Rachel began to cry uncontrollably, sobbing and holding her sides. "Judah Bar David gave it to me! My Judah!"

Isobel hastened toward the hysterical woman and, taking her by the shoulders, shook her firmly. "Rachel! Enough! We know the girdle is yours! Debra is only trying to have you sent back again—don't you see! You must stop this—now!"

The weeping subsided and Rachel looked at Isobel in horror. "Oh, no! They wouldn't send me there again, would they? Please, Isobel, I cannot live if I go there again!"

Mary, who watched the drama in bewilderment,

wondered to what place Rachel might be sent and who "they" were who might send her.

But instantly Debra interrupted, jousting at Rachel with pointed accusation. "Of course you'll go there again! The cell is the only proper place for lunatics!"

"Debra!" Isobel warned.

But in sinister rage she howled again. "Rachel is lunatic! She must be lunatic to believe Judah Bar David would waste his affections on such a pale weakling as she!"

At this, once more Doe-eyes gave way to uncontrollable weeping, and though Isobel reached for her, holding her close to soothe her, the cries would not be silenced.

With the witness of all this, Mary's ordeal of emotional and physical exhaustion suddenly overwhelmed her. Empathy for Rachel served to emphasize her own plight and she could not restrain the trembling despair which surged within her. Shaking, she too cried aloud, holding herself and rocking back and forth, not calculating the risk she took.

Instantly, all eyes were upon her. Even Rachel's weeping ceased, and amazed silence filled the chamber. "A child!" Doe-eyes whimpered, momentarily forgetting her own misery. "Isobel! It is a little child!"

The great lady of the chamber went immediately to the dark corner where Mary hid, and bent over the small pile of blankets and girl. Her wise eyes were filled with wonder and compassion as she carefully reached for Mary and stroked her hair.

"There, there, little one.... Where have you come from?" she soothed. "How did you get into this cathole?"

Mary's weeping subsided a little, and the shaking steadied, but she could not reply. Isobel lifted her face and wiped the tears away with her long silken sleeve. She studied Mary's perfect features and immediately her intuition answered the questions for her.

"Ezra!" she whispered. "This is Ezra's doing!"

CHAPTER EIGHT

The moment Isobel discovered Mary, she offered her some bread and cheese which had been stored in her own compartment of the room, and Mary downed it ravenously. But just as soon, hope for further nourishment was squelched. Hannah entered the chamber, inquiring as to the source of the commotion which had been echoing from the room. Seeing the attention Mary was receiving, she growled, "Isobel! That child is none of your concern!"

Isobel turned to her with flashing eyes and countered, "I am making her my concern! What cruelty do you intend for her?"

"I have no intention regarding her," was Hannah's reply. "I only follow orders."

"Ezra's orders!" Isobel snapped. "So he has finally done it. He's talked of it for years. A child trade! Hannah, how can you allow this? Bringing children into this business!"

Though Isobel was much taller than Hannah, the shorter woman matched her in temper. Stretching to her full height so that she almost wavered for top-heaviness, she hurled a cutting response. "One child, Isobel! There is only one, no more! Besides, at least she will be paid for her labors—unlike you, who were trained as a child by your own father!"

Isobel's face went white at this reminder, and she had no reply for a moment. Mary studied her and an instant empathy grew within her for this woman.

But when Isobel found her voice again, she was indignant. "Tell me, Hannah! What good can come of starving this girl? She has not eaten all day long. What use will a skeleton be to you?"

Hannah eyed Mary and said very deliberately, wanting the child to catch each syllable, "She will eat in time, but when *I* allow it, Isobel, and not before. And she will sleep when I say so. She must understand that her life is not her own, and that all good things are hers when she obeys."

Whispers coursed through the room, and Hannah turned a threatening face to the spectators. "No one is to violate this arrangement!" she warned; and the women were silent, looking at the floor or at each other so Hannah would not single them out for rebuke.

But Isobel was not so compliant. "Are these Ezra's orders alone, Hannah? Since when do you operate only at his command? This place and all its business are yours as well as his!"

Hannah pointed a finger in Isobel's face. "Your mouth will one day be your ruin!"

Isobel, not to be put off, stared intently at the madam of the inn. "Tell us, Hannah," she said, motioning toward Mary, "Why *this* child? She is so young . . . so lovely. . . ."

Hannah smiled triumphantly. "What better qualifications could she have?"

Once Hannah left the chamber, the women busied themselves again with dressing and grooming for the evening. While they occasionally glanced Mary's way, they were helpless to know what could be done and were afraid to offer solace for fear of offending the establishment. Isobel, however, spoke repeatedly to her. "Little one, we will have to leave you alone in a while," she explained in a low voice. "We work outside on the streets a good part of the evening."

Mary studied her apprehensively.

"Child," she continued, looking cautiously over her shoulder, "I will be back as soon as possible. Until then, do whatever Hannah tells you. Do not fight her. Do you understand? It will go better for you if you do not resist."

The girl trembled and at last felt the urgency to speak. "Isobel, what will happen to me?"

The woman stepped over to her and bent down, holding her hand. "Child, I cannot stay. If I stay with you this evening, it will go hard for me, and I might not be allowed to be with you at all. Trust me," she pleaded. "I will return as soon as possible."

As she stood up, a mocking laugh was heard behind her, and Isobel turned to confront the cold face of Debra. "Are you too good for us tonight,

Isobel?" the woman sneered. "Do you have a vaca-
tion from work this evening, or does the child pay
your wages?"

As Mary and Isobel had been talking, the room
had emptied. All the other women had exited for
the streets. But Isobel confronted Debra un-
daunted. "Since when do you make my business
yours?" she countered. "You had better get moving
yourself. Clients do not come so readily for you as
they once did."

The words rankled. Debra glanced at Mary and
turned her vindictiveness on her. "Youth and
beauty!" she snarled. "It seems Ezra is forgetting
the value of *experience.* Men prefer experienced
women!" But there was a bit too much protest in
her voice.

"Leave the child alone!" Isobel commanded. "She
is none of your affair!"

"But she is yours?" Debra laughed.

"I have made her mine, yes! She is my affair!"
And then, grasping the hawk-faced woman by the
arm, she held her in a grip of pain. "To the street
with you, whore!" she growled, thrusting her toward the door.

Wiry Debra headed for the hallway, but as she
did so, she turned another glance to Mary. "Youth
and beauty do not last long here, little one!" she
warned. "In time you will learn the truth of that!"

Isobel turned to her charge, who watched the
harasser's departure with trepidation. The sturdy
woman knelt beside her and stroked her head one
more time. "Child, rest easy if you can. Debra is
more noise than nuisance."

But Mary was vacant of hope, and when Isobel turned to leave, they both wished for morning.

Mary soon learned that the darker the hour, the more frantic the pace and noise about the inn. While the girl wondered what hideous purpose the proprietor and his partner, Hannah, had for her, there was no respite for her weariness and hunger. If the activity of the place had not kept her awake, it was apparent that a purposeful program of sleep-deprivation had been planned for her.

Whenever she dozed off, someone was there to rouse her. And always it was with the accompanying words, "Rahab, you must not sleep."

Once when this happened, Mary opened her red eyes and looked into the face of Ezra. Her body stiffened, and she drew back. Again it came, spoken by the one who represented her enslavement. "Rahab, you must not sleep."

Hunger, fatigue, and trauma cast a peculiar haze over the room. It was as if Mary were slipping into another dimension—a dream world shaped like a descending shaft, through which she tumbled headlong. But somehow she protested weakly, "Who is Rahab? I am not known by that name. I am Mary!"

"Mary?" he feigned a quizzical expression. "Why, Mary has run away. Didn't you know? Rahab has come to take her place. Mary was weak, but Rahab is strong and likes this place and all that happens here."

"No, I am not Rahab! I am Mary!" the girl appealed.

"Ezra did not love Mary. Ezra loves Rahab," the

captor asserted, stroking her gently on the shoulder.

Mary shuddered and shook her head. "No. . . ."

"Yes, little Rahab. Ezra loves you."

For a long time Mary said nothing, closing her eyes helplessly, and at last Ezra inquired, "You must be hungry, little Rahab."

She looked up and gave a mute nod. "You must learn to tell Ezra such things." He smiled. "All good things will be provided by your keeper, if you are good. Rahab is loved very greatly." At this he looked over his shoulder, snapping his fingers at Hannah, who watched from the shadows. Instantly she handed Ezra a plate of spiced meat, candied fruit, nutcakes, and other delicacies.

Ezra held it before the child, who reached for it eagerly.

"Ah-ah!" he warned, pulling the plate away. "First, you must tell me your name. I must be certain you know who you are."

Mary eyed him desperately. She knew what he wanted, but could not bring herself to comply.

"Ah, well," Ezra sighed, handing the plate back to Hannah. "I guess I have the wrong girl. I thought for certain this was Rahab. I must have been mistaken." At this he began to rise, and Mary watched Hannah finger the food with tantalizing strokes. The child grasped at Ezra's robe and clung to it tightly.

"Who is this child?" the innkeeper shrugged, inquiring of the madam. "Do we know her?"

"Rahab!" Mary cried.

Ezra turned to her with a gleam in his eye. "Did

she say something, Hannah?" he mused.

Again Mary tore at his garment. "Rahab!" she repeated, tears of submission flowing down her face. "I am Rahab!"

Ezra knelt beside her, and Hannah placed the food on his lap. Piece by piece he fed the morsels into her birdlike mouth.

"That's my girl," he crooned. "That's my Rahab."

Once Mary had finished her meal she was left alone and fell into the deepest sleep of her life. Any observer would have known that exhaustion alone could not account for the near-comatose quality of her slumber; he would have known that the food had been drugged. But as it was, the wild music and dancing which had spilled from the main hall all evening did not invade the girl's consciousness, and no one came to rouse her.

Finally a loud scuffle directly beside her woke the child and reintroduced her to the reality of her surroundings.

The room was empty except for Isobel—and Ezra, who was accosting the woman bitterly. It seemed she had returned early from the street and had brought no client with her. "The first time in five years!" Ezra cried. "It seems you are all of a sudden taking your security here very much for granted!" At this he drew back and threw a hard slap against her face, sending Isobel reeling across the floor.

"No, Ezra! The traffic is light tonight, that is all," she declared, shielding her face miserably.

He was unconvinced. "Hannah has told me of your attachment for our little girl here. Perhaps you were too anxious to return to her. Perhaps your mind was not on your business!"

"No, Ezra, it was not like that. . . ."

But again he struck her, this time sending her to the floor, and Mary stifled a cry. Then, bending down, he lifted the woman to her feet and flung her toward the door. "Go and work in the kitchen until morning!" he commanded. "And stay away from the child!"

He watched her depart, and then turned to Mary in frustration. "The best woman in my chamber being ruined by a little trollop! You'd better not be more trouble than you're worth."

At early dawn, just as Isobel was returning to the chamber, Mary was sent to replace her in the kitchen. All day long she worked, scrubbing pots, washing floors, doing laundry, until at evening, just as the women were waking from their "night," Mary was allowed to go back to her lonely corner.

It was apparent, from the timing of things, that she and Isobel were not allowed to be together, for Mary went back to her little blanket pile just as her friend was departing for the streets. Though Isobel caught her eye and offered her a fleeting smile, there was no opportunity for communication, and Mary faced the dark hours alone.

But she was not to spend them any more peacefully than she had the night before. Again she had been deprived of food all day, except for gleanings in the kitchen. And it seemed the time for sleep was to be programmed just as the previous eve-

The Abduction

ning's had been. Once more, every time she dozed, she was wakened; and twice, when she gave way to hysterical crying, she was left in total darkness.

At some point in the night hours, she drew from a remnant of consciousness the memory that Ezra had brought her last meal, and she called out for him.

Soon he was by her side, feeding her, "comforting" her again, and reminding her that he was her provider as long as she called herself Rahab.

It came to be, this night, that the girl could not discern reality from dream. Her consciousness was so altered that she could not be certain what transpired and what she only imagined. Her hearing seemed to amplify the slightest vibrations. Her senses lapsed into one another, mixing impressions of smell, taste, touch, and sound. She seemed to swing in and out of a black haze, a deep tunnel and groundless shaft. And always, within that shaft, it seemed the walls rushed upward past her, or she fell helplessly through the dark tunnel—grasping wildly at its side, hoping to catch hold of something, anything, to break her fall.

But at last reality became vividly clear. Sometime in the darkest hours before morning, she was wakened by the hand of a woman. Thinking it must be Isobel, Mary roused expectantly.

But it was not Isobel who greeted her. It was Hannah. And behind her stood Debra and the manservant. Hannah looked deep into Mary's drug-glazed eyes.

"Child, we have something for you this evening.

79

Something you will like very much." She smiled. "Debra and Levi have come to initiate you into the business of the chamber."

The girl trembled, sensing nothing but evil in the woman's pronouncement. But it all happened too quickly for her to fully comprehend. She knew only that Debra and this "Levi," the manservant, were lifting her from her pallet and escorting her down the corridor toward the dining hall. When she entered the riotous room, which she had glimpsed only in passing when she first arrived, she saw that it teemed with men, all laughing and calling out to her. Here and there the familiar faces of the chamber women peered at her, most of them sympathetic but powerless spectators. All other faces displayed, at best, curiosity—at worst, jeering heartlessness. No one lifted a hand to help her as her escorts took her to the center of the dance floor, where Ezra waited.

Mary looked frantically about for Isobel. But Ezra had seen to it that the grand lady was kept away, and Mary pulled against her captors in a vain attempt to flee whatever lay ahead.

She did not take it all in clearly, but Ezra was presenting her, "Rahab," to the onlookers as a "new attraction," a novel introduction to the pleasures of the inn.

With this, Debra and Levi took her forward, pushing her to the floor. Debra held her down and the crowd looked on as the manservant stripped her and demonstrated the use to which she would henceforth be put.

The music, the wall flares, and the laughter all swirled over and under her. Her tears and her cries were ineffectual. At last "Mary" was no more. Only "Rahab" remained.

PART II
The
Alabaster Flask

Stay me with flagons, comfort me
with apples: for I am sick of love
(Song of Solomon 2:5).

CHAPTER ONE

A heavily laden camel train from the Mediterranean wound its way slowly down the western hills toward Magdala. Though its rich young caravan master had made one of his most successful ventures into Sicily and Cyprus, he was very happy to be home. The moment the train had reached the crest of the hill behind the city, and the moment his eyes had rested upon the familiar sandstone buildings within its walls, a smile of relief and anticipation lit his face.

The man walking beside him, while only one of his many servants, had been his best friend since childhood, and he studied the caravaneer's expression with the insight of long acquaintance. "Judah, I have never seen such eagerness in your face at a glimpse of our little Magdala. Surely your travels have not wearied you of the greater world at twenty-five!"

Judah only laughed, his snapping dark eyes aglow with pleasure. "Magdala has its benefits, Isaac," he assured him. "Need I remind you?"

The servant nodded knowingly. "Certainly not. You have spoken of it often enough since we left three months ago."

"Not of *it,* Isaac. Of *her!*" he corrected, his aristocratic features softening with feeling.

Isaac shrugged as they walked, and he kicked at a pebble in the path.

"You disapprove, I see," Judah noted.

Isaac was silent, but at his master's prodding he at last admitted, "It is somewhat distressing, Judah. Why, she is only a common...."

"Careful!" Judah interrupted. "Would you risk our friendship on a word?"

Isaac curbed his tongue and stared angrily at the road ahead. Judah, who cared more for his servant's feelings than was typical of a master, at last grew uncomfortable with the strained silence between them. "It is more than her status that troubles you, is it not? You may be open with me, friend."

Isaac eyed his master warily. "How open, exactly?"

"Speak your mind," Judah offered. "Only be careful with your designations."

"Very well, then," Isaac began. "I will start with the incident five years ago, when you began frequenting that Magdalene tavern."

Judah winced, but let him continue. "I felt it was no good when you, a Bar David, took to trafficking with ... such women. Do you recall my warnings?

And then, to become the subject of an ongoing feud between those two . . . what were their names? Ah, yes—Rachel and Debra." With this last phrase, his upper lip curled in a sneer.

"The girdle was not worth so much as they thought—at least not to me," Judah defended.

"The girdle? The girdle was not the issue! *You* were the trophy for which they vied, Judah!" The servant shook his head. "Oh, master, you are to be admired for many reasons. But you seem to have a blind spot when it comes to women."

Judah chuckled good-naturedly, but Isaac was not amused. "I find it no laughing matter, sir. Many men are so stricken; but that you should always have found your taste tending toward . . . harlots. And you—a Bar David!"

The master was instantly sobered, and his eyes flashed angrily. "So this is the source of your indignation! Bar David, again! At times the family name is a curse rather than a blessing!"

Isaac curbed his growing outrage. "Sir, my father and his father before him have served your family. The Bar Davids are a proud line. . . ."

" 'Stretching back to the king himself,' " Judah interrupted. "Yes, Isaac. How many times have we heard it since our youth?"

"But it is true, Judah! Most Galileans use the given name of each father for every new generation. And thus the son of Matthew Bar So-and-so becomes So-and-so Bar Matthew. But your family has retained the king's name all these hundreds of years." His fervor grew with the assertion. "Indeed, you should be proud of your heritage—just as my people have been proud to serve you!"

But when he stopped his exhortation, Judah was no more reverent than before. "Ha!" he laughed. "Listen, if my father and his proud ancestors had not pushed me to pursue the family's business aspirations, I would have married at eighteen, like most good Galilean boys. As it was, I was forced to turn to these 'ladies' or deny my manhood!"

Isaac was unconvinced. "That is not reasoning but rationalizing, Judah. It is because of just such thinking that lads are encouraged to marry young. If every man thought as you do, the land would be utterly polluted!"

Judah mimicked his fervent gesture and then slapped his friend on the back. "You do get carried away, Isaac! You sound like a regular street evangelist."

Isaac took offense and drew back. "An evangelist would do the Magdalene streets more good than your women do them!" he declared.

By now, they drew close to the western gate, and Judah's feet picked up pace. Isaac's last comment would have earned a harsh rebuttal, had the handsome young master not found his thoughts increasingly upon the object of his affections who was now, surely, not far from reach.

"Oh, Isaac," he smiled. "I would take all your warnings to heart, but I cannot be so morose. Life's pleasures are too sweet! Besides," he said, pressing on ahead, "my lady is no common temptress. She has not had to set foot on the street since Ezra took her in."

The view from the roof of the Magdala Inn could be truly beautiful on a clear day, especially from the height of the small but exquisite pavilion erected only a year before. The sea was visible, with its border of fine white sand and its watery expanse of lapis lazuli blue stretching far to the east. But the young woman who gazed upon it from one open arch of the elevated chamber did not study the scenery. She watched the roadway which curved out of the Galilee hills from the west and wound through town directly past the establishment.

When she was not studying the road, her eyes traveled to a hand mirror held before her. The face reflected there was not the same as it had been when she had come to this place five years before. While it had always been beautiful, its beauty was now more defined by blossoming womanhood and by means of cosmetics. The brown eyes were deepened and highlighted by the subtle artistry of paints and brushes, the lashes lengthened to their fullest by black powder, so that the whites seemed larger. This gave the eyes themselves as much illusion for size as for reality.

Indeed, "illusion" was the point of the art—illusion of quality, proportion, and balance. While the face had always been exquisite, it was now devastating. For illusion did not stop with the eyes. It traveled to the temples, the cheekbones, the lips, the chin, the neck. The temples were high and white, the cheekbones high and rouged, the lips full, like dark wine; and the chin was contoured by design so as to appear haughty, no matter the mood of the heart. The neck was lengthened by means of shadow effects, of white and dark sculpting. And all was done so that it did not seem to have been done. The face did not appear to have been painted, but to have been bred just this way.

Except for the eyes. Here the obvious cosmetic alteration could be allowed. It added to the mystery. And it lessened the possibility that other stylization might be detected on the face. A captivating woman admitted of mascara. It was her hallmark of temptation, and therefore was allowed to be noticed.

When the face was finished, the articles of the craft had been replaced one by one in a small cedar chest which Isobel had presented to Rahab on the day the pavilion was opened. This box was the girl's special treasure and was always to be found in a place of honor on the dressing table. Lined with red velvet, its lid was inset with a polished brass mirror, which cast an almost perfect reflection. Numerous little compartments separated brushes from colored powders, creams from oils, perfumes from spices. This door hid a small jar of staining color for nails on toes and fingers, this corner housed the pencils of antimony for brows and lashes, and yet other drawers concealed other prizes.

And on that same day, Isobel had shared with Rahab some of the finer points of the trade.

"Are the spices for my bath?" Rahab had asked.

"Yes, you may use them for that. But there is another use. Come, let me show you." Isobel smiled. Taking a pinch of cinnamon and saffron, she led her to the bed and pulled back the fine, satiny coverlet. She reached beneath the pillows and deposited small amounts of the fragrant powder in the folds and then did the same beneath the bedclothes.

"Men are greatly moved by the sense of smell," Isobel explained. "The Greeks would call this an 'aphrodisiac.'"

Rahab laughed with delight. "Of course!" she exclaimed. "But Solomon speaks of such things, too. 'I have perfumed my bed with myrrh and aloes'!" She clapped her hands as she sang the verse. "I don't know why I never thought of it!"

Isobel studied her quizzically. "You know the Scriptures?"

At this Rahab shrugged bewilderedly. "I guess I learned them somewhere," she said.

Isobel drew close and stroked her cheek. "My poor lamb," she sighed, noting her saddened expression, "sometimes you look so lost. I promise you that one day we will find where you came from and who your family is."

But Rahab was determined to enjoy the moment and suddenly laughed a very adult laugh. She turned to the box again and lifted a small door in the upper portion. Her eyes lit up at the sight of a beautiful alabaster flask with a ruby stopper. Taking it out carefully, she stroked the golden surface. The bottle was no longer than her outstretched hand, but it displayed the most exquisite etchings she had ever seen. Birds, dolphins, and unicorns peeked from beneath leaves and garlands, chiseled with delicate detail. Rahab turned the flask over and over and asked, marveling, "Tell me, Isobel, what is this?"

"The most costly of ointments," Isobel whispered. "A very fine aloe and spikenard mixture. You may use it for your bath, but," and here she looked about secretively, "it is best kept for the anointing of your favorite clients."

Both women giggled, and Rahab put her finger to her lips. "Hush, Isobel. Wouldn't Ezra be angry at such a waste of money?"

"He would. But he does not earn the living around here. We do!" she replied, a private twinkle in her eye.

"True. . . ." Rahab smiled. "But to think *you* would use such a gift on a customer, when you have always scorned men to their backs! Perhaps you do not despise them so much as you let on."

"Ha!" Isobel corrected her. "You misunderstand. We use any means necessary to coax men's favors. That does not mean we care one shekel for their hearts!"

Isobel's haughty pride appealed to Rahab. Often she wished she could be like her. And in large measure she did manage to reflect Isobel's attitudes. She set about, from that day, to use her cedar box and her oils to greatest advantage. Isobel kept the containers replenished as they ran low, and Rahab practiced the art of anointing with flair and abandon. Road-weary men looked forward to the soothing touch of her hands upon their heads and shoulders, and to the cooling massage she worked upon their feet.

While she had numerous ointments for this purpose, the little alabaster flask was kept for the rarest of clients—usually for those who were most moneyed. But despite Rahab's agreement with Isobel that men were generally despicable, there was one who received the special anointing, not because of his wealth, but because he held Rahab's heart.

She thought on him now as she studied herself in the mirror, her face already perfected; it was the heavy mahogany hair which was now being treated. It had already been shampooed, and due to the harshness of the soap, oiled—though not enough to weight the fine strands. It had been perfumed delicately and dried in the sunny breeze that flowed through the arch, and was now being brushed, again and again, as Rahab sat on a low, cushioned stool. Her hairdresser, who could be seen in the looking glass, bore a scowl upon her face. "I do not have to do this," Isobel complained. "It is only that no one else does it so well, and I cannot bear to see it done half-heartedly. But you could help by leaning back a little. You are about to fall out of that window, you press so hard against the sill."

"Oh, Isobel," the young woman laughed. "Judah should be returning today. I only hope to see his caravan the moment it enters the city."

"But you are sure to sunburn your face, sitting there all day. And besides—it would not be good if Ezra knew how you focus your thoughts upon one customer."

"Customer? Judah is not just a customer to me!" she retorted.

"Hush, child."

"Let Ezra hear! I do not care if he hears," she declared, a flippant pout contorting her face.

Isobel said no more and continued to brush the long hair. Gradually the young face in the mirror showed a more somber mood.

"I had another strange dream last night," Rahab reflected.

Her friend grew concerned once more, but this time for a far weightier matter than a sunburned face.

"About the woman and the children?"

She referred to a dream the girl often experienced, in which some gentle lady would appear, accompanied by two small twins, a boy and a girl. Though the woman never spoke, she seemed to beckon to Rahab, pleading with her to care for the little ones. The dream could not be termed a nightmare, for it was quiet and gentle, but Rahab always awoke from it terrified and weeping.

"No, not this time," she answered. "This dream was far more horrifying. Oh, Isobel—I cried out. But no one heard me!"

Isobel laid the brush aside and turned Rahab about by the shoulders. "Child, I was sleeping in the next room. I would have known. You did not cry out."

"Well, whether you heard or not, I did. At least, in my dream I did."

"Very well, Rahab. Calm yourself. Now tell me, what was the dream about?"

"There were seven men. . . . Oh, Isobel! It was horrible!"

"And what did the men do?"

"Seven! Seven men!"

"Yes, the seven men, child. Do you want to tell me what they did?"

"No, Isobel! I cannot speak of it!"

By now, it was clear the subject was so upsetting to the girl that Isobel must not pursue it. But Rahab's nighttime traumas, and her own powerlessness to help, distressed the woman's motherly heart.

"Child, the next time you are awakened by one of these visions, come, let me be with you in the night," she pleaded.

Rahab looked at the multicolored floor tiles, lost in thought. "Isobel, why can't they tell me?"

"Tell you what, child?"

"Why can't anyone tell me where I came from, what my life was like before I arrived here?" Then, turning desperate eyes to her friend, she cried, "Why can't anybody tell me who I am?"

Isobel reached for her and held her close, but did not say what came to mind. Only the thought, "Ezra could tell you," fought to be voiced.

Suddenly, however, Rahab's demeanor changed and the swift alteration in her mood sent a chill across Isobel's shoulders. The girl pulled away from her embrace and stood straight as a poplar, tossing her glorious head with careless abandon. As quickly as that, her face lost its pallor and she turned to the window, leaning out. "Judah will be coming very soon!" she announced.

CHAPTER TWO

As Judah had pointed out to his servant, Isaac, Rahab had never been forced to earn her living on the streets. From the night of her initiation into the chamber, she had been groomed to be a "special attraction." And she had not failed Ezra's expectations. With an almost frantic, and, Isobel feared, self-destructive zeal, she had plunged into her role. Within a couple of years, when she could be considered a woman, she had become the most sought-after female in Magdala. Of course, the fact that she had begun as a child, and was still barely more than that, added a certain spice to her forbidden fruit. With the ensuing months and years, she had so perfected her art that she had become one of the only such women in town to operate during the day. No longer did she keep the strange hours customary to her profession; and, because clients sought her out, she did not need to ply her trade upon the street corners.

As Ezra had seen her willingness to accommodate him, he had allowed a handful of other women to be her handmaids. She had especially requested Isobel, who had eagerly accepted the post and had served these past years as her beautician, friend, and confidante.

And then, the rooftop chamber had been built. Due to Rahab's price, her clientele tended to be of a higher class than those who normally frequented the inn, and therefore they merited, in Ezra's eyes, a finer environment for their pleasure. So did Rahab, to Ezra's mind. He was pleased to pamper her, and took unusual joy in lavishing finery upon her—finery he could now afford.

The fact, therefore, that Rahab was today upon the street was not related to her business. She had caught a glimpse of Judah's caravan just as it had rounded the palm grove north of town. And she waited now with a number of her maids for the train to draw near the inn.

Because it was unusual to see such a party as hers in public daylight, passersby were quick to notice; and while few in this Jewish society would admit it, they were curious and not a little attracted. This was no ordinary streetwalker, their instincts told them.

As she cast her gaze above the crowd, hoping at any moment to see Judah perched atop his haughty camel, she was a study in sophisticated feminine perfection. As a child she had always been tall for her age, and now that she had reached nearly her full growth, she was graceful and slender as a birch in her supple white tunic. The simple gown, of the finest soft linen, was cinched in to her narrow waist by a wide jeweled girdle, and from this were suspended a mesh coin purse and a tiny perfume flask—very delicate items, intricately crafted, and never missing from the wardrobe of a fashionable lady. Rahab's awareness that her native beauty was her greatest asset was pointed out in the simplicity of other adornment. While many women strung layer upon layer of beads, baubles, and pearls about their necks and down their torsos, Rahab wore only one gold chain; and while it was customary to pierce the nose with a ring, she did not distort her face in this manner. Two narrow bracelets emphasized her slender upper arms, rings adorned her hands, and a thin tiara was woven through the edge of her veil—a gauze of nearly transparent silk, soft rose in color, which served more as a token of modesty than a cover. Since it was unusual for a harlot to wear white, as she did today, the veil's hue was necessary to identify her profession.

Beneath this fine fabric, which flowed simply down her back where it was caught lightly into the girdle, she moved without restriction, her lustrous hair a natural covering and her most outspoken summons.

Today, however, she was not summoning anyone but Judah. She strained on tiptoe to get the clearest view above the crowd. As she did so her only other ornaments, two delicate anklets adorned with small golden bells, tinkled against each other. But they went unappreciated in the din of the street.

It was a noisy place to be, the street corner. One did not discern sounds separately, but in chorus—as a grand cacophony. Wagon wheels bumping over cobbled pavement; a thousand voices chatting, bartering; the braying of donkeys and bleating of sheep—all blended into one another to produce either nerve-jarring tension or elevating excitement. For Rahab, however, no one sound was important, nor was the sum of them. Today she was unaware of anything but the hoped-for arrival of her paramour.

Unaware, that is, until a single voice reached through all the other sounds to catch her ear and arrest her spirit. There was nothing especially noteworthy in the voice's quality nor in its strength or projection. There were a hundred hawkers in the market booths of greater dramatic talent and vocal force. But they did not catch the breath or stop the heart.

"The tower of your city has become an eros pillar!" it was crying. "The symbol of God's protection is defiled by your lewdness! O Magdala—hear the word of your God and of his servant David: 'Hear my cry, O God; give heed to my prayer. From the end of the earth I call to thee, when my heart is faint; lead me to the rock that is higher than I. For thou hast been a refuge for me, a tower of strength against the enemy. Let me dwell in thy tent forever; let me take refuge in the shelter of thy wings.' " Here the voice broke with emotion, and the Psalm was allowed to sink into listening ears before the cry began again: "Return to your God, Magdala. Give up your harlotries and let your tower represent God's strength before this evil generation! Purge the pollution from your streets, and let the sweet, cool waters of Dalmanutha speak the purity of your city!"

As Rahab took in the words, her face grew warm and red. There was something strangely familiar in these images—haunting, like some deep-buried memory.

A shudder went through her, and something like fear. But it was not fear in its normal sense. It was more sadness, loneliness, as though something or someone deep within her cried out to be . . . remembered.

She had shifted her gaze toward the sound of the voice, but in this crowd she could not see the source. Instead her eyes focused on one young man who stood taking in the words with a somber face. As the psalmist was quoted, he studied the crowd, a peculiar expression of sorrow marking his countenance. He was a handsome fellow—probably in his late twenties—with weather-browned skin and even features. But it was not his tall stature or his modest good looks which drew Rahab.

As he surveyed the market populace, his gaze traveled to the gathering of chamberwomen on the corner and at last fell on Rahab herself.

She had grown used to the scrutiny of men. She was accustomed to glances—admiring, lusting, disdaining. But she had never been looked upon as he looked upon her.

Something in his blue eyes penetrated her—seeming to expose her more surely than nakedness. But the gaze was not erotic. It was soul-searching.

It did not speak of the flesh, but of the spirit. And she stood transfixed by its haunting compassion.

Her maids may have wondered at the change in her, but they asked no questions. They need not have bothered, for the interlude was short enough. As Rahab's attention had been focused on the man, Judah had arrived; and, slipping from his saddle, he had caught her from behind, his strong arms encircling her waist.

Pulling her face toward him, he tore her from the spell. The gentle prick of conscience lost its sting, and whatever power the stranger possessed was pushed aside.

The warmth of Judah's touch was all she felt. And for now, it was enough.

CHAPTER THREE

A light spring breeze blew down from the western hills, wafting across the rooftop of the Magdala Inn as it descended toward Galilee's moonlit waters. No light was necessary in the little garden adjoining the penthouse pavilion. The moon was sufficient to illumine the small court, centered among potted palms and fragrant Damascus rose bushes, where the two lovers, Rahab and Judah, strolled this evening. The pavilion was unoccupied now, Rahab having sent Isobel and her maids downstairs for the evening, but through one arch it could be seen that the chamber nearest the garden had very recently been used. Upon a low stand was the alabaster flask, open and empty. And a low couch, richly dressed in silk and velvet bedcovers, indicated by its disheveled appearance that it had lately been cohabited. Across the foot lay a man's cloak—Judah's—

and beside it the jeweled sandals of his mistress, where Rahab had carelessly loosed them.

Judah was the only client Ezra ever allowed to spend the night with Rahab, and this was only because her lover had petitioned for it. Against his better judgment, Ezra had permitted her favoritism. But then Rahab was the *innkeeper's* favorite, and he indulged her at every turn.

She walked now beside her lover barefoot, her arm wound through his intimately, her sleek body loosely garbed in a simple tunic. From the inn below could be heard the music of the main hall, and with it was mixed the laughter of the customers in gradually increasing volume. As long as Rahab had been at the inn these sounds had affected her strangely. She did not know why, but they called up fear; though she had displaced it with work and frivolity, she had never become comfortable with the noises.

Judah did not seem to mind them. In fact, his mood was charged with their effect whenever he stayed the night, so Rahab did not tell him of her uneasiness. There was much, in fact, that she had never told him.

He spoke freely with her this evening, as he always did, of his work, his business, his travels, his fortunes. He spoke proudly of his hopes, his inheritance, his properties, and his dreams. In truth, he reveled in the release which such sharing provided. And Rahab was flattered to be more than a plaything—to be a listening ear, a partner of sorts to his inner man.

But what did he know of her? The fact that he

had never inquired of her past, her family, her life did sometimes sadden her, but she did not dwell upon it. All men were like this, she assured herself.

And then the hollow reality would flood over her —that if he were to ask her anything, she would have no answers. Rahab had no memory before the inn. All was a void—an impenetrable blank. Rahab had begun with Ezra—her consciousness had been born of Ezra and was a continuum of him.

Suddenly she shuddered, and Judah ceased to speak. They had come to the balustrade. He held her trembling hands to his cheek and wrapped his arms about her bare shoulders. "You are cold," he whispered, pressing his body against hers and her back to the low wall. "It is a warm night. Even the breeze is mild," he said, scanning the night sky. "Why do you shiver?"

The young woman had lost track of Judah's conversation. She looked shyly into his dark eyes and he chastised her with a teasing smile. "Where are your thoughts, my lady? They have not been on me. Don't you want to share my dreams tonight?"

At this Rahab turned and stared out to sea vacantly, the nightmare of the seven men racing through her mind.

"Yes, Judah," she sighed, turning again and grasping him close. She buried her head in his arms and pleaded, "Quickly, tell me of your dreams. They are far happier than mine."

CHAPTER FOUR

The faces of the woman and the two young children were especially contorted with unhappiness tonight, as they swam in and out of Rahab's sleeping thoughts. The woman, apparently the mother of the two little ones, held out beseeching hands, repeatedly beckoning to the dreamer. The children did not cry, but only stared at Rahab with dreary, pleading eyes.

Always before at this point in the vision, Rahab had awakened. But tonight, for the first time, the dream slipped uninterrupted into the other episode with which the girl had contended repeatedly in her sleep. And tonight, the dream of the seven men was more vivid than ever before.

As always the shadowy figures converged upon her from behind a dark curtain and the sounds of their coming were as the trampling of a hundred feet, so that the dreamer felt her head must burst with the reverberation. All the faces were grotesque, mocking—and the first character was of overpowering size. She felt she knew him—as much as a dreamer can know anything. And then, as the seven set upon her, all acts were of violence, and there was no love.

Even now, though she beat vainly against her oppressors, she would not have awakened, had a new face not been added to the scene. She had never noticed him before. But there he stood, just beyond the curtain. She reached out to him vainly. Surely he would help. But he did not move to rescue her. He only watched.

Suddenly Rahab was awake. Two arms were trying to hold her close, and she wrenched herself wildly against the embrace.

"Rahab! Rahab. It is I, Judah!" her captor insisted. "Please, my lady. It is only a dream. Only a dream."

Rahab relaxed somewhat as her lover's voice reached through the morbid veil of illusion.

"Judah?" she whispered.

"Yes, Rahab. What is it you have been seeing? You have thrown yourself about the bed like a madwoman."

He had a smile on his face as he said this, but his concerned manner indicated fear of the word. Rahab surveyed the couch upon which they reclined. Blankets were all in disarray, pillows scattered about the floor.

She stood up and stepped to the window where she had watched for Judah's train. She ran a hot hand across her forehead and wiped away her tears. The dawn street was empty and gray. No voices rose to break the silence, and only the Tower of Migdal was shrouded in fog. Studying the specter—Rahab's fortress—she said, "Judah, I heard an evangelist in the market yesterday. He spoke of purity and prayer. He preached that God is a refuge." Rahab took her eyes from the blind tower and looked sadly at the man who had given her the few moments of joy she could remember. He listened in silent bewilderment as she insisted, "For me God stands behind a veil. If I cried out to him, he would only watch—and never raise a hand to help."

CHAPTER FIVE

Rahab had not often seen Doe-eyed Rachel since the pavilion had been erected. The delicate woman had never been strong, and her health had declined badly over the years since Rahab had first come here. Though Ezra still maintained her, as she appealed to a certain clientele, she had not been among those chosen to operate out of Rahab's quarters. Therefore she still worked at night, and kept to the bedchambers of the inn below.

Rachel was emotionally vulnerable and highly susceptible to spells of nervous anxiety and even hysteria. Though she had never shown a sign of a rash or falling hair, some of her sisters said she had the "bad blood" which would eventually lead to insanity. Ezra would not permit the rumor to be spread, as it would drive off clients and give his whole business an evil name. The "bad blood," everyone knew, was infectious, and no inn could survive a reputation for it. But on more than one occasion Rachel's emotional weakness had constrained Ezra to have her put away—confined for a while. Heartless as he was, the innkeeper would long ago have thrust her into the street without protection or livelihood, had it not been for the outcry of Isobel and others who cared for her welfare.

It was only because Rahab did the rare service of accompanying a man to the street door this morning that she happened to encounter Rachel. As the two lovers, Judah and his lady, said good-bye, Rachel came upon them, and the reaction was instantaneous.

In the profession of these women, it was always a dangerous thing to fall in love with a client. Though Rahab's favored position had allowed her to get away with favoritism, Rachel had never been so blessed. This did not mean she had conquered her feelings, however. And today when she saw Judah, the blood rushed to her face.

Rachel had been walking down the corridor from the back of the inn when she encountered the pair. Stealthily she had slipped into a corner, hoping she would not have to confront the man who held her heart. But she was not quick enough.

"Rachel!" Rahab called out. "It is good to see you!"

Caught in mid-exit, Doe-eyes was forced to face the couple, and she shuffled awkwardly under Judah's scrutiny. It was clear from his pleasant but cool civility that there were no sympathetic stirrings within him. If she had ever entertained the notion that he cared for her, such illusions had long ago passed. He had never thought her anything but a commodity for fleshly indulgence.

She raised her hand to her midriff, as she half-consciously remembered the lovely girdle he had once given her.

"Are you well?" Rahab inquired, thinking this gesture a sign of pain.

"I am well, Rahab," the woman answered, casting her gaze to the floor.

But Rahab was not convinced. "Step out of the shadow," she insisted. "What bruises are these on your wrists?" she asked, holding her friend's hands to the light.

Rachel did not answer, but quickly withdrew her arms and folded them against her stomach.

"Oh, Rachel, you have been confined and shackled again, haven't you! Ezra put you in that awful place beneath the inn once more!"

Tears rose to Rachel's eyes. "It is well, Rahab. Ezra knows best. It did me good. It helps me not to cause so much trouble for him when he puts me there for a time." Doe-eyes had never looked more like a frightened wild creature than she did right now. Rahab reached out and held her close.

"Why did he do it this time?" Rahab queried. "What kind of 'trouble' could you have caused, to have been put there again?"

Rachel trembled a little. "Oh, I cry too much. It happens without warning. I don't know why I cry. The tears just come up though I try to keep them down. And Ezra can have no use for me when I do this."

Rahab turned to Judah, who only shook his head and motioned her to follow him to the door. He seemed to have very little interest in Rachel's condition or needs. Rahab studied him incredulously, but quickly reasoned that he must be on his way, for business awaited him.

"Is there nothing we can do?" she asked when they had reached the exit.

Judah only shrugged. "This is none of my affair," he commented. "Ezra manages this place."

Rahab looked over her shoulder at the quiet woman who stepped back into the shadow; then she embraced Judah one last time before he departed.

It was at the sight of this embrace that Doe-eyes' suppressed feelings cried out. The punishment she had just undergone in the dungeon was not sufficient to discipline her response. The misery of her life had been made even more apparent by her recent isolation; and now, to see the one she loved above all others in the arms of this girl brought a torrent of despair.

She began to sob uncontrollably, swaying like a crazed dog and pacing the hall with a wild stare. From that point events tumbled upon one another so rapidly that Rahab could only watch in helpless bewilderment.

The few daytime customers left the dining room and peered into the corridor, wondering at the strange weeping. And then Hannah rushed upon the scene.

"Quiet! Quiet, you fool!" she warned the woman.

Had it not been for the onlookers, the exasperated madam would have struck Doe-eyes. But in a few moments Ezra was there to assist.

Seeing him, Rachel calmed herself, but not to his satisfaction. With marvelous composure, he assured the customers there was no alarm, that they could go back to the main hall, where a round of free drinks awaited. As they complied, shaking their heads and murmuring among themselves, Ezra turned angry eyes on Hannah.

"Can you never tame this one?" he demanded.

"You know her nature. She has always been incorrigible!" the madam objected.

"Incorrigible, indeed!" he ranted, grasping the frail creature by the arms. "I've had enough of her! My sympathetic nature has been strained too far!"

At this he dragged the balking female toward the street door. Rahab reached for her when she drew near, but could not help. As the crazed woman was hauled past Judah, she grasped at his robe and pulled him to her, pleading with her eyes that he do something. But he only wrenched himself free, his lip curled in disgust as he wiped his wrinkled garment where she had defiled it.

Rahab observed this silently, then pushed past her lover, following Rachel to the street.

She knew it was no use to plead with Ezra, but she cried out, nonetheless. As the innkeeper reached the thoroughfare fronting the hostel, he did not bother to survey the passersby. Brutally he cast the dejected harlot into the gutter, where she lay in a convulsive heap. As he turned back to the inn, he saw that Rahab had been a witness and his eyes softened.

"Don't waste your time mourning her, little one," he insisted, caressing Rahab's cheek with meaty fingers. "Just warn your sisters that they must all be as good as you, for Ezra's patience is not beyond measure."

As he retreated down the hall, she smudged away the feel of his hand, fighting back stinging tears and a heart full of hatred. "Oh, Judah," she whispered, turning for comfort to the only warmth she knew.

But Judah was not there. She rushed to the door just in time to see him disappear down the crowded street. Then her eyes fell on Rachel.

Citizens who passed by shunned the rejected woman, drawing their robes close and giving her wide space. But Rahab went immediately to her. Kneeling down and embracing Doe-eyes, she wept.

Even this gesture was cut short, however, as Hannah was quickly upon them.

"Rahab! Shall you be the next to find a home out here?" she threatened.

"Go, child!" the outcast cried, shaking her off. "There is nothing to be done for me."

"An ounce of reason still resides in your brain, Rachel!" the madam sneered. And then, turning to Rahab, she warned, "You would do well to heed your friend. Now get back to your garden house, before Ezra plucks your petals!"

Reluctantly Rahab stood up and turned for the inn, casting one last look at Rachel. The memory of that broken fawn, that dejected heap, would remain forever with her.

CHAPTER SIX

Isobel was not fond of men. A woman need not be fond of men to be in such a business. Rahab had always known of Isobel's antipathy toward the male gender. She had often expressed it, in crude jokes regarding her clients, in ribald stories about their ineptitudes in the bedchamber, and in general disrespect for their dominant and oppressive position in society. Of course, all her backhanded remarks were kept to the confines of the women's quarters. No prostitute could be more endearing or patronizing of the customers than Isobel. Her talent at flattery had been honed to a fine art. And her salty wit, which was used against men when they were not present, turned into a captivating feminism which only added to her allure in their presence. The fact that the men never seemed to recognize when her jabs traversed the line between innuendo and outright mockery was the subject of many a laugh "after hours" in the chamber.

Rahab had never heard Isobel in such a hate-inspired tirade as she exhibited today, however. Ever since word had circulated that Rachel had been evicted, Isobel had not ceased to make her opinions known.

"Now, I am no more in favor of Rome than any decent Jew should be," she was presently asserting. "But Roman women have been so far ahead of us in the battle against male supremacy that we are left to eat their dust like road turtles!" Her eyes snapped, and her buxom chest heaved with conviction. "In fact, what battle has any Jewess ever waged against a Jew?" she demanded. "Oh, certainly, we have all fought in clumsy ways—in the inarticulate ploys of uneducated womankind—with whinings, pouts, withdrawal of favors, or neglect of personal attractiveness. But to what end?"

Rahab was present in the large chamber that housed the women. It would normally have been their sleeping time, but no one could sleep knowing what had happened to Rachel. In fact, the high window which was usually curtained during daylight was exposed, and a sunlit breeze wafted through the room where all the women sat upon their beds or on the floor at Isobel's feet. The youngest female in attendance, Rahab listened in rapt silence to the oration. She had always admired Isobel's intellect, but today her friend's words were positively eloquent. And all who listened must have felt the same admiration, for while no formal meeting had been called, the women, having been exposed to Isobel's zeal, were congregated attentively about her.

"To what end?" she repeated her question.

Of course it would be Debra, her perpetual rival, who tossed back a flippant reply. "Why, to the end that the men simply turn to ladies like us. If their silly women ever realize that their wifely stupidity is our greatest advertisement, we will be in serious trouble!"

This sparked a round of laughter from the majority, for it assuaged their latent fear and resentment of the threat posed by "wifely" women who inhabited the day and slept at night. The laughter died away quickly, however, as Isobel set Debra squarely back. "The men turn to us, you say? No! They do not turn *to* us. They turn *on* us!" At this Isobel stood up from the low stool where she had been sitting and began to pace back and forth. "Look at us! How have we benefited? Have we homes or families? Have we lovers who nurture or encourage us? How many of us will abort unwanted babies? How many must contract disease—even, as Rachel discovered, lose our *sanity* for this 'business'?"

"But it has always been this way," someone interjected. "Even in Rome there are paid women."

"Certainly," another agreed. "But are they stoned by the religious leaders when they are found at work?"

"No!" yet another responded. "Many of them are part of the religious system in Rome and Corinth and Ephesus! And their work is part of the people's worship."

"I care nothing about the religion of the Romans!" Debra sneered.

"Nor I!" Isobel asserted, taking the lead again. "Any more than I care for the religion of the Jews!"

At this a tide of laughter surged once more through the audience, for these women had only been alienated by the Judaic system. But Isobel was continuing: "In fact," she said soberly, "no form of our trade elevates any female—Jew or Gentile; for whether it be cloaked in sacred mystery or scorned as depravity, it is bondage—bondage to men and their way of things!"

So saying, the speaker shook her head, punctuating her words with a pointed finger. "Truly, the fact that the Romans accord their temple women a holy position only keeps the poor creatures more enslaved than we, for their vision of their true situation is clouded."

The room grew quiet as the gathering contemplated Isobel's insight. "So, how have the Roman women surpassed any Jewess in this struggle?" Debra challenged her. "If we are 'road turtles' by comparison, how has the hare raced ahead?"

"By rising up!" someone shouted.

"Well said," encouraged Isobel. "Such a thing has been done!"

"By wealthy Gentile women, Isobel!" Debra objected. "And not for two hundred years! Haven't we heard your Roman stories often enough? We tire of them!"

There was no formal education which taught Jewish women of their sisters in history. Any sense of womanhood past had been preserved by legend and word of mouth. The tale of the great women's march into the Roman Forum two centuries before was not extolled openly among Jewesses. Though it was passed from generation to generation of mothers and daughters throughout the Mediterranean world, it would have been forgotten entirely in Israel, had it not been for a few Isobels who kept it alive in their own small circles.

How much was fact, and how much fiction, could only be surmised. But it was true that a group of Roman freewomen had invaded the male domain of the empire's capital, demanding the repeal of the Oppian Law, with its strictures on feminine attire and life style. It was true that, though the men had objected loudly, predicting the ruin of Rome by rising "female despotism," the women had laughed them down, maintaining their obstinate stand until the law was eradicated.

And the tidal wave of revolution had only begun. More laws distasteful to women were repealed; divorce became a female prerogative, as well as male; childbearing became less popular among trendy women in an era of overcrowded cities and warlike imperialism. It became common to speak of the "New Woman," who moved about as freely as a man, who dressed luxuriously, studied philosophy, owned her own business, practiced law and medicine, and even wrote manuals on abortion which were used by females of every stratum, from prostitutes to society dames.

"You are right, Debra," Isobel admitted. "There have been no marches for two hundred years. But Roman women have never been the same since that day."

Debra was laughing now. "You have been too

good a teacher in the past, Isobel! You told us yourself that the men didn't let the women get away with much for long. What do you want us to believe?"

It was true that as recently as the rule of Augustus Caesar, only two decades before, sharp censures had been enacted to curb the "New Woman." Augustus's "Julian Laws," which would one day be considered the most important social legislation of the ancient world—while certainly beneficial to family values and "the sanity of society," as Augustus called it—had effectively squelched whatever advancement women had made toward equality. Though a woman could be freed from the power of her husband under these edicts, this could happen only in the event that she produced three children. And the death penalty was still enacted in Rome, as it always had been in Israel, for a woman caught in adultery—though the same punishment was not imposed upon a straying husband. And while a man could visit a prostitute freely, a woman could not attend an athletic contest; so a man's life was free, and a woman's bound.

"Your point is well taken, Debra," Isobel conceded. "But we can learn by the example of a few brave predecessors."

Isobel would not be allowed to continue, however. A peculiar scuffle outside the window had pulled the others' attention away from her argument.

A small shower of pebbles and rocks was being thrown against the sill, and a few fell through the grate onto the chamber floor. A rowdy chorus of boyish laughter followed, and then, "Come see, ladies! Men are throwing rocks in the street!" Though the young voices were mocking, the meaning was perfectly clear to the women inside.

"Rachel!" Debra cried. And instantly, all present were on their feet and racing down the corridor toward the main door.

Rahab followed the group, not really comprehending. But it was not long before the explanation came. One of her sisters, seeing her push toward the front, held her back. "Don't go out there, little one," she warned. "It would not be a pretty sight."

From the street could be heard the shouts of a dozen men and the cry of a gathering mob. The screams of a woman in terrifying pain were quickly obliterated, leaving the sound of stone upon stone buffeting her and hitting the pavement.

"Rachel!" the girl shrieked. Her frail friend had been caught with a client and so had not lasted a day without Ezra's protection. Apparently the religious leaders of Magdala were seeing to it that the Mosaic penalty, death by stoning, was enforced.

This time no one would be able to rush to Doe-eyes' side. Isobel reached for Rahab and held her close, helplessly silent.

Debra looked on, but even at this grisly moment chose to take advantage of her rival. "So now, tell us, Isobel," she snarled, "What shall we learn from our 'brave' Roman sisters? Shall we learn to smile on the day of our death?"

CHAPTER SEVEN

Rahab stood alone at the balustrade that hemmed her rooftop garden, watching the dark night sea where it caught the moon between clouds. It was an unusually cool evening for a Magdalene spring. It seemed to the young woman that nature had shrouded itself in mourning for Rachel. Even the breeze off the sea bore a certain eeriness, seeming more somber and determined than usual.

Ezra's favorite had asked to be alone since the terrible incident of the afternoon, stating that she would be incapable of credible professionalism this day. He had not questioned her. Almost anything she wanted was hers for the asking. But how she loathed the viper! Everything within her recoiled at the thought of him. Strange, but she did not really know why she felt this way. To her memory, he had always treated her kindly, as his most highly favored woman.

To her memory. . . .

That was the limit of her conscious mind. The hatred, the revulsion arose from that dark space, that fathomless void that occupied the vaults of time before Rahab had arisen.

Yes, even Rahab knew that she had replaced someone—that nameless memories swam ever closer to the surface, yet remained inscrutable, more real than the illusion which she represented.

But she must not dwell on this. Whenever those dark places came close enough that she felt she might at any moment see into them, she tensed. Her very body reacted with cramping in the stomach, sweat on the palms, pain in the temples. And sometimes she could barely breathe.

Eventually her mind turned to other things.

The "other things" tonight, however, were Doe-eyes and the stoning. And these things all bespoke Ezra—Ezra and his brutality—Ezra and his. . . .

"Rahab," a voice interrupted, "shouldn't you try to sleep?"

It was Isobel, who had come to check on her. Rahab turned dreary eyes her way.

"Do you feel it in the air, Isobel?" she asked.

"Feel what, child?"

"The heaviness? The dark spirit?"

Isobel glanced seaward and a sadness such as she could not express filled her. "Yes, child. It is as you say. The night is heavy—for Rachel."

"For us all, Isobel. All of us in this terrible place," she said, scanning the inn. And then, shuddering, she continued, "Oh, Isobel, I cannot sleep tonight. I am afraid to sleep. . . ."

"What is there to fear, Rahab?"

"The dreams. I fear that the dreams will come stalking tonight."

"I will stay nearby," Isobel promised.

Rahab embraced her, seeking comfort. "How is it that you are always so confident?" she whispered. "When I heard you speak today, I wished to be like you, to know your strength and will."

Isobel stepped aside and studied the garden for a long moment. "I may appear to be confident, Rahab," she explained, "but my spirit arises as much from anger as from strength."

"You are angry at all men, aren't you, Isobel?"

"They have given me no reason to feel any other emotion."

Rahab perused the beloved face of her friend. "Tell me about your life—before coming here. You must have been a very great lady. . . ." But the instant she said this, Rahab feared she would be misunderstood. "Oh, I do not mean that you are not great *now,* Isobel. You are the very finest, the noblest lady here. . . ." But this seemed another inadequate statement. "The finest lady" in a whorehouse? As Rahab stammered yet again, Isobel smiled broadly.

"Child, thank you. Your thoughts are very kind. And, yes," she asserted, throwing back her shoulders and raising her sturdy chin, "I was a great lady—once. . . ." To this she added an affirmative chuckle, but it settled quickly into somber reflection. "That was a long time ago . . . so long ago it seems like a dream."

Rahab leaned forward intently. "Yes, go on, Isobel . . . tell me where you came from and how you learned so much. You are wiser than the most learned men who visit here."

"Ha!" Isobel interjected, her laugh hearty and full-blooded.

Rahab was stunned by her cynicism.

Isobel perceived her uneasiness, and quickly reassured her. "Don't mind me, child. I know what you mean to say, and your observation is well taken."

The story that was forthcoming was another of those things, like the death of Rachel, which Rahab would never forget.

"I am a Jewess, but I was not raised in the orthodox tradition. My family lived in Rome and I was raised there," she began.

Rahab was aware of a faint foreign accent in Isobel's speech, but she had never thought much about it. In such a crossroads city as Magdala, one grew used to a variety of inflections and tongues. Nevertheless, *how had a Roman woman come to be in this place?* Isobel read her thoughts.

"It is a simple story, really," she continued. "I was abandoned here."

"Abandoned?"

"By my husband."

Rahab's eyes flashed wide. She had never imagined that Isobel had once been married. She never thought of any of the women here as having had husbands or families. "Who was he—your husband?"

"He was a Roman like myself. And very wealthy, like my family. But he was not a Jew—not when we married. As I told you, I was not orthodox, and it did not trouble me or my parents to have a Gentile take me for his wife." At this, Isobel's expression grew wistful. It was apparent that she had loved the man very much.

"What happened?" the girl gently prodded. "You say he was not a Jew when you married. Did that change?"

"Yes," Isobel replied, rousing out of her sentiment. "He was very fond of one of his servants, a fine Jewish man. He often discussed matters of religion with him, and was convinced to join the faith."

"So he was a proselyte?"

"Yes. Which was all fine, to my way of thinking. If he found comfort in Judaism, I would not hold him back. I was proud of my heritage, and it pleased me that he should embrace it, though the faith was quite meaningless to me."

"But I still do not see...."

"I am coming to it, Rahab." Isobel nodded. A shadow crossed her face as she explained her husband's treachery. "For many years, we were quite happy. Claudius, my husband, was a most kind and tender man. He encouraged me in many pursuits which most men, even in Rome, found objectionable for their wives. You see, some men even refused to marry because of what they considered the forwardness and extravagance of the 'New Woman.'"

"The kind who marched into the Senate?"

"Yes. Women had changed and the men were uneasy with it all."

"But not Claudius?"

Isobel took on that faraway look again. "Not Claudius. There never was a more liberated man than he." She sighed deeply and reflected. "He was not threatened by my studies, my involvements. I had a business, you know—purples and dyes. I worked out of our own home, and had many servants. Claudius benefited greatly by my endeavors, financially and socially."

"Then how. . . ."

"It was his obsession with the faith that pulled us apart."

For a moment, Isobel was silent, stepping into the garden and dwelling upon her own tale. It was as if the recounting brought back such pain, she must cease speaking. But at last she went on, her voice at first soft and sad, but gradually taking on intense emotion and bitterness.

"For a long time, Judaism lifted him up. And with him, myself. In fact, I was drawn to the spirit of his zeal and began to reach out, in my own way, to Jehovah. Then his fervor took a strange turn. He became involved with some men of the synagogue who espoused a much harsher interpretation of the Torah and God's laws than he was accustomed to. It was at that time that he decided to make a pilgrimage to Jerusalem. I accompanied him. And, oh, how I wish I had never made that trip!"

Rahab could not imagine regretting such a journey. To the young woman who had never left Magdala, Israel's capital represented the whole wide world. "What happened?" she marveled. "I have always wished to go there."

"Oh, Jerusalem was wonderful. It was not Jerusalem I feared. It was the strange alteration in Claudius that troubled me. From the time we set out until we started home, I watched him withdraw from me more and more. His friends from the Roman synagogue had arranged the pilgrimage and were in charge. I knew that they were somehow to blame for his behavior. But I did not know how. Until, on the return trip, we reached Galilee. . . ."

"Yes? What happened then?"

"Claudius abandoned me."

Rahab hardly knew how to respond, but her amazed silence asked the obvious question.

"Why?" Isobel echoed her thought. "If I tell you why, perhaps you will understand my hatred for all men, for both my husband and my father, the two who should have been closest to me, are responsible for my being here."

"Do explain!" the girl urged.

"Claudius came to despise me for something I could not help and could not change. The fact that I was not a virgin when we married had never troubled him until then, because I had not chosen my condition. It had been forced upon me—by my own father."

Isobel's face burned with the memory of those early incestuous abuses.

"Child, such a thing is not unusual in Roman society—not even among Jews if they are unorthodox. It is no respecter of societies, and the pain is as great in all cultures. It was Claudius' unquestioning love which had brought me healing. . . . But suddenly his love was no longer so unquestioning. It was, in fact, irrelevant in the face of his new religious life."

"He left you because of this?"

"His friends and their way of righteousness considered me a marked woman—a fallen creature. There was no redemption for me, no sacrifice great enough. I was fortunate that they did not have me stoned—like Rachel."

The young listener shook her head and gripped the low wall with tense fingers. "What did you do when he left?"

Isobel's face showed lines of stress and bitterness. "A woman alone on the shore of Galilee, not knowing the language, homeless and hungry—a Roman woman—I was fair game for the first gang of rowdy sailors to come upon me. Within a matter of days I had been reported to Ezra—and the rest you can imagine."

Rahab shuddered. The recurring dream of the seven assailants slammed into her consciousness afresh. "Dear Isobel!" she cried. "Did they hurt you badly?"

"Had they not vouched for my attractiveness, Ezra never would have paid a shekel for me. When they brought me to the inn, I was a sorry sight."

"They sold you to him?"

"Like so much chattel."

At this Isobel grew silent again. She turned her eyes to the sea once more and sank into a private pit of misery. "Perhaps," she whispered, "we are nothing more than chattel, after all. Perhaps women like us were marked before the world began—cursed by God to be cursed by men. . . ."

Rahab had never heard such fatalism voiced by her spirited friend. The girl followed her gaze seaward and shivered, drawing away a little. She thought of Judah, and how she had always longed for a secure knowledge of his love. Was she nothing more to him than . . . chattel?

"Perhaps," she said hesitantly, considering Isobel's sentiment.

But Rahab's dejection shook her friend from her self-pity. "Child," she offered, donning a jovial aspect, "don't take my ramblings too seriously. I am only very tired and irritable. We both know life will be better in the morning."

"Morning?" Rahab reflected. "To get to morning one must go through the night—and I fear the night."

Isobel did not question her. She knew her young friend dreaded the repeated dream.

"I will stay close by, Rahab," she assured her once more. "With the dawn *all* this will be but a dream."

CHAPTER EIGHT

"Chattel . . . chattel." The word still haunted Rahab hours after Isobel had left the garden and gone to sleep in her own corner of the pavilion. The young woman had never found the rooftop bower to be so bleak and unfriendly. A thousand thoughts circulated through her mind. Scenes of Rachel in the street, the sounds of the mob and the cries of their victim . . . Judah and his insensitivity to Rachel's distress—his seeming disregard for anything beyond the flesh.

"But what should I expect of him?" Rahab pondered. "What are any of us to any man but objects to gratify desire? *Chattel.* . . ." The word hung in the air. "O God!" she longed to cry out. But God had never been there for her. Perhaps long ago in that part of her which was no longer—for that girl who had died at Ezra's hand—sometime, perhaps

God had been known to that little girl. But Rahab did not remember. Whenever she pondered it, she bumped headlong into the impenetrable void which was her past. And with the collision always came the same sense of panic, of flight more terrifying than anything present. The past must be so horrible, she reasoned, that she could only collide with it and never reenter it.

Rahab wandered the garden for a long while. It was three hours past midnight, the "soul's midnight," she had heard it called. She had never been sure of the reason. Perhaps it had gained this designation because it was the dead center of blackness on earth. And it was the testing time of the minds, the hearts, the souls of all who slept not—the hour when light was most spent and most distant, and when God (if he be real) seemed farthest away.

"God giveth his beloved sleep. . . ." The words came back to her from somewhere in the past, and she shivered. "I must not be one of his beloved. My sleep, if I have it, is full of terror," she whispered—to the air, to herself, to the God who was not there. "And tonight, I do not sleep at all."

She pushed her way through a narrow path of greenery, and the rustling branches echoed "chattel" again. She turned about to see who spoke, but no one was there; as her garment caught in the slender limbs, it rustled "chattel" again.

"Who is it?" she called faintly, almost afraid to move.

For a moment all was silent. Even the sea breeze which had wafted across the roof all evening seemed to still. But then, though she moved not, though the branches were silent, she was certain she heard it once more. It was not so much a clear word this time, as the simple sound of a distant voice . . . or voices. They were very low and far away, like the rattle of locusts' wings, and seemed to ascend from the stairway which led up to her apartment.

As they drew nearer the door of the pavilion, she could discern mocking laughter in their tone—derisive, plotting. Rahab could not imagine the source. Ezra had never sent men to her in the night. She was his day lady—his lady of light. And surely, even if there were some unusual change of policy, he would not enforce it *this* evening. Hadn't he promised her no visitors until tomorrow?

"Who is it?" she called again, her skin rising in gooseflesh. Whatever Ezra had in mind, he had never imposed more than one man on her at a time—not to her memory. . . .

But this appeared to be his intention tonight. As her eyes froze upon the stairway curtain, a group of men were entering. Their faces were familiar, for they had haunted her a thousand times.

"But I am not asleep!" she cried. "You cannot be here, for I am awake!"

Still they approached, their eyes glowing with cruel desire, their aspects human but inhuman. "Who are you?" she demanded, her chin raised defiantly. "I shall call Ezra!" she threatened. But they were not dissuaded. "Isobel!" she called, but there was no reply.

The leader grasped her by the arms, his hands like hot brands about her wrists. And this time, though it was a reenactment of the dream, it was no dream.

When he had finished with her, he continued to pin her wrists down as his followers turned the bed into a menagerie of acts unnamable. As in her nightmares, the abuses were of every nature. But tonight, toward the end of the ordeal, she was aware of something new: the searing pain where the leader held her was becoming more intense and with it came the odor of burning flesh.

When they were done, the men—the beings—stood up and left the room. How they left she was not certain. They seemed simply to be no longer there. But the broken girl could not think on anything for long. She lay upon the bloodsoaked couch wracked with sobs of despair and pain.

That no one had heard her all this time was beyond belief. How her voice had not raised the dead was inexplicable.

It was dawn before anyone found her. But not even Isobel's horror at the sight could match its reality. And when she brought Ezra to the scene, his face grew pale—even *his* face.

"First Rachel and now Rahab!" was all he could say. "First Rachel and now Rahab!"

The girl, who lay dazed upon the bed, stirred at the sound of his voice, and she questioned him in tones so soft he had to put his ear to her lips.

"Why did you send them?" she pleaded. "How could you?"

"Send who?" he replied, bewildered. "I sent no one to you!"

Isobel drew near and scrutinized her ward with terrified eyes. "See here, Ezra," she insisted. "What are these wounds upon her wrists? See, here, upon both wrists!"

The innkeeper was a hard man with a strong constitution. But he shuddered at the sight.

"They appear to be burns—like brands," Isobel stammered. "The mark of someone—or something. . . . She could not have done this to herself. It would be impossible!"

Ezra turned his head away, clutching his robe with shaking hands. His sincerity, for once, was untarnished as a child's. "There was no one here last night," he asserted. "I may not always be kind— but I keep my word, Isobel. I promised Rahab no visitors. No man came to her by day or night."

PART III
The Years of the Locust

That which the palmerworm hath left hath the locust eaten (Joel 1:4).

CHAPTER ONE

It had been nearly a year since Rahab's nightmare had taken flesh. In all that time, the beasts had not returned and the dreams had become but an awful memory. Though the strange brands were yet visible upon Rahab's wrists, she wore wide bracelets to cover them, and tried not to look too closely at them in private. But for this grisly reminder, the incident would have seemed but a dream in itself.

It had also been nearly a year since Rahab had seen Judah. He had been away on business in Rome and Corinth for months, and time had somewhat mollified the sting of his behavior the day of Rachel's death.

Rahab had heard that he was returning today, and she hoped he would call on her. She had grown weary of watching for his train from the rooftop and had gone down to the dining hall to chat with the servant girls, whose perpetual activity was a source of diversion. It could be said for the inn that it was the cleanest establishment of its kind on the Magdalene coast. Here the floor was being scrubbed, there the tables polished, and across the room candles were being trimmed. Rahab almost envied these girls the simplicity of their labors. They were not required to be glamorous or exciting, to develop skills at conversation, to pretend infatuation where none existed. In fact, Ezra knew that in a business like this the servants must be just that: servants. They must not cross into the field which his other ladies occupied, for the confusion of roles would stifle efficient management.

When Rahab considered her work, she knew it was role-play. With clients there had never been a genuine emotion displayed, an honest word spoken. Yet she also knew life as a harlot was not the real essence of her being. That reality lay buried somewhere outside the inn, and her life with Ezra was as shrouded in alien garments as her past life was in mystery. It was as though every time she acted here, she took on a guise, and with the guise, further darkness concealed her true identity.

Yet, what could she do? To confront all this might expose the mystery—fulfill her memory. And that must never happen. After all, surely even in this life there had been *some* sincerity. Hadn't she truly loved Judah? To her mind, her part of the relationship had never been harlotry.

As she sat in the dining hall, her eyes wandered repeatedly to the hall door and her pulse quickened. At any moment her lover might appear. She had once learned, in her buried girlhood, that a watched pot never turns to steam. And she knew that if she could only occupy herself with other things, the time would pass more quickly.

Rahab had asked Isobel to coif her hair several different ways before she settled on its present arrangement—myriad slender braids falling about her shoulders and down her back. Now she questioned once more if this were the best design. Was it too stiff, too formal? Wouldn't she appear softer, warmer if the hair were loosed?

Quickly she began to undo the plaits, allowing the hair to lie where it would. The strands, having been crimped, were full of wavelets; and as she loosed the last rope of hair, she shook her head, letting the profusion of curls drape her like a wooly mantle. Then, detaching one of the small hand mirrors from her girdle, she surveyed herself. She had never been blind to her own beauty, but today she was especially pleased with what the mirror depicted.

As she had hoped, time had passed quickly this way, for just as she was attaching the mirror once more to its chain, her name was called by one of the servant girls.

"Rahab, a man asks for you."

"Judah?" she inquired, standing up and turning for the door. But before the girl could reply, Rahab saw that it was someone else who sought her.

A small, slender man, dressed not in aristocratic garb but in the robes of a commoner, waited in the hall. Must she entertain this stranger, when Judah might come at any minute? Her heart beat dully as she approached the man, and though she attempted to wear a pleasant face, she knew her disappointment was not well hidden.

Summoning every ounce of femininity she could muster, she gazed at him with feigned appreciation. "Sir, I am flattered that you should request me, but my day is already quite full. I await a client presently who has an appointment in advance."

The little fellow bore a strange expression. Rahab read anger in his look, and assuming he was unprepared for this rejection, tried to appease him. "Believe me," she whispered coyly, placing a hand on his sleeve, "had I known *you* were coming, I would have arranged my day differently."

Now the stranger's eyes snapped, and he drew back from her touch as if offended. "You are mistaken, young woman!" he declared. "I have never set foot in such a place as this, and I am not here to avail myself of your services!"

Rahab studied the man incredulously. "Why, I only thought. . . ."

"You thought amiss!"

"Then, why *are* you here?" she asked.

The newcomer looked about uncomfortably, quite ill at ease with his surroundings. "My name is Isaac," he explained. "I am the personal servant of Judah Bar David."

Rahab's heart sped. "Judah? He sent you?"

"No, madam. He did not send me. . . ."

"Then why are you here? Is he well? Has something happened to him?"

"Madam," Isaac said, shaking his head, "my master

is well. In fact, if he knew I had come to talk with you, he would be very angry."

Rahab was visibly relieved to know her lover was all right. But now she grew anxious regarding this man's intentions.

"What is it you wish to say?" she asked hesitantly.

"I know that my master comes to this place whenever we pass through Magdala," he began. "He has done so for years, since before *you* came to the inn." The point that she was but one in a long line of Magdalene harlots to capture Judah's heart penetrated all too sharply.

Isaac was not a cruel man, however. Angry as he was with his master's choice of women, he took no pleasure in hurting this young girl. "I must say, though," he added, "that my lord speaks more fondly of you than of any other 'lady' here." The designation stuck somewhat to his tongue, and he shuffled awkwardly.

Rahab lifted her head, a smile working at her lips. "Does he?" she asked.

"Indeed," Isaac assured her, softening a bit. He had not been prepared for her charms, and his masculine heart could not help but be affected. Clearing his throat, he went on coolly. "Now, madam, I am here to serve my master in the best way I can."

"Yes?" she urged, overlooking his stern demeanor.

"I see that you misunderstand me," he insisted. "I tell you he speaks of you, and you think I am here to bring you a bouquet!" Then facing her squarely, "I am here to say that if you care for my lord at all—if a woman . . . like yourself . . . can have such feeling—you must turn him away!"

At first it seemed Rahab had not heard. But as the command took conscious hold she rebelled instantly. "Turn him away? You cannot think I would ever turn Judah away!"

"If you care for him . . . if you 'love' him, you will do just that." He spoke the word "love" as though it could not accurately be associated with Rahab. But she did not challenge his tone.

"I *do* care for Judah, sir," she declared, realizing that her voice was carrying into the dining hall. "And for that very reason, I would never do as you suggest."

" 'Suggest' is too weak a word, madam," Isaac went on. "I insist upon it. Do you realize that Judah is a Bar David, in the princely line? It brings him down to frequent this place. And if you love him, you will help him to find himself, to be true to the stature of his name!"

At this Isaac turned on his heel and walked toward the street door, looking back once. Rahab watched his departure numbly, and when he called to her again, she slumped silently against the wall.

"It is within your hand to help my lord," he cried. "He is a Bar David! Not a Magdalene scavenger."

CHAPTER TWO

The sun filtered in strips through the reed blind covering Rahab's chamber window. She was no longer watching for Judah's train in the street below. She sat alone in a dark corner of her room trying not to think of her lover or his servant.

But the more Rahab defended herself, the more she involved her thoughts with the subject she wished to avoid.

Could Isaac be right? she wondered. *Was such a sacrifice indeed necessary to Judah's well-being?*

The event she had so eagerly anticipated this morning, the arrival of her love, was now a fearsome thing. She preferred that he not come today, for she did not know how to deal with him just yet.

Presently, however, the sound of Judah's voice was rising from the stairs, and involuntarily her breathing stopped short. Before she knew it, she was on her feet and running to greet him.

She had not remembered his being so tall. She was certain he had never been so strong, as he swept her into his arms and kissed her fervently.

"I have thought of you every day for a year!" he exclaimed. "Oh, Rahab, how I have needed to be with you!"

The girl was carried away with his proclamation, and the two lovers embraced passionately. But then Rahab drew back. "Every day for a year? When there were Roman women all about?" she teased. "Come, Judah! I have learned a great deal about those ladies and their liberation. You must have found them quite sophisticated."

Judah studied her with a twinkle in his eye. "Where have you acquired this new education, Rahab?"

The girl stepped away with a coquettish toss of the head. "I am not entirely cut off from the world up here, my lord. Besides, it would be silly to assume you see no one else when you are away."

"I see only you when I am here," he crooned, reaching for her. "That is what matters for the moment."

Had she expected him to deny anything, to proclaim her his only lady—his only . . . harlot?

Rahab fended off the thought and displayed one of her most convincing smiles, as Judah held her two hands close to his face, caressing them with his cheek.

Suddenly his eyes were caught by the unusually wide bracelets upon her wrists. "Where did you get these?" he asked, fingering the ornaments. "I recall your wearing bands about your arms, but not upon your wrists."

Rahab quickly withdrew her hands and answered, "It's not unusual to wear bracelets. Don't Roman women wear bracelets?" And then, laughing nervously, she turned toward the garden.

Judah had not missed her reaction, however, and for once decided to question her about herself. "Do you remember the last night we had together?" he began, stepping up behind her.

"Yes," she replied hesitantly.

"You had some kind of strange dream, Rahab. Is such a thing common for you?"

"Oh, that!" the girl shrugged, a twitch working at the edge of her mouth. "It has been nearly a year since such a thing has happened." She hoped he would let the subject pass, and quickly grasped for another topic. "Speaking of a year ago, my lord, I wish to ask *you* something."

She had turned to him now, and her face was intently serious. "Of course . . . ," he offered.

"Why did you leave as you did? Do you know what became of Rachel?"

Judah was struck by her self-possession. She had never been so forthright, and her directness called up the guilt he had tried to suppress since that awful day. But he did not fumble for a response. With a debonair and sympathetic smile he approached her again, enfolding her in his arms, and whispered, "Yes, I heard about it, Rahab. But let's not speak of such a painful thing now. It has been so long a time since we. . . ."

"Yes, a year. A year since my friend Rachel cried out to you—the one she loved above all others—and you abandoned her!"

There. It had been said. Judah's face grew pale. "It was none of my affair," he stammered.

"It was anyone's affair who could have helped. You are one of Ezra's favored clients! You *could* have done something!" Her courage mounted with each syllable, and she turned coldly from him.

For a long moment, silence reigned. Judah stared helplessly at Rahab's unfriendly back, and then at the floor. When she turned again to face him, his pained expression melted her.

"Oh, Judah," she sighed, stepping close, "perhaps you truly did not realize the consequences of your choice that day."

She knew she covered for him—that she excused the inexcusable. But the relief in his eyes rewarded her, as did the warmth of his arms. She would have let all else pass for now, yielding freely to his love, but. . . .

"Judah, there is yet more to discuss," she whispered, choosing to ride out her momentum of courage.

He sighed with dismay. "More, Rahab? But why . . . ?"

"A man calling himself Isaac visited me today."

Judah drew away angrily. "My manservant? Why would he come here?"

"Is it true that you are of the royal household—a descendant of King David?" she inquired, her eyes wonder-filled.

Suddenly Judah assessed the reason for Isaac's

strange act. "You must understand Isaac, my lady," he explained. "He has always been the zealous religious sort, and of late his blood has been stirred by tales of the wilderness preacher."

"Wilderness preacher?" Rahab asked.

"Surely you have heard of the peculiar 'prophet' at Bethabara—the one they call 'the Baptist.' "

When Rahab only shrugged her shoulders, Judah laughed again. "Well, I thought news traveled most quickly to the brothels. But perhaps Isaac was the first of his hearers to set foot in this place. Anyway, it seems this is no typical street evangelist. He's quite a showman, actually, parading around the Jordan waters in nothing but camel skins. I personally don't know what a sensible fellow like Isaac sees in him."

Despite Judah's irreverence, Rahab's curiosity was piqued. "What does he preach?"

"Oh—something to do with preparation. . . ."

"Preparation?"

" 'Preparing the way of the Lord!' " Judah mocked, thrusting his arms wide and lifting his face heavenward. "You'd think a great prophet could be more original. Isaiah was saying things like that seven centuries ago!"

Rahab smiled with him, but found the story more than amusing. It had the same effect on her as the message of the Magdalene street preacher a year before, and she longed to hear more.

Judah, however, was in no mood for it. In singsong he intoned, "As part of his 'preparation,' Isaac will save my reputation." And then with a merry twinkle in his eye, he pulled his lady close, and his laughing eyes softened. "Tell me, Rahab, are you going to send me away?"

But she maintained resistance. "Judah, you *are* a Bar David."

"So! That is it!" he laughed, his head thrown back. The young lover sighed and pushed her away in frustration. "So I am," he muttered, "and sometimes I fear it is a curse rather than a blessing."

Rahab was offended. "How can you speak so of our king and nation?" she demanded.

Judah could see that she was indeed troubled and resigned himself to an explanation. "Rahab," he began, "I am as proud to be a Jew as any man should be. But it is not such a marvelous thing to be a Bar David. The king had many sons, you know. Many women, many sons. And somewhere in my ancestry some obscure descendant took the name into Galilee. Galilean Davids! Can you imagine? *Bar* Davids! Not respectable Judean *Ben* Davids. There are probably *Bar* Davids all over Galilee, but they had sense enough to leave the kingly reference to our Judean cousins. What royalty could ever arise from Galilee, after all? It is a sick man with a sick mind who insists that his connection with a king long dead be clung to in this province. As for me, I see no honor in it. I am Judah Bar David only because my family insists on it. I should be Judah Bar Helez, after my father, as any proper Galilean would maintain."

Rahab listened carefully but was still perplexed. "I know little about such matters, Judah. It only seems to me that to be a son of David is a very great thing. Why, the street preachers may also lack originality, but they quote your ancestor all the time. And it seems to me that you must be closer to Jehovah than most men because of your lineage."

At this, Judah's eyes flashed even more mockingly, and his head shook with laughter. "Closer to Jehovah!" he cried. "Oh, my lady! Of all women, you have led the sheltered life!"

A blush rose to Rahab's face and she studied the floor tiles without a word. At last, her lover quieted and drew her close again.

"Enough of this, now," he said, pulling her head gently to his shoulder, and surveying the twilight sky. "Enough of times past and menservants. Enough of street preachers and wilderness prophets. Feel the beat of my heart close to yours, my breath upon your cheek. Let the night be ours, and yourself be mine, while we still have the night and each other."

CHAPTER THREE

Why it should happen again this night, of all nights—when it had not happened for a year—that would seem the cruelest of mysteries. To be tormented and lie helpless against the onslaught of her demon oppressors *in the presence of her lover*—that would be too cruel! The fact that her cries did not stir the sleeping one beside her, that the screams which filled the chamber did not bring a single soul to her aid, would be a mystery as well. But not the most important.

For now, however, mystery and justice were less the issue than the fiery pain in her groin, and the blood that stained the sheet.

She need not have counted them. There were seven, she knew, but they seemed a legion. And their hands were scaly, their breath a sulfurous stench.

Tonight she did not strike out against them. She struggled briefly, but despair paralyzed her—their luminous eyes and ravenous grins struck her dumb. Her very physical form was being invaded—not only by the defilement of rape—but by the entities themselves, who would not stop at ravaging it, but wished to possess it, to enter it!

With the final convulsion which sent her writhing across the bed, across Judah, and onto the floor, her lover awoke.

The scene terrified him. He had witnessed something similar on their last night together. But as he quickly surveyed the bed and the extent of his lady's agony, he knew this night was worse than the other—that the "dementia" had escalated.

And then something in Rahab's twisted form, in the terror of her eyes, and the silent scream which seemed to have stuck in her throat—all this proposed to him that more than dementia wrenched his lady's soul.

Leaning down from the bed, he reached desperately for her hand, hoping to pull her to himself and away from her torment. But the instant her coal-hot eyes discerned his gesture, a sound—guttural, unearthly—arose from the core of her. He had caravaned through wilderness places, where wild dogs shouted and mountain cats cried, but this was unlike anything he had ever heard.

Terrorized, he drew back and leaped from the couch, grasping his cloak and throwing it quickly about his shoulders.

He began to inch his way toward the door, fearing to turn his back to the creature who swayed now upon her knees, reaching for him and wailing.

She opened her mouth. "Judah!" But dread and awe flooded him. The voice was not Rahab's.

"Lord Jehovah!" he cried. "Away with you!" But she crept toward him, using her hands and crawling.

Just as the young man found the exit, however, the pitiful creature slumped forward, as though her very breath had gone, and she fell, limp, to the floor.

Judah stopped and stared at her, bewildered and fearful. He did not move through the door nor back into the room, but stood rigid, afraid to do either.

And then his name was called again: "Judah. . . ."

This time it was Rahab's voice, weak and frail, beseeching him to help her.

He studied her carefully, as one might study a stunned viper, wondering if it would at any moment rise up and strike.

"Judah," she called again, lifting herself on one elbow and reaching for him like an alms-seeker.

He surveyed her sweat-covered body, her blood-soaked tunic, and his stomach wrenched. Fighting nausea, he turned his head away.

"Oh, Judah!" she pleaded. "You are a Bar David! A son of David! Help me!"

At this, a kaleidoscope of emotions ran through him. He had never felt so helpless. Shaking his head violently, he turned and flew down the stairs, a cry of revulsion coursing up from his inner man.

"Judah!" the girl repeated. "Son of David, save me!"

She lay silent for a moment, wondering if he might return, hoping against hope that he would.

When she heard footsteps on the stairs, her anguished heart raced.

"Judah?" she inquired, raising herself a little from the floor. But the sandaled feet were not those of her beloved, and when she peered above, she grew faint.

"Ezra—no . . . ," she whispered.

The innkeeper's eyes flashed ominously and he brandished a leather whip in one hand. Unleashing his anger, he overturned tables and chairs, flinging her little cedar chest to the floor. And then he wheeled on her.

"Between you and Rachel I shall lose every customer I've ever had!" he bellowed. "This insanity shall cease, though I must drive it from you!"

The cruel strap came crashing down, biting into Rahab's ravaged flesh, and the dark night grew darker still.

CHAPTER FOUR

To ply her trade on a Magdalene street corner after hours—or upon any street corner at any hour whatever—was a new thing for Rahab. But such was her occupation tonight.

She had left the inn with her sisters of the chamber, and had at first clung close to them, afraid to step out on her own. But as they had, one by one, strolled down the street or gone off with customers, Rahab had found herself standing alone, with only the amber glow of street torches for security.

She folded her arms across her midriff and grasped her elbows. Her skin was gooseflesh, though the night was warm.

Had she been more conspicuous, she would have been the first harlot approached this evening. Since the group had dispersed, however, some time had elapsed since a man had passed down the walk.

And in the solitude she reflected upon the past days.

Ezra, in an atypical move at restitution, had allowed Rahab to recuperate from her bout with "dementia," and from the infliction of his harsh temper. But the respite had been short-lived. Still the most beautiful of the innkeeper's ladies, she had found her zest for the paint pots and coiffure lacking of late. The competitiveness which had gained her a favored slot had been hard to muster since the night Judah had run away. And so, with her "recovery" had come a new life style. Just this morning she had been informed that, while she would continue receiving men in her pavilion, she would also be relegated to the street with the other solicitors.

Her heart ached at the thought of Judah. Such a monstrosity she must have seemed to him. She would never forget his pale, fear-filled face, the revulsion in his expression.

As she stood here tonight, remembering Judah's eyes, it occurred to her that not so long ago she had waited in this very place for her lover's train. And the memory of another young man's eyes returned like a haunting goad. Time could not obliterate that stranger's penetrating gaze, the way he seemed to read her soul. No matter what had transpired since that afternoon, the recollection remained vivid. And though she did not think of it often, when the image returned, it captivated her.

She pondered who he was—what power he had to strip her heart. And she wondered if she would ever see him again.

A strange thrill went through her at the thought. What would she say if he ever spoke to her—if he . . . ?

But as quickly as the fantasy suggested itself, it was pushed aside, for somehow she could not envision him engaging her services.

She had not been alone for long, before she heard footsteps down the way. Assuming it to be a potential client, she smoothed her dress with a nervous hand. She did not like this manner of working. The shadows and sounds of the night street had always frightened her.

Always? When? What had the night sounds of Magdala meant to her buried self, that they should suggest such terror?

Instantly, the memory that tried to emerge was forced back into its cage. The little glimmer of revelation was quickly absorbed into the quicksand of her subconscious.

But now, the sound of feet. She must ready herself to lure any oncomer. Until this moment, her customers had been handpicked by Ezra. They had been moneyed men of the world—not among the riff-raff who used the services of the inn. And Ezra had seen to it that she was treated well by those he sent.

Now she was on her own. Anyone might be coming her way.

Though she tried to imagine who it might be, she never would have expected a boy. The footsteps were much too firm, too self-possessed. But boy he was. And Rahab grew apprehensive as she watched his approach, for just as he saw her, he stopped. Eying her for a moment, he cast a glance over his shoulder and gave a shrill whistle.

Instantly a horde of youths rounded the distant corner behind him, running eagerly to see what he had found. None of them was any older than the first, who looked to be about twelve years of age. And several of the dozen or so lads appeared to be even younger.

"What have you found, Josiah?" one surly little fellow inquired.

"It is my father's day lady," the leader replied, his eyes wide, as though he had stumbled upon some coveted prize for which he could take the credit.

"Ezra's day lady?" another queried. "What would she be doing on the street at night?"

By this time, the boys had congregated behind Josiah in a huddle, their unscrubbed faces awe-filled and their boyish mouths agape.

As for Rahab, she recalled hearing that the inn-keeper had a son. The boy had been born to Ezra's wife after he had divorced her for burning his supper one evening. The poor woman had been returned to her aging parents in shame, and after carrying the child to term without any support from her husband, she had died giving birth. The elderly grandparents, incapable of caring for the boy, had shunted him from guardian to guardian, until at last, helpless to cope with his incorrigible nature, they had sent him back to Ezra. The authorities, encumbered by complaints from citizens regarding his antisocial behavior, had insisted that Ezra maintain him. So from the time he had been about eight years old, he had hung around the inn—an embarrassing obstacle to his father—while he acquired the most carnal of educations on the Magdalene coast.

Rahab knew that his gang of rowdies, notorious for vandalism and cruelty, heartless as mountain bandits, could have no good in mind. They were the same ones who had thrown pebbles at the women's chamber the day of Rachel's death.

"Father sent her to the street because she is. . . ." At this Josiah raised a finger to his temple and rolled his eyes.

"Lunatic?" a comrade interpreted. "She is lunatic?"

"Right, Machem. She has strange spells," Josiah explained, jerking his arms and body spasmodically, his face contorting into grotesque caricatures.

The gang laughed uproariously, several mimicking Josiah's pantomime. But Machem, who seemed to be the deputy of the bunch, stepped forward a little and studied Rahab with caution.

"She is beautiful," he insisted, shaking his head. "How could such a beautiful creature be lunatic?"

"Lunacy is no respecter of persons!" Josiah laughed, slapping his companion on the back. "Does it not add to her mystery?"

At this Machem chuckled nervously and drew away, eying the harlot warily.

"Ah, come on fellows!" Josiah challenged. "The lady came out here for company. Let's not disappoint her."

And suddenly the boys were charging toward

the lonely woman who stood vulnerable in the torchlight.

Rahab wanted to run, but her feet were lead, her throat constricted. A dewy sweat covered her face and the palms of her hands. Some awful stirring rose up from her buried being. She knew she had felt this fear before—the fear of being accosted on a Magdalene street. That long-ago time, she had fled valiantly—but tonight her demoralized body was helpless to move.

As the boys drew near they encircled her, as wolves would surround a stunned gazelle.

"Where are your men tonight, lady?" Josiah demanded. "Have you frightened them away with crazy talk?"

"Ha!" Machem spurred the torment. "Perhaps you scratched them with your claws."

"No . . . ," Rahab answered.

"We are young, but we understand a great deal!" Josiah laughed. "We understand that if my father were not so kind, you would be starving on this street."

"Or," cried another, "you would be dead!" And with this, he hurled a small pebble at her, like a member of a stoning committee.

Instantly, a fever gripped the gang and several were picking up small stones, throwing them at the terrified woman.

"Stop!" Josiah commanded, seeing the game was being carried too far. "Do you want Ezra to have our necks?"

A few more pebbles were flung, but quickly the

mania ceased, and the boys looked sheepishly at their leader. "She may be mad," Josiah growled, "but she is still my father's finest lady. Leave her alone!"

Subdued, the small crowd studied first their victim, and then Josiah. Parting a little, they began to disperse, until Ezra's son and Rahab stood alone upon the street.

"You have been much trouble for my father," the boy snarled.

Rahab surveyed his hardened features silently. Somehow, despite her own fear, she was aware of the dirt-smudged cheeks, the unkempt tunic of this street rover, and fresh hatred for Ezra twisted her stomach.

For a moment her eyes locked compassionately on Josiah's. "Your father—" she whispered. "Do you love him?"

The lad could not discern the intent of the question, and Rahab was not sure why she had asked it; but with its voicing, something of a kinship was born. Tears glinted along the rims of Josiah's eyes, but were just as quickly blinked away. Bending down with a quiet moan, he grasped a handful of pebbles and dashed them at her skirt. Then, without looking back, he tore for the darkness of the alleys.

Rahab stood silent for a long while, watching the vacant place where the gang had surrounded her. The reality of her condition, the fear that some awful destiny awaited her, had never impressed itself so pointedly as it did just now.

She looked at her gravel-stained gown, at the little welts which the pebbles had raised upon her arms, and she remembered Rachel.

"O God!" she cried out, tears spilling down her cheeks. "I am afraid!"

She took a few stumbling steps backward and then ran as fast as she could for the inn. Childlike, she was spurred by the sound of her own feet, by the hollow dimness of the street light, and by the fingers of the unseen which grasped at her flying skirt.

It was not until she was about to round the last corner that she was forced to slow her pace. The fine carriage of some aristocratic Magdalene was passing late toward home, and Rahab, not wishing to attract attention, tapered her run to a walk.

The carriage nearly filled the narrow lane. As it drew alongside, she was obliged to press against the closest building, and her proximity to the travelers put her in touch with their conversation.

"Now, see, here is an example," an austere voice was saying. "The soul who displeases Jehovah will be homeless and despairing. If your wilderness prophet would confine himself to preaching against the evil in our streets, it would be well!"

With the press of the vehicle, Rahab held her breath. She was exposed clearly to the riders, and it seemed the voice spoke of her. As she waited to move on, she could not help but see that the curtain was pulled back a little. The street light across the way showed up two figures in dark silhouette, and it appeared that an old man and a young woman were conversing.

"Yes, Father," the woman was saying, but her voice betrayed frustration.

"I only point to this poor creature as an example of Jehovah's grace," the man continued. "It is a wonder that any harlot lives a day in Israel!"

The words burned Rahab like a brand. But just as she thought the exposure had ended, that the carriage was on its way, the curtain was jerked further open.

"Father!" the female passenger called. "Tell the driver to stop! I know this girl!"

"Nonsense, Suzanna," the old man corrected. "You have never known a prostitute." And then, "Move on!" he ordered the driver.

"I know this girl!" Suzanna cried. "Mary! Is that you, Mary Bar Michael?"

At the sound of that name, a bolt of anguish ripped through Rahab's breast. As though she had been slapped across the jaw, her head spun backward and a cry of inhuman proportion tore from her throat.

What power the word had to terrorize her she did not comprehend, but neither would she think on it. Instantly she was fleeing toward the inn—the inn where Rahab had been born, and where Ezra fed her.

CHAPTER FIVE

The finger of revelation which had reached out to Rahab on the street had become a hand when the girl in the carriage spoke that foreign name. And the hand seemed even now to grasp Rahab by the ankle as she approached the inn.

She would wrench herself free of it. Her buried self would not be resurrected as long as she had the sanctuary of her pavilion.

But the pavilion was not to be her retreat tonight. When Rahab entered the hallway alone, Hannah met her with snapping eyes.

"So you bring no client," the matron snarled, oblivious to the girl's shaken state. "I told Ezra you would never succeed upon the street! I knew you did not have the constitution for it! He has kept you a hothouse plant all these years, and you cannot function outside your artificial garden!"

Grasping Rahab by the arm, she led her down

the corridor toward the women's chamber.

"Well, little flower," the madam growled, "we have always provided your clients before. I'm certain we have someone for you tonight. Wait here!" she commanded, thrusting her into the empty room.

Already the wild music and carousing of the main hall were in full swing. Rahab could smell the aroma of free-flowing wine as it mingled with the odor of many bodies jostling about the tables and dance floor. And she could easily envision the scene inside. Though she had never been obliged to work at night, she had occasionally watched the activities of the big hall as she passed the doorway while seeing some late client out to the street. She had always been relieved to retreat to her quiet rooftop—relieved that she need not traffic with the same crowd which her sisters entertained.

But tonight, Hannah had other plans for her.

Within minutes the matron had returned, leading a customer toward Rahab's dark station. The moment the girl laid eyes on her "man of the hour," she knew Hannah had purposely selected him as a punishment. Though he was a stranger, Rahab could discern enough about his character at first glance to send a shudder through her. He was a short, squat fellow with an immense belly and bloated face. Something resembling the bristles of a prickly pear claimed to be his beard, and set within this frame were yellowed teeth—what few remained to him. Bleary, besotted eyes and a blotched complexion told how he had spent the past few days, and only his foul breath competed with the odor of his body.

"This lovely lady will show you a fine time, Lemuel," Hannah assured him. And placing him in Rahab's charge, she glanced catlike at the girl. "There is an intimate little nook down the hall," the matron directed. "Do enjoy yourselves."

Rahab watched miserably as Hannah strode triumphantly back to the dining room. It was not until the grimy creature at her side had cleared his throat several times that she moved to fulfill her assignment.

"Yes," she whispered, the word catching in her throat.

A clammy sweat and a sick pallor crept over her as she led her companion to their little roost. The light was very dim at this remote end of the corridor, and Rahab fumbled with the latch upon the door.

"Here, little lady," the stranger offered, bending close. "Let me help."

With this, he reached for the lever, intentionally placing his flaccid hand directly on hers. She trembled, but controlled herself until she felt his oily lips and the stubble of his chin upon her bare shoulder.

"O Lord God . . . ," she groaned.

Suddenly she was pushing past him through the dark shadows and beyond the main hall. She had nearly reached the street door before she was stopped. Two strong arms encircled her, and she grew faint.

"Rahab, it is I," a warm voice reached her. "It is Isobel, little one. Are you all right?"

"Isobel?" she cried.

"The same," her friend assured her. "Where are you going?"

"Help me!" Rahab pleaded. "I cannot stay here another moment. I shall die if I do!"

Quickly a crowd gathered from the dining room. It seemed Lemuel had reported his prostitute's rude rejection, and Hannah had been sent for.

Too much happened at once for Rahab to comprehend it all. She saw the madam addressing the group, saw Lemuel's irate expression. "Dementia," "strange fits," "our apologies"—snatches and phrases were all she heard of the hasty exchange. But, slick as that, the clientele were appeased, and Rahab, Isobel, and Hannah were left alone.

The girl clung to her friend, her guardian, burying her head on that woman's sturdy shoulder. Yet through her own wracking sobs, she caught the one word she had always dreaded.

". . . dungeon . . . ," Hannah was saying.

The dark of night and the dark of Rahab's soul would join together there.

CHAPTER SIX

L evi, Ezra's manservant, rattled the key in the iron lock apprehensively. For two years it had been his duty to incarcerate the "devil-woman," as she was now called, and to release her when she was sane. Each time, he asked himself why the innkeeper retained such a miserable creature. While she still managed to attract clients, she was nothing like she once had been. Following every bout with "dementia," her youthful beauty was more hidden, her ability to refurbish herself more taxed.

Tonight, as Levi cast a hesitant torchlight into the dungeon cell, he found a being less like the lovely child-harlot than he had ever yet encountered. Years of dealing with the chamber women had hardened him, and he had developed a quick tongue, a ready wit. But now, as he peered cautiously across the dark room, his eyes falling upon the huddled mass of rags and hair called "Rahab," he was speechless. He remembered having kept the woman Rachel in this hell-hole—but at her worst, she had never frightened him.

No sound had been heard from the dungeon for three days. The "devil-woman"—who was known to spend equally long periods in raving mania, her seemingly inhuman stamina allowing her to throw herself madly about the hold, shrieking demoniacally—had been silent for thirty-six hours. No one knew whether she was alive or dead, but Ezra had waited this long before sending Levi so that Rahab could "contemplate" her situation.

The manservant set a tentative foot inside the cell and drew the torch across the room to light up the figure in the corner.

As he did so she raised her head, the tangled mahogany hair parting to reveal a distorted and haggard countenance. Dirt covered her cheeks, divided by little streaks where tears had eroded it, and her eyes were swollen nearly shut from crying. She shrunk back in pain as the light glared into her dark-accustomed vision, and a faint groan rose from her dry lips.

"She is alive, then," Levi whispered, his face awe-filled. But straightening his shoulders, he attempted indifference. "Well, you've been busier down here than any other lady of the inn," he laughed. "Seven clients all at once, and for nearly a week, eh?"

At this he bent down and fumbled for the ankle band that attached her to the wall by a long chain. Pulling from his cloak another key, he nervously inserted it into the latch and began to unshackle her. She watched him wearily, saying nothing. When he was done, she lifted her knee slowly, bringing her ankle close to her body and massaging it with a cold hand.

He studied her briefly, and though he fought it, a shudder went through him. A twitch worked at his mouth, and he stood up, wiping his hands on his robe and turning the key over and over between sweaty fingers. "Well," he repeated, "too bad for Ezra they weren't paying clients." He laughed again, but when his eyes met her hollow gaze his expression cleared and he looked toward the door.

"So . . . it's away with you now—back to Hannah and Isobel," he instructed.

Rahab turned lifeless eyes toward the exit, and raising herself, took his hand for support. Once to her feet, however, she preferred to stand unaided, and after a shaky moment, stepped toward the heavy gate.

"You are to go to the pavilion," he explained. "But take the back stairs. No client should see you like this."

It seemed a lifetime since the woman had set foot in the pleasure chamber that had been her special domain for four years. In reality, it had been only a few days since she had received a client here, but each time she emerged from one of her "spells," the world of her everyday existence seemed more foreign. Rahab, who had always sensed the loss of a previous identity, now found that even her own personality was slipping away as the seven invaders became increasingly dominant over her mind and body.

Today, as she entered the glistening room, she found she had to consciously direct her legs to walk, her body to go forward. She braced herself against the white-plastered walls and gazed upon the garden foliage absently.

She was relieved to find the pavilion unoccupied. Levi had said Hannah and Isobel awaited her, and she had not looked forward to the cruelty in the eyes of one or the pain and concern in the expression of the other.

"What a disappointment I must be to Isobel," she considered. "How worthless I am to anyone!" Rahab thought, as she spied the sofa where she and a hundred men had indulged their appetites.

Throughout the years she had steeled herself against any pangs of guilt for her profession. To acknowledge guilt might expose the truer self—the hidden person. And so the chin had been trained to lift itself, the hair to be tossed in wanton seduction, the hips and the thighs to beg a following.

But when she saw the sofa, the one emotion she could not completely resist was of the broken heart Judah's memory evoked. However, she also remembered Rachel, and she knew that if she allowed her heart to overcome her so soon after being released from the cell, she could as easily be abandoned to the street as that poor, unrequited lover had been. Judah's rejection would not catapult her into that trap—not Rahab.

Her look of determination, the haughty tilt of

the head, was almost comical, given her present appearance. But no one was here to observe her, so no one laughed.

Quietly she passed through the rooftop bower and approached her favorite viewpoint along the balustrade. She shielded her eyes from the blaring post-winter daylight that framed the garden's cooler shadows and peered below to the familiar avenue.

In the past she had been grateful she need not solicit upon the street corner. Ironic, she thought, that she now more often worked out there than in this pleasant penthouse.

She remembered her first night upon that pavement—how frightened and incompetent she had been. She recalled the menacing boys who had abused her, and she was certain the leader had often brought his friends as spectators when she was confined to the cell.

Of course, she could not remember that first night upon the street without reliving the strange incident of the carriage, and the young woman who had called her by an alien name. What had that name been? To this day, she could not recapture it. It had been buried with too much else in her hidden mind.

But none of that mattered now. Nothing really mattered, and nothing ever had, since Judah had been lost to her. She had found it necessary to survive, to cling to whatever sanity was left. She had used her rational hours to pursue her vocation, to study the ways of seduction, the fashion and cosmetics of desire.

And when the seven possessors would leave her to function, she functioned well.

Rahab lifted a hand to her haggard face and felt the dirt upon her tear-stained cheeks. No one on the street or elsewhere would think her beautiful at this moment. She must find strength to bathe and dress. But the very thought was overwhelming. She had not eaten for three days, and she leaned heavily against the low wall until her keepers should come to care for her.

As she watched the boisterous traffic of the marketplace, her eyes stopped where she had long ago awaited Judah's train. And with the memory returned the vision of the gentle stranger who had captured her whole being that afternoon.

As she watched the site, however, something else drew her attention. A group of people was forming on that corner. Shoppers wandered toward them in curiosity, listening to their excited conversation.

Rahab could not hear the words, but the audience showed a variety of responses, sharing the talk with confirming nods, outright joy, or scoffing laughter. A few of the Magdalene religious, designated by their robes and phylacteries, murmured together in disapproving anger. And still the crowd grew.

For a long while Rahab was caught up in the scene, wondering what it meant and how she could find out. But as she studied the gesticulations, the postures, she heard footsteps behind her.

"Get her cleaned up!" Hannah was ordering.

Isobel was left with the task, as Hannah cast scornful eyes upon the "devil-woman" and walked toward the stairs. "Food will be sent up," she called over her shoulder. "See that she eats it!"

Isobel studied Rahab sadly, saying little as she helped her undress, then poured a basin of warm water.

Rahab responded accordingly, and followed her friend's directions in meek silence.

But as the kind woman began to wash her tangled hair, Rahab could refrain no longer. Bent over the soapy water, she asked, "What is the stir in the marketplace, Isobel? Have you seen it?"

Her companion shrugged. "Something to do with that wilderness preacher, I guess. The inn is buzzing with it all. How much to believe, I cannot know."

"What do they say?" the young woman prodded.

"Something about a strange voice, and a shaft of light—one of his penitents being called the 'beloved son,' or some such thing, by some thundering voice from the sky. . . . How should I know? I never spent time on fantastic tales."

CHAPTER SEVEN

It was late afternoon, and Rahab was very weary. Several days had passed since she had been released from the dungeon cell, and she still had not recuperated from the ordeal. Because she was making a poor showing on the street, she had served fewer clients lately than ever, and Ezra was working her overtime to make up for the slack.

Just now she had done the unthinkable. She had fallen asleep at midday, alongside a snoring client on the pavilion couch. When she roused herself, she had been relieved that Hannah had not found her.

She stood stiffly beside the low lounge and drew the stranger's cloak over his naked body. How many times she had performed this service she could never count. As long as there was time between customers a man was allowed to sleep if he wished.

But for his paid lady to do the same was not permitted.

Rahab pulled on her own tunic and stepped to the dressing table. Her eyes lit on the little cedar box and she ran her fingers sadly over the long gash left by Ezra's tantrum the night he had beat her. The velvet-cushioned contents of the box had been spared his temper, being securely locked within. She raised the lid, looking fondly on the alabaster flask, which she had not used since the night Judah left.

Tipping the box back, she surveyed her face in the lace-framed mirror. The eyes were hollow, she noted, the skin too pasty. She exercised her facial muscles, but no color rose to her cheeks. The reflection was alien, and she shut the lid with a sigh.

Turning about, she leaned on the edge of the table and watched the client on the bed. He was a big man, nicely constructed, though a little too well fed. As he sprawled now, he filled nearly the whole divan, and she marveled that there had been room for them both.

His face twitched in his sleep. She wondered what he dreamed, and what was indicated by the slight, boyish smile at the corners of his mouth. She wondered also who he was and where he had come from—if his wife knew of his dallyings and whether she cared.

It occurred to Rahab that this man, like all who came and went, was as alien as the reflection in her mirror. He was no more to her than one incident within a history of such experiences. She would not remember him when he left, unless it would pay her to do so. And then she would have to remember him by some relative comparison to the others.

Yes, the client would pass quickly from mind once he left. Not so the dream that had just roused her from the forbidden slumber. It was the vision that had haunted her for years—of the woman and the two small children who reached out for help. Today, however, it had taken on another dimension. The children were calling her by name. But the name was foreign to her, and she shut her mind to it. She would not let it penetrate, and when she woke, it was powerless to touch her.

After some moments the man in the chamber stirred. He sat up lazily on the couch and looked about the room through sleepy eyes. When he spied Rahab, who had by now entered the garden, he called softly to her and held out his arms with a broad smile.

Rahab went to his side, also smiling, but shaking her head. "Enough for now," she said, her eyes feigning an excited twinkle. "Time for you to go, or your wife and babies will come looking for you." She reached over to coax him from the divan, but the little verbal jab, which usually worked like magic to hasten a man from the room, had only encouraged him. He gave a wicked chuckle and, instead of rising up, grasped her to him.

"You *are* a devil-woman!" he laughed, kissing her with hot lips. "You can't compare with my wife. Let her come looking!"

The years had taught Rahab skills in handling such cases. She did not struggle but, winking deceptively, stroked his shoulders, sliding her hand down his spine; and then, without warning, she dug her nails into the small of his back.

Suddenly the client was sitting up and preparing to leave. The gesture—was it purposeful injury or rough play? He could not be certain, and that was the beauty of it. It would urge him to comply, but would not destroy his goodwill. Client and agent had been served.

No more than a half hour later Rahab was on the street. She moved like an automaton through the press of the crowded boulevard, which seemed unusually busy today.

At seventeen years of age she could have passed for twenty-five. She was still very beautiful but, like Debra, she had been used beyond her years. And the spiritual torment of her oppressors had robbed her even further of youth's freshness.

Rahab was closed in on herself today. She could not seem to walk just right, to cast her eyes about in the manner that would catch another's glance. She reached a slight opening on the walkway and lifted her braceleted arm to lower her headcovering, a certain sign that she was "available." Though she had chosen a shady spot, knowing that the early-spring sunlight would show up the weary lines about her mouth and eyes, the heavy gold bands she must always wear upon her wrists collected heat against her skin. She fumbled with them, attempting to bring circulation to the perspiring flesh. She took a tiny flagon of perfume from her belt, touched the contents to her neck, and waited. As she did so, a heavyset woman and her young daughter passed close by and, upon seeing Rahab, the woman quickly escorted her child away, shielding the girl's eyes and muttering something to her with a shake of the head.

The incident hardly fazed Rahab, who had become used to such reactions over the years. All she cared about at this moment was the hope that some flesh-hungry male would take her back to the inn. Her feet were already weary with the pavement, and her heart was not in the marketplace.

As she stood there, knowing Ezra would expect her to call to the passersby—to mince about with the jangle of chains and tinkle of anklebells—she had energy only to caress her red-black hair and roll her eyes. The mouth could not even pretend a smile, but had formed itself into a permanent expression of hardness. For boredom had become the hallmark of her face, just as hollowness characterized her soul.

And as a shimmer of realization brought home the recognition of her state, she remembered the one time when her soul had been exposed—when the light of probing truth had once entered. She remembered the stranger with the penetrating eyes, and she shivered.

Her skin was gooseflesh and she stepped out of the shadow into the warming sunshine. Perhaps here, though the light was less flattering, her body would cast off the spiritual fear which the memory stirred. She lifted her face to the massaging glow and stood, eyes closed, amid the flow of pedestrians.

She might have stayed in this position indefinitely, drinking in the fire of noonday, had she not been jolted by the touch of someone's hand upon her arm.

Expecting a client, she opened her eyes and looked down into the face of a young woman.

"I cannot believe it!" the girl was saying. "I have found you again!"

Rahab drew back, surveying the unusual blue eyes and the wisp of golden hair that peeked from under the lady's veil. She could not recall seeing this woman before, but her heart raced strangely.

"Oh, don't you remember?" the girl cried, clutching Rahab's arm, her face radiant. "I am Suzanna—don't you know? You used to call me 'Lily.' You were my very best friend when we were small, and I have prayed for you all these years! Mary! Oh, Mary Bar Michael, you have returned to me!"

Rahab loosened the woman's grip and jerked herself free. "I do not know you!" she growled, looking anxiously about. "What do you want with me?"

"You must remember!" Suzanna insisted. "I know you are my Mary! I saw you on the street one night, two years ago. I knew you then and I know you now! Oh, Mary, whatever may have become of you, I know who you are!"

Rahab's knees grew weak, and the chill returned, despite the sun. "This name I do not know!" she cried. "You have nothing to do with someone like me! You are mistaken!" She withdrew, pushing through the crowd, her face flushed and tears rising.

But Suzanna called after her, "Will I prove it if I speak of the twins? Of Tamara and Tobias, and of your mother who died?"

At that reference, the haunting dream of the woman and children leaped to mind. A horror of rising consciousness swept through Rahab, and a subhuman groan pushed up from her throat.

"Leave me!" she howled, her eyes fiery, her hands clenched. "Leave me!" And she turned, hastening through the puzzled crowd to return to the inn.

In all her young life, Suzanna had never willfully disobeyed her father and mother. But this evening she would not return home from the marketplace in time for supper. Nor had she ever gone into the quarter of town that housed the brothels. But to-night she would venture there, unescorted, to find the one whom Jehovah had returned to her.

Suzanna was not a "brazen" woman. She would never have passed for a harlot. But the way she searched the avenues near the inn was a sight to behold. Despite her characteristic limp, she displayed boldness befitting a Roman trooper, questioning every stranger, every woman of the street who watched her from the doorways.

"The beauty with the long, dark hair—the woman in white with the scarlet veil—has she passed this way? Do you know her?" she queried. "I must find the Magdalene . . . the harlot with the beautiful hair!" she told anyone who would listen.

Some kind of providence kept her as she entered doorways no "decent" woman would venture through. Some protective guard seemed set about her, as men on the prowl stepped aside, eyes lowered, at her approach.

The sun was just dipping below the horizon when Suzanna found Rahab. The tall beauty was among a group of Ezra's ladies stationed at the entrance of the inn, where they solicited passersby. She did not notice Suzanna until, as the girl drew near, the scarlet gathering received her approach with suspicion and bewildered murmurs.

A rush of anxiety swept over Rahab, and hoping that Suzanna had not seen her, she slunk back through the doorway, hiding inside the darkened hall. But the pursuer had spied her immediately, and spoke now with Isobel on the street.

Rahab could not hear their conversation but saw Isobel shake her head and attempt to usher the girl away. When it appeared that Suzanna would not be dissuaded, and when Isobel's expression turned from one of concern for her welfare to anger at her persistence, Rahab at last stepped forward.

"There she is!" the pretty blonde declared, elevating herself on her good foot. "You say her name is 'Rahab'? I know her by another name, and whatever spell you have cast to make her forget friends and family shall one day be broken!"

At this, a small crowd began to gather on the street, and Rahab hastened to Isobel's side. "Please, let me deal with her," she pleaded. "I don't know this girl or what she wants. But she will apparently not be silenced until I see her."

Isobel's eyes were snapping, but she agreed. "All right. See what can be done," she sighed, fearing the onlookers. "Hannah will hear of this if the girl is not appeased, and then we will have more trouble."

Rahab escorted the young woman quickly from the door. As spectators watched the unlikely pair with curiosity, the two disappeared around an alley corner.

"I tell you, again—Suzanna, did you say? I do not know you!" Rahab asserted, holding firmly to her arm. "Whatever business you think you have here is wasted on me!"

The blue-eyed virgin faced the renowned harlot squarely, her chin raised at a bold angle. "I know your memory is gone, my friend," she acknowledged. "Your eyes show that you truly do not remember me. But," she searched Rahab's countenance, "are there never stirrings within you? Strange proddings that say you have lost something precious? That there is a great part of you concealed by the life you now live?"

Rahab grew flushed, and a tremor worked at her fingers. She released the girl and stood silent, staring at the ground. "I . . . I do not know what you mean," she stammered.

"But I think you do," Suzanna persisted. She studied Rahab for a long time, and then with a faraway look she stepped into the street, peering past the rooftops of the close-quartered buildings. "I am remembering our favorite place, my friend."

"Our 'place'?"

"We used to go there every chance we had . . . the watchtower of Magdala."

She waited a moment to see if the reference took hold. But Rahab was unmoved.

"Ha!" the harlot at last responded. "Our favorite place, then, is the 'eros tower,' the 'high tower of Baal.' Perhaps it is not I who have missed my calling, but you!"

Rahab meant offense, but Suzanna took none. "Yes, I have heard such labels used by the street preachers. But not everyone sees it that way. You and I, when we were small, felt close to Jehovah when we went to the tower. Those who built it considered it symbolic of God's protection."

"Protection, indeed!" Rahab scorned. "It has done little to keep Rome from our doors, or to assure morality in our streets. Sailors watch for it when they seek our port, as much for the pleasure it represents as for the safety of its harbor. Magdala, my dear, is owned by women like myself, and not by Jehovah!"

Suzanna's face grew warm and red, and tears appeared along her lashes. "So, you are determined to be lost to me," she whispered. "But Jehovah is moving in this city, as he is throughout Israel. I have been to see the prophet at the Jordan, the one they all speak of," she declared with fiery eyes. "I was there the day the thunder spoke, and the one he heralded is unlike any man who ever walked this land!"

Unprepared for this turn in the conversation, Rahab drew inward. "You have seen both the prophet and the. . . ."

". . . the 'Messiah'!" Suzanna asserted. "That is what he is—I am certain. Jehovah *is* moving," she repeated, studying the somber face before her, "and Magdala shall not be overlooked. *You* shall not be overlooked!" Suzanna's voice softened now, and her gaze locked on Rahab's. "For years I have prayed for you," she whispered, "and you shall be reclaimed . . . Mary."

At the sound of that name, all the emotion that played beneath the surface of Rahab's heart began to rise up. And in her practiced way she fought the revelation of her inner self. "What do you have to do with me?" she cried, her voice picking up volume. "I am Rahab, Ezra's Rahab!" she wailed. And now a peculiar light flashed in her eyes and her tone began strangely to alter. "Do you not know who I am? The 'devil-woman of Magdala'! They call me the devil-woman!"

An eerie sensation crept up Suzanna's spine, and she stepped back, scrutinizing the one before her carefully. "Devil-woman?" she faltered with the words.

"You have heard of me!"

"Yes. . . ."

"So, you'd be wise to flee!"

The voice was completely alien now, as were the eyes. And Suzanna reached for the alley wall as she hobbled away from the advancing creature.

Had Rahab been conscious of the young woman's reaction, she would have relived the scene of Judah's retreat—but for one thing: Suzanna, as she watched the contorted features of her lost friend, as she studied the writhing form of Satan's victim, was not without confidence.

"Very well, Rahab," she conceded. "I will go. The victory, for the moment, is yours. But it shall not always be so!"

Interlude

Little Caleb, who had brought the phallic device from his father's store of secret treasures in the grown-ups' bedroom at home, wished now that he had never been so daring. He regretted he had ever heard Josiah speak of the devil-woman and he wished he had not been so anxious to impress the gang of street boys.

His terrified flight from the alley where he had just seen the renowned dungeon creature did not slacken until he was blocks from the place. And when sufficiently distant from the horror to regain himself, he slumped against a lamp post and closed his eyes.

Where were the other boys, he wondered, and what would he tell his father when he returned with blood-streaked hands and singed garments? His heart pounded madly and his throat hurt from strained breathing. Would his father suspect him when the implement was found missing?

Such matters would grow in importance as he

neared home, but for now, the spectacle he had just witnessed and the close call with danger he had just survived filled his mind and twisted his nerves.

The boy stood up shakily and turned homeward with trepidation. But the memory of the crazed eyes, the snarling teeth behind the bars, and the yellowed claws which had ripped his flesh would remain an indelible impression of his childhood, long after father and gang had ceased to govern his life.

The Magdalene harlot, the one who had become famous throughout the Galilee coast for her rare beauty and demonic alter ego, sat slumped upon the cold stone pavement of Ezra's dungeon cell. She had been confined there for two months, but time was immaterial to her. She had spent more hours in her demented state all these weeks than in her "right" mind—the mind of "Rahab."

She studied the silver shaft of the phallic device which had been tossed into her chamber by the boys at the window. She had found it upon emerging from the hideous heart-pit of her demon oppressors—upon emerging into her Rahab consciousness. And it moved her strangely.

Something in the way it caught the moonlight that found a path through the window grate . . . brought a swimming series of hazy images across her psyche. The images, which rose from yet another part of her—that part which had existed before Rahab—were the most tangible reminders of a time past that had ever surfaced.

A pile of dung with a silver fish upon it—three young children kneeling before it. . . .

What did this picture signify?

Was it a memory?

She shook her head erratically and lifted her fingers to her temples. Instantly the vision was gone, but in its place came yet other phantoms: the gentle face of a motherly woman, the tower of Migdal, and the laughing blue eyes of a little blonde girl.

"No," the demon-harlot whispered, rocking to and fro. The visions must be driven back. They were coming too close, staying too long, appearing too clearly now.

She surveyed her cell once more and then studied her ravaged body and crabbed hands. One large tear slid down her cheek and onto the pavement as she raised herself, her joints aching in the dampness, and stood solitary, staring up at the small aperture that opened onto the street. For a long time she waited in silence, as if anticipating someone's arrival. Yet how she hoped they would not return to torment her again—those slippery little street urchins who took such pleasure in her misery!

Perhaps she would be able to withstand them now. Perhaps their return would not send her back into an altered state—her "dementia." But more likely it would—for even now, at the thought of their grinning, leering faces, at the memory of their tauntings, she felt the demons within begin to stir.

She wrapped her arms about her stomach and held on tightly. Sometimes it seemed she could feel the beings move about, feel their very arms and legs, feel them crawl up her throat with inching claws. And at such times, she knew, her eyes were theirs, her voice was theirs, and she had no control over her own self.

The best thing to do then was to move as little as possible—better yet, to seek out a quiet corner and sit stonelike for fear of aggravating their activity.

And so Rahab looked toward the darkest spot in the room—the far niche beyond the sewer—and she turned to go there, to sit out yet another night in hopeless loneliness.

Many times during the past months, it had appeared the demons wished to kill her. That was what Ezra, Hannah, and Levi had thought when they found her battered and bruised from being flung against the walls and about the cell. No personal power could have done such damage, they realized. She had been acted *upon*. She had not been the actor.

But Rahab knew the demons had no intention of killing her. Such an outcome would have been too merciful. No, they would not destroy their host. They would torment and cripple her, but they would not crack the shell that housed them.

And so, hers was a living death, and she sought the darkest corner in which to live, or to die.

No sooner had she sat down, however, than the dreaded fear descended. Footsteps could be heard coming down the alley, and she braced herself for the return of the adolescent hounds.

She had never made much note of their faces.

Except for Josiah, whom she had encountered on the street over three years before, she could not distinguish one boy from another. But the youngster who appeared at her window now was surely a newcomer. Perhaps it was her more composed state which sharpened her awareness, but she was certain she would have remembered this fellow's shining dark hair and perfect features. Her heart pounded for fear of his intentions, but even through her apprehension, she could see that he was not like the others who frequented this place.

The boy was silent as he scanned the dank cell. He carried a small torch, which he seemed hesitant to put through the bars. But when he at last did so, illuminating the hold, Rahab shielded her vision with a cry.

For a long moment nothing was said, until the lad addressed some unseen companion. His voice was dry as he whispered, "Oh, please, no . . . this cannot be the one!"

Rahab fully expected that he would be joined by the same gang who always came. But only one figure closed in beside him to peer through the high grate.

And at the sight of the new arrival, the devil-woman drew back further, if possible, against the stone wall and covered her eyes once more with shaking hands.

It was a young, fair-eyed woman who knelt with him, and as she identified Rahab, a tremor passed through her. She placed a comforting arm about the boy and nodded, "Yes, Tobias . . . I fear it is."

"But she is nothing like the Mary I remember.

Nothing like anything I have ever seen," he said brokenly.

"Oh, Toby," Suzanna choked back her own horror, "we knew what we would find would not be pleasant. We have heard stories of the 'devil-woman.' But we must remember that this is our Mary. I have seen her on the streets, and I know it is your sister."

The boy only continued to stare with frozen eyes into the ghastly vault.

"Come," Suzanna urged him. "I know your fears, but we must not think of ourselves now."

The youngster turned slowly to his companion and, drawing courage from her determination, placed his hands upon the window grate.

The creature within watched him apprehensively. He was a sturdy fellow, she could see, as he ably gripped the bars. He gave a tug and then said, "It's pretty solid, but the frame is a little loose. We'll have to use the rope."

Quickly Tobias drew a large hemp cord from his cloak, and the pair tied the ends about the side bars. Then the boy stood up. With Suzanna's help and a hefty pull, he began to dislodge the grate. One more jolt and the bars, frame and all, clattered to the alley floor.

The devil-woman gave a terrified howl and began jumping about the cell, swaying like an ape upon her haunches and growling up at the couple. Her keepers had long ago given up on chains and shackles. Her superhuman strength had grown each time she was confined, and she was capable of breaking any fetter.

Suzanna watched the sudden squall with trepidation; but at last, with the same forthrightness she had displayed in her trek through harlot-town, she leaned through the window and called to the creature.

"Enough, Rahab! Enough, whatever your name! We seek our friend and we have found her. You will not delay us in our business!"

Her boldness set the creature back a moment, and in that interlude of stunned silence, Tobias reached into his cloak, withdrawing a large ripe apple. They had heard tales of the reactions induced from the bedeviled soul at the sight of decent food, and they were counting on this manipulation to coax her out.

Tobias handed Suzanna the fruit and stood back. The pretty woman held it forward, turning its shiny skin in the torchlight. Rahab watched it ravenously, and began to move quietly toward the outstretched hand.

The couple were breathlessly silent as they retreated inch by inch from the oncoming creature. When Rahab drew within reach, Suzanna began to woo her with soft and gentle words, encouraging her to try climbing from the cell.

Tobias hesitated to offer Rahab any assistance. He knew that any sudden movement might send her into a fury once again.

But as the bedeviled woman reached up, hungering for the retreating apple, he was able to place a hand upon her arm and help her through the exit.

The stench of her rags and the vermin tangle of her hair were enough to repulse the strongest stomach. But as she came close enough that Tobias could scrutinize her features, a tenderness stirred within him. As long ago as it had been, young as he had been when she left, and distorted as her features now were, she was familiar to him. He knew this was his sister, the kind girl who had cared for him in his early years, and a lump formed in his throat.

He handed the ravenous being the wet, red apple, and Suzanna watched the one-sided but poignant reunion with hope amid sadness.

Between the creature's voracious bites into the fruit, Tobias slipped a looped end of the rope over her branded wrists. After an initial tug, he kept the cord slack so she could eat. And when the couple led the ravaged one down the alley, she barely seemed to notice, for the apple fulfilled its role, keeping her absorbed and silent on the trek through the sleeping town.

Only at night could a woman and a boy manage to escort such a creature through the streets of Magdala. And even with the darkness, they took care to follow the most vacated route.

Their destination was a small, well-lit house at the end of a narrow lane near the sea wall. Suzanna and Tobias moved as quickly as possible with their charge, who had by now finished the apple and was engrossed in yet another piece of fruit the boy had offered her. As they drew near the small abode, they heard the sound of several voices and could imagine that the place was well occupied.

As they approached the door, Suzanna stepped up to it cautiously. She had been severely chastised by her father for her disobedience the day she had pursued Rahab to the inn. Now, for him to find out, as he surely would, that she had slipped out this night to go after the devil-harlot once again, and to knock upon the door of a houseful of men, would bring a discipline more severe than anything she cared to imagine. She was not, and never had been, a willful daughter. Her recent escapades were based on one thing only—her concern for her old friend and the knowledge that if she did not act, the woman might never receive help.

And it seemed help might be available. Jesus of Nazareth was in Magdala—within this very house before whose door they stood. When Suzanna had heard he was staying here, she, like hundreds of others, had determined to seek him out. The fact that there was not a crowd stationed right now before the house, awaiting a glimpse of him, was due only to the protectiveness of his disciples. Jesus needed some privacy, they had told the throng that had dogged him all day. The people must go home for the night. The Master would be speaking upon the seashore tomorrow.

Suzanna would never forget the first time she saw Jesus. She had accompanied her father and mother to the Jordan site where John the Evangelist was baptizing. Simon, a member of Magdalene commission of Pharisees, had gone to evaluate the strange rumors of seditious activity on the part of the "holy man." What neither he nor anyone else had expected was that an unprecedented event would transpire that day. The much-discussed thunder and mysterious "voice" from the skies had seemed to designate one young man in the congregation the "Beloved Son" in whom the Speaker was "well-pleased." And then, as the stranger yet stood in the shallows, everyone watching in awe, a shaft of light and a form like a white dove had descended, settling directly upon him.

Suzanna had been close enough to catch a glimpse of his face, and the eyes, especially, impressed her. While he was above average in height, and while his strong shoulders and weathered complexion spoke of manly vigor, there seemed to be nothing else striking about him—except his penetrating gaze, which appeared to part the crowd as he left the scene. Unmistakable determination was written on his features as he made his way to the far side of Jordan and into the distant wilderness.

It had been well over a year since that day, and the excitement he was creating throughout Israel had grown beyond reporting. The man who now worked miracles of healing and seemed to have power over nature itself could not go anywhere without a crowd. Hundreds from throughout Palestine and adjoining countries perpetually thronged him, listened to him, and sought his touch.

Now that Suzanna stood before this house, knowing the very one she could not forget was quartered within, her hands were cold and her knees shaky.

But as she glanced back at her little friend Tobias, who stood wide-eyed and just as fearful, waiting with their charge—as she looked at the pathetic, hunched form in rags who was also once her friend—she knew she must not let reticence deter her. With a determined step she approached the door and rapped, at first lightly, and then more boldly.

It was not long before light from the entrance was flooding the street. And silhouetted in the doorway was a young servant girl.

"We seek Jesus of Nazareth," Suzanna said simply.

"There is no room," the girl replied, peering past her at the strange pair behind. When she caught a good glimpse of Rahab, her face grew pale and she shook her head quickly. "No room at all!" she insisted, and hastily shut the door.

Suzanna turned to Tobias, who shuffled nervously now. "My sister is done with the fruit," he whispered, holding firmly to the cord with which he led her. "She will not remain calm much longer!"

Suzanna nodded and knocked once more upon the door. This time when it was opened only a little light filtered out, for the man who stood there nearly filled the portal.

"What do you want?" he demanded, his voice suited well to his size. The dim light from Tobias' distant torch caught the stranger's face and Suzanna detected rugged features above a heavily bearded chin. The piercing eyes challenged her boldness.

"We seek Jesus of Nazareth," she repeated faintly.

The big fellow glanced into the street, and when he saw the poor creature they had brought with them, a slight twitch worked at his jaw.

He need not be told their mission. Such petitions were a daily occurrence in his life; but it was also his duty to protect the Master's privacy when the day drew to a close.

He opened his mouth to send them away, but before the words were spoken, the devil-woman began to stir strangely. Having become aware of her surroundings, she studied the large man uneasily and began to draw back, tugging against the rope.

Something in the sight of him seemed to fill her with terror, and a blood-chilling cry rose from her throat.

Instantly the murmur of conversation within the house ceased, and the entryway was crowded with men seeking an explanation of the eerie sound.

The big man stepped outside to see if he could bring matters under control. But as he came closer to Rahab, her terror intensified and Tobias could not restrain her. She was determined to break away, to flee the stranger, and the boy was flung about at the end of the rope like a useless anchor.

When the man reached out to help, Rahab ceased her retreat and took the offensive, lunging at the big fellow and snapping with her teeth.

Quickly some of the onlookers joined the first to see if they might assist him, but at the sight of them, six in all, the woman grew even more violent. Her voice was shrill. "Ezra!" she howled, designating the big man. "Leave me alone!" And then, turning on his six companions, she swayed before them like a monkey, hissing and defying them to come closer.

"My name is not Ezra," the man responded. "I am Simon, called 'Peter,' and these are my friends." Patiently he named each one: "James, John, Andrew, Philip, Nathanael, and Matthew."

"No friends!" she cried, terrorized. "My enemies! My masters! Ezra, go away!"

The men who had joined him watched, helpless, as Peter tried to reason with the woman. The closer they drew, the deeper her anguish—until her eyes fell on yet another figure—this one in the door of the house.

She relived all her nightmare in that instant, for this seemed the shadowy figure of her dreams, who always lurked just out of reach and never answered her cries for help.

"Papa!" she shrieked. "Save me! Don't you see? They are coming for me. Oh, Papa! They will hurt me! Won't you help?"

Peter was bending over her now, taking the rope from Tobias' hand. Though he made no move to harm her, to her mind he was the first to attack. The other six would soon be upon her, and her heart was racing with painful throbs.

But in that instant, the scenario changed. The shadowy figure in the doorway responded.

The woman ceased her raving and watched his approach incredulously. For a long moment she stood still, panting and shaking. A flicker of hope seemed to spark within the tormented eyes, and the creature reached out a tentative, childlike hand.

But then, just as quickly, her temperament altered. Suddenly she was howling, rearing back, and tugging against the rope with more strength than even Peter could manage.

The figure from the shadows motioned to the other six to assist the big fellow, and then he stepped close, eying the creature silently. All at once, a multiple-voice echoed from the maw of the ravaged being. "What have you to do with us, Jesus of Nazareth?"

"Come out of her, sons of perdition!" the Nazarene commanded.

Instantly, the woman was convulsive, slain to the ground and writhing in anguish. But the first throe was the most intense, and the following six spasms freed her.

The body lay still upon the street for some time. Suzanna, terrified of making a move, watched helplessly for a sign of life. The Nazarene too surveyed the quiet form, but no sign of helplessness showed in his bearing. At last he knelt down beside the figure, and placing a cool hand upon her forehead, spoke one word.

"Mary."

Now the eyelids fluttered, and presently the woman looked up into his face. She reached out a limp hand, and for the first time in more than nine years, a smile of peace touched her lips.

Somehow, she knew it was safe to be Mary Bar Michael with this Man.

PART IV
The Anointing

While the king sitteth at his table, my spikenard sendeth forth the smell thereof. . . . He brought me to the banqueting house, and his banner over me was love (Song of Solomon 1:12 and 2:4).

CHAPTER ONE

It was Suzanna's relationship with her father, Simon, that allowed Mary Bar Michael to be sitting in a warm chamber, bathed, clothed, and fed that night. It was not any great sympathy toward the "devil-woman," nor was it any conviction regarding the Nazarene that spurred the Pharisee to harbor her in his home. But he had, much to his daughter's surprise, been present at the house where the healing had occurred, and seeing Suzanna's earnestness, he could not in good conscience turn the woman away.

The involvement of his daughter with the recent healing had, however, prompted him to make yet another overture. It was now rumored in his household that he had invited Jesus to dinner the day after next, so that he and his fellow Pharisees might have an opportunity to learn of his doctrine.

So it was that while Mary sat resting upon a low

bed in Suzanna's room, even before dawn she could hear a bustle of activity among servants downstairs, as they already prepared for the event.

She had been left alone to sleep, but she could not. Her heart was full of too many things. She looked about the chamber, but she was not really seeing it. She was remembering the Nazarene, and she was discovering a sense of her own body—for it had not been her own since she was nine years old.

It seemed she was just emerging from some long night of gloom, just rising out of a dreadful sleep, in which the images were not clearly crystallized. She was left with that shudder of relief one experiences when finding that what torments him is a departing nightmare—incapable of harming him.

Dream and reality still blended, however, almost indistinguishable from one another—except that now light appeared to be the essence of life, whereas before, darkness had enveloped her.

Mary stood up from the bed and looked down at her feet. She could not remember ever feeling so tall—yet she knew she had been this tall for a long time. Her legs were weak from the ordeal of the dungeon and from the Master's purifying touch, but she made her way across the room toward a low stand on which Suzanna kept a brass hand mirror. She had seen it when she first entered the chamber, and it had caught her attention repeatedly since she sat there. It had seemed to beckon her, and she had avoided it, fearing to see herself— fearing that she would not know herself at all anymore. Her hand shook as she reached for the pearl handle and raised the dark glass before her.

As she had sensed, the eyes were childlike, wide and searching, but they peered from behind a face much older than it should be. She remembered being beautiful—and she was beautiful now, but her skin was too drawn. Dark circles beneath her eyes and creases at the corners of her mouth had distorted her before her time.

For a long moment she stared into the glass. She took it to the bed and sat down with it, peering into it all the while. It was easier to handle her disorientation while sitting down; yet even so, she found she must close her eyes against a slight dizziness tickling at her temples. The face in the mirror juxtaposed against the face in her mind challenged her equilibrium, and she raised her hand to her cheek, hoping touch would ground her in the present.

Still, images of a time past predominated. She saw herself a vibrant young girl running along the Galilee shore. She heard her own laughter and she felt the breeze in her windblown hair.

Looking once more into the mirror, she shuddered. Past and present were becoming more defined, and a tear ran down her cheek.

"Where have I been?" she whispered. "Jesus, the years have flown without me. I am healed, but the years have flown."

CHAPTER TWO

The demons were gone!

The sun broke brilliantly through the chamber window onto the freshly waking form of the young woman occupying the bed, and as it poured over her long-agonized body, it affirmed the miracle.

Yes, she was awkward with her new self; yes, the image in the mirror had confounded her, bringing with it the dawning and detestable reality of what life had been for her.

But—the demons were gone!

Mary did not want to move for fear of breaking the spell of this moment, for fear of dispelling the joy of her new condition. She had not worn it long enough to trust it, this new identity. She would just lie here a while, savoring it—the peace of it, the rest from struggle. And she hoped that avoiding too tight a grasp on it might mean she could keep it.

Her head resting on her pillow, she silently watched the branches of a white-blossomed storax outside Suzanna's window. With slight swaying motions the branches bent to the massage of a breeze off the beach, and something in their unquestioning cooperation brought a smile to her lips. They seemed nature's arms, flung open to the blessings of heaven, and they spoke of faith.

She thought of her own arms and the times they had been restrained by shackles and chains. Ezra had never allowed her to wear her golden bracelets in the dungeon cell. He feared she might destroy them in a fit of mania, and so her wrists were now bare. Curiosity drove her to lift them to the sunlight. As she did, her eyes glowed. Not only the demons, but the scars too were gone!

As she reveled in this additional confirmation of her healing, a knock was heard at the door and Suzanna poked her head into the chamber.

"Mary?" she called softly.

"I am awake."

The blonde angel stepped quietly up to the bed. She peered down at her through the sunlight and almost seemed a vision. "Is it well with you, Mary?" Suzanna inquired, her voice betraying the same tentativeness which Mary felt.

"It is well." She smiled, looking again at the branches outside the window. "I was thinking of the Nazarene."

Suzanna reverently followed Mary's gaze. "He will be here tomorrow evening," she announced. "He is coming to visit Father."

"Yes, I know," Mary said. "I overheard the servants last night."

Suzanna sat down beside her and took hold of her hand. "I do not know what you remember of me," she began carefully. "I hope that in time you will recall our years together and the joy of them."

Mary turned her face away as little wells of tears filled her eyes. "I have had moments of remembering," she whispered. "Even when I was not myself, the past would call to me. But . . ." her voice broke off and a lump formed in her throat.

"I think I know," the girl nodded.

The ravaged one only stared through the window, and Suzanna studied her quietly. Then, with a determined sigh, she summoned a smile to her own face. "Well," she laughed, "we must get you ready for the day. Do you wish me to prepare another bath?"

"That would please me . . . 'Lily,' " Mary replied.

Suzanna was struck by the reference, and her smile brightened. Without hesitation, she left the room and headed for the kitchen where a great kettle of hot water was always simmering.

Mary drew the covers back slowly and surveyed herself. Indeed she was whole. Although the emotional scars of her brutal past would not disappear immediately, her strength would be returning daily. The gift of wholeness was already hers, bestowed before she could even ask for it.

The instant she pulled her legs from beneath the covers, however, she remembered when she had first felt her body was not her own. She remembered how it was to be a nine-year-old, forced to discover in one wrenching night the internal chambers of her being. She remembered the rape by Ezra and his six hounds.

Reflexively she sought the womb of the bed. Unnameable terror swept over her, for the ugly reality that had threatened to seize her all these years—which had been pushed into the pit of her subconscious, time and again—had suddenly asserted itself and now laid hold upon her.

Buried in the blankets, she fought the images that flashed before her. With a pitiful cry, she clutched the pillow about her head like a helmet.

But Suzanna had heard and flew to the chamber, throwing herself across the weeping huddle, holding her close.

"Whatever it is, you must not be afraid, Mary! Let it come. It cannot harm you!"

Still the agony increased, and the huddle became a flailing dervish.

"It's all right, Mary! Scream and kick, if you must! Nothing can harm you ever again!"

The ruckus was heard by servants downstairs, and soon the chamber was filled with onlookers.

"She is possessed!" they insisted. "She is not whole, after all."

"No!" Suzanna asserted. "This is part of the healing. It must be this way!"

And now the daughter of Simon held her friend even closer.

"Remember, Mary! Remember the Nazarene, and let it come. For now nothing can harm you!"

The whirl of arms and legs gradually calmed, and the mahogany head appeared above the covers.

Tear streaks glistened on Mary's flushed cheeks and she clung to her rescuer like a little child.

"Think on the Nazarene!" Suzanna repeated.

The heaving sobs subsided into shudders of relief, and the fearful one glanced about the room in a daze.

"Leave us, now!" Suzanna commanded the servants. "She must be alone!"

As the people turned to go, Mary continued to cling to her friend. But behind her wild eyes, a hope prevailed.

"Nothing can harm you!" the gentle girl whispered. "What has been given you cannot be taken away."

Mary studied that confident face a long while and then, once more, drew the bedcovers back. She lowered her feet to the floor and took a deep sigh.

"Help me, Suzanna. I want to stand before him tomorrow."

CHAPTER THREE

This would be an unforgettable day for Mary, not only because of the Nazarene's anticipated visit, but because its few hours would hold a series of purging episodes similar to that which had marked the morning. None of them would be so violent or intense as the flashback to the brutal initiation by Ezra and his men. But each surfacing memory would demand something of Mary, emotionally and spiritually.

There seemed to be no pattern to the revelations of her past. They focused haphazardly on her life at the inn and on her growing-up years. Personalities and faces swam in and out of her memory, and any little thing might trigger a recollection: a passing servant who bore a resemblance to so-and-so; a familiar odor; a word or phrase. But with each remembrance, Mary was called upon to examine it, face it, and relegate it to its proper perspective in her mind.

It was as though a lid on the box of her history had been opened. Some memories leaped at her, some slithered forth, and others poked a tentative foot over the edge and quietly tiptoed out.

It was increasingly apparent that while her time at the inn had been characterized by loss of memory, her new life would not spare her even the worst of realizations. The seeming waste of her past would serve to enrich the soil of her seedling faith.

Indeed, as later on the Master would teach her, he would be the Gardener, the Husbandman of her soul. And he would use the cast-off years of her existence—the years the locust had eaten—to enhance her hardiness, to spur her growth and add to the fiber of her life.

But today she did not see this. Today was painful. The planting and the sprouting, the weeding and the digging were agonizing.

Often, therefore, as she wandered about Simon's home, or mused quietly to herself, she called to Suzanna—sometimes with tears, sometimes with a smile.

"Is it true that we did this?" she would ask. "Do you remember this neighbor or that? Can it be that such a thing happened? Hold me close, Suzanna!"

And her friend remembered with her—affirming, marveling that the realities had been endured.

But no one had been fully aware of the abuse Mary suffered, either as a child or a young woman. Suzanna suspected, with all the neighbors, that

Michael Bar Andreas was a neglectful father, but not until Mary disappeared had the suspicions been confirmed.

And then it had been too late. Magdalene society was so constructed as to allow a child to slip irredeemably through the cracks. The "touch not," "handle not" mentality of the "good people" had allowed such a tragedy.

It was inevitable that memories of Mary's father should be among the last to surface in her emerging consciousness. During her years at the inn, when her childhood threatened to reveal itself in dream or daytime vision, Michael Bar Andreas had always remained a shadowy figure. He stayed just out of reach, hidden around a corner, the greatest symbol of her hopelessness.

Even now, when she spoke with Suzanna, Papa was not mentioned. Her friend wondered how long it would be before he emerged from the pit of Mary's repressed self.

When he did, it was in response to the most natural stimulus.

That afternoon Mary sat in the courtyard reminiscing over images that tumbled forth with dazzling speed. Most appealing, for the moment, was the memory of the last trip she had made to the Tower of Migdal. Her eyes brightened and she eagerly clasped Suzanna's hand. "Soon, very soon, let's go again!"

Simon's daughter recalled having mentioned the lighthouse to the "devil-woman" in the Magdalene alley. "Eros tower," Rahab had called it. But Suzanna would not remind her of that remark.

And now Mary reflected quietly. "We did not go there alone that day, did we?"

The listener shook her head, anticipating what would come next, and wondering what its impact would be. "No, we were not alone. Two others went with us."

"The twins . . . ," Mary whispered.

Suzanna studied her carefully. Tears slowly washed over Mary's cheeks. "What became of them —my babies?" she inquired.

Her friend was about to reply, when suddenly the room became markedly absent of noise. The bustle of the servants ceased, and all eyes turned to the street door, where two youngsters, a boy and a girl, had just entered.

The girl, sun-cheeked and raven-haired, hung tentatively behind her robust, handsome brother. They both stood at the edge of the court, eying Mary, and wondering whether or not to approach. Suzanna gestured to her servants to get on with their work, and they, understanding the drama, obeyed reluctantly.

"There is your answer, Mary," she directed. "Your heart must tell you who they are."

Mary's eyes grew wide, and a smile worked at her full lips.

"Tamara . . . Tobias," she whispered, calling them to her.

"Yes," Suzanna nodded. "My parents took them in shortly after you . . . went away. My mother, who died five years ago, always worried about them— remember?"

Tobias took a step forward, then reached back for his sister, drawing her with him.

"This is our Mary," he explained to her softly. "Don't be afraid."

The girl's stare implied a whole range of emotions, and she held her brother's arm tightly.

Mary wanted to speak a soothing word, but it caught in her throat. All she could do was motion for them to come near.

When at last they were beside her, she reached for both at once. "Oh, my babies!" she cried, holding them close.

Despite their comparative youth, they understood the depth of her feeling and could sense her love, for they had never forgotten her in all these years. When she released them the twins had tears in their eyes and smiles on their lips.

Mary drew back now, and held them at arm's length, surveying their features and their stature. "So big you have grown!" she laughed. "Oh, there is so much to know about you!"

She stroked Tamara's silky hair, and then she focused on Tobias. "I know you helped me, little brother. It was a very brave thing you did, coming after me."

The boy studied her quietly, and then looked shyly at the floor.

"How you remind me . . . how you look like . . . Papa," Mary whispered.

Suzanna surveyed her expression hesitantly and Mary turned to her. "Papa!" she stammered. "Whatever became of Papa?"

CHAPTER FOUR

Mary stood alone at the rooftop balustrade of Simon's home, watching the sun set beyond the sea wall. A little breeze was working up from the evening shore, and she was glad for the light shawl Suzanna had provided.

It had always been one of her childhood joys, in visiting this house, that the roof afforded such a grand view of the beach and the lapping tide. She remembered those visits clearly now.

In fact, since this morning her memory had continued to clarify even more aspects of her past. In essence, her life had "flashed before her eyes," a phenomenon often reported by those facing imminent death. But in her case, it was new birth which had brought the lines of the tapestry into sharper definition.

She thought now of Papa, and the report Suzanna

had given of his last known whereabouts. It seemed that his deterioration had become more pronounced and rapid after he had sold his daughter to Ezra. Though he had apparently been receiving remuneration in foodstuffs, and perhaps even money, the neighbors knew he could not long maintain himself and the twins in his condition.

Some months after Mary's capture, Ezra evidently ceased to honor the "deal" struck with Michael, and so even that income was withdrawn. Eventually, seeing the neglected condition of the children, Suzanna's family had taken Tobias and Tamara as their own, threatening to go to the authorities if Michael did not comply. And hence, when he could no longer support even a corner of the house, Bar Andreas had abandoned it. He was said to be living outside the town walls in some kind of makeshift shelter, from which he ventured forth once a day to fish along the shore and scavenge whatever he could.

Mary surveyed the beach and wondered if he still dwelt there. Somehow a picture of him failed to form distinctly in her mind. When she had seen Tobias today, Papa's image had flashed before her, but something within her would not allow her to retain a permanent portrait.

Even now, as she scanned the shore, her eyes skimmed it gingerly, fearful of really lighting on him.

It was, of course, highly unlikely that along the evening beach any particular person would be spotted at a glance. This was the fisherman's hour. As the profession called for night work, sunset brought a bustle to the shore, while the sailors readied their boats and gear.

Mary watched the gathering activity and yet another thread wound its way into her mental tapestry. "Mama," she whispered.

The picture was hazy, blurred by sadness. She longed to recall, yet staved off the full impact of the memory, letting it dawn upon her slowly. She could see herself as a little girl, standing with her mother as they watched Papa set out to sea with the other sailors. And then, flashes of the dream of the woman and two children burned anew into her consciousness. She remembered her mother's death, and her heart ached desperately.

Surveying the sunset, she recalled how her gentle mama had spoken with her upon their shoreline walks, about the strength and vulnerability of men, about modest womanhood and the love of God. Suddenly, large tears rose to her eyes and spilled over her cheeks. She gripped the balustrade and trembled.

Looking down at her tall self, she lifted one hand to touch the long fall of dark, unveiled hair which draped her bosom. A blush reddened her face and her heart pounded. But once again, she studied the beach and the busy sailors, and suddenly she rebelled.

"Mama, you do not know men as I have known them!" she argued.

At that moment she could see her mother's face more clearly than any other remembered image. And the tears along her lashes grew hot and persistent.

She fingered the wide scarf about her shoulders and fought the exhorting voice.

At last, with a sigh, she raised the shawl over her head, covering her luxurious locks as she scrutinized the industrious men below. "For you, Mama," she whispered. "I do this only for you—and not for them."

CHAPTER FIVE

The morning was one of the most glorious of Mary's life. The purging hours of the day before had been a fuller's soap—lifting, exposing, and washing away filth and debris—so that the young woman would never again look upon herself or the world in quite the same way.

There was more healing to come—much more. The wounds had only been scraped and exposed to the open air. Time would be needed before the rawness subsided and the pain was gone.

But she was a recovering woman. And the sunlight of this morning touched her like stirrings along a sweet-sounding chord.

When she had passed through the courtyard last night after visiting the balustrade, no one had mentioned the fact that the shawl draped her hair, but everyone noticed. And only when she saw their surprise at her sudden modesty did it become apparent to Mary that the household had disapproved of her going about unveiled. As a harlot, she had grown so hardened to her impact upon the "righteous" that disapproval had ceased to affect her. The fact that she now experienced shame at their reaction seemed to be significant.

Why hadn't Suzanna said something about the family's expectations? she objected. The guest had been in no condition to think of such things on her own; but then, of course, it was not like Suzanna to be judgmental or directive.

And so, upon descending from the roof, Mary had only noted the spectators with her own quiet surprise and hastened to her room to avoid scrutiny.

Since dawn she had again lain upon her back gazing out Suzanna's window, and she thought on the vision of her mother and her own rebellion against her early exhortations. It was, she considered, not so much a rebellion against custom as against the catering to men's vulnerability. It was, in fact, a rebellion against men in general. A well-founded rebellion, she told herself, as there was very likely only one man on earth who could be trusted.

He was coming tonight, and while her loathing for his gender was mixed with ambivalence when she thought about him, she need not analyze that ambivalence just now.

She rose from bed and pulled on her outer garment. It was still early, but she wished to help prepare for this evening's visitor.

As she opened her door, Suzanna was moving

toward her down the gallery. "Mary, I was just coming to wake you," she explained. "A woman has come to call on you. She waits in the courtyard."

Mary could not imagine who would be seeking her at this house. All her acquaintances, male and female, were at the inn. And so it was with apprehension that she went to greet the visitor.

The woman sat upon a low stone bench facing the courtyard, her back to the gallery stairs. But Mary could tell by her dress and by the way the servants avoided her that she was a lady of "reputation."

Somehow, the caller had been worldly wise enough to cover her head, showing that she knew how to cross the line between the two Magdalene cultures. She was a harlot, though, unmistakably. Her shiny silken gown, decked with trinkets and bangles, its color a muted scarlet, would not let her pass as anything else.

But it was none of this which revealed her identity before Mary looked on her face. It was her build—robust, buxom, even from the back—which betrayed her. And it was the way she carried herself before the questioning glances of the household which told Mary her name.

"Isobel!" Mary cried.

Instantly, the friend of her misery stood and faced her. She paused a moment at the sight of Mary, wondering what she would find in her. But, past that, she flung her arms wide and the girl rushed for her ample embrace.

The servants, who still were not used to having

Mary in the house, were even more baffled that
another streetwalker had been admitted. Had
Suzanna not been nearby when Isobel knocked on
the door, and had Simon not been away, the caller
would not have gained entrance. But the Pharisee's
daughter had not hesitated to welcome "Rahab's
old friend," as she introduced herself.

The women's embrace was fervent and clinging,
but at last Isobel pulled back, brushing tears from
her mascara-decked eyes. "Child!" she exclaimed,
holding Mary at arms' length and surveying her up
and down. "You look wonderful!"

"How did you find me?" the girl laughed.

"Word gets around," Isobel replied, the old crafty
twinkle in her eye.

"Of course." Mary smiled, remembering her
friend's repeated contention that women of the
street always know more than any common gossip.
After all, she maintained, when a man's guard is
down he reveals more in an hour than a tattling
female in a fortnight. And where did men let their
guard down but with women who were paid to be
sympathetic listeners?

"But, who . . . ?"

"Ah . . . no," Isobel refused, shaking her head.

The "who" among the Magdalene upstanding that
had informed Isobel of Simon's houseguest would
never be revealed to Mary now. She knew that
Isobel must have heard the entire story of the
Nazarene and the miracle he had bestowed. But it
struck her strangely that she was no longer privy
to the doings of the inn. Her instant emotion was
one of sadness and alienation, that her confidante

Isobel would not let her in on a secret. However, the feeling was mixed with a sense of confirmation: indeed, she was entering a new life, and the old must fall away, completely.

But must that include former friendships? Would she lose them, too?

Suddenly she grasped Isobel again and sighed, "Friend, I am so glad you have come! It means a great deal to me." And then, releasing her, she offered, "Come upstairs to my quarters. We must visit."

At this, the servants, who had been occupying themselves with their tasks and pretending not to eavesdrop, were visibly troubled. But they said nothing, only watching incredulously as Mary led the harlot up the stairway to the gallery, the most private family area.

As Isobel followed, she took from the bench a small parcel which she had brought with her and now carried beneath her arm. Mary did not inquire as to the contents, assuming her friend would reveal it if she chose.

When they entered Suzanna's room, which was still given over to Mary, Isobel stopped just inside the door, as if afraid to go further.

"Come in," Mary urged, turning about in the center of the floor. But Isobel stood alone, looking quietly upon the chamber as though it were a chapel.

"Oh, Isobel," the girl offered softly, "I think I know how you feel. I felt the same when I first came here."

It was not the room itself that held Isobel back. There was nothing unusual in its modest furnishing. It was definitely feminine; but for style and comfort, it could never rival the chambers of the inn.

It was the spirit of the place, and not the form, that had struck both Mary and Isobel at first encounter. The chasm that separated their world from Suzanna's was somehow sensed upon entering the room. An impersonal observer might have pointed to the Jewish menorah in the corner, or the small scroll of Scriptures on the night table. "This is the cause of their hesitation," he would have deduced. But these were only part of the picture. The women's reluctance was due to something greater: a spirit of godly contentment and wholesomeness, which no amount of religious paraphernalia could evoke. One who knew Suzanna better would realize that the white-flowered branches rustling at her window and the spray of field flowers in a solitary table vase were more to the point. And he would know, instinctively, that her face in the brass hand mirror each morning was one of grace and peace.

But at Mary's urging, Isobel at last entered farther and sat with her upon the bed.

"Tell me," the girl prompted, "are things well with you . . . and the others?"

"They are well," Isobel replied, still feeling like an absurdity in this setting. She fumbled with a trinket on her scarlet chest and shuffled against the simple fringed carpet at her feet.

But finally, despite her awkwardness, she focused on Mary. "Little one, I have thought of nothing but your whereabouts and your welfare since I learned you had escaped the cell. When I next heard about this strange Nazarene and his . . . helping you—I—I had to find you." The words were flowing freely and color rose to her face. "Rahab, I can see that you are well. What will you do now? Will you return to us?"

At the sound of that name, which until two nights ago had been hers, Mary shuddered.

"I—I am not 'Rahab,' " she whispered.

Isobel leaned close. "What? Speak up, child."

"I am *not* Rahab," she repeated, remembering how she had defied Ezra with those words years ago.

Isobel scrutinized her carefully. "Of course, child. . . . Then you have learned your real name at last?"

"Yes—'Mary.' . . . I am Mary Bar Michael!" she announced, tears trembling at her lashes. "Oh, Isobel!" she exclaimed, in a sudden rush of relief. "I will never be 'Rahab' again. I have been set free and I know who I am!"

With this, the girl's eyes traveled to the window in a gaze which transported her beyond the walls. The visitor was silent, feeling a peculiar strain. She was genuinely happy for her protege, though she sensed that the dramatic change had put a distance between them, a gulf which said, "This one has been where you are, but she has moved on."

Isobel's face burned with the tumult of her own heart, and she cleared her throat anxiously. "I brought you something, dear," she said in a husky whisper. "I thought you could use it—might want it or ... need it ... somehow. I figured you might not return for it."

Mary was brought back to the immediate with those words, and she turned shining eyes to the parcel.

"Oh, dear friend. You needn't have brought me a gift."

"Not a gift, Rahab ... 'Mary.' It was already yours. I just thought you would miss it."

Suddenly the girl knew what it was. Tearing the wrapper off excitedly, she found the cedar treasure —the ointment box Isobel had given her years before.

Her throat grew tight with memories, as she touched it lovingly. "Ezra tried to destroy it once," she recalled, fingering the deep scratch along its side where he had left his brutal mark.

"Yes ... ," Isobel remembered.

Mary turned aching eyes to her friend, reliving her lover's abandonment that night. "Judah ... ," she whispered.

Isobel had not meant to bring unhappiness, and she apologized quickly.

"No, it's all right," the girl insisted. "Somehow, I had not thought of him since I'd been gone. Some-how. ..."

"I am sorry," Isobel pleaded.

Mary pondered the box another moment, and then carried it to the night table. "I shall treasure it always," she said, donning a bright face for her caller. "Thank you."

The sturdy harlot now stood to go. "I will see myself to the door," she explained.

"But . . . ," Mary stammered, holding out a beckoning hand. "You have only just arrived. When will we visit again?"

The woman tried to reply, but had no credible answer.

"Well," her hostess laughed nervously, "we will see each other often!"

Isobel managed an acceptable smile, and then exited as unexpectedly as she had come.

"You do not live so far away!" Mary called after her. But when she was left alone to absorb the experience, she knew the distance between them was great.

CHAPTER SIX

For a long time after Isobel left, Mary sat in the bedroom looking at the cedar box. It, more than any other material object, represented her past. And the very sight of it stirred in her a multitude of feelings.

She lifted the container once more and set it upon her lap, running her hands over its smooth golden surface and fingering the perfect parquetry of the lid. Automatically she reached for the latch and opened the box.

Inside were the familiar vials and jars containing precious ointments. Myrrh, cinnamon, aloes—all were here as they had been replenished innumerable times over the years. She thought of the countless male bodies she had soothed and wooed with these oils and jellies. The recollections were not all repugnant. Part of her considered her past with pleasure and fondness, and she wondered what that meant.

Most poignant of the memories were those of Judah. Even now her heart ached at the thought of him, and she wondered where he was, what he was doing—whom he was with.

Her fingers shaking, she lifted the little door that protected the alabaster flask. Yes, it was here—still beautiful, still her finest treasure.

She took it out and removed the ruby stopper. Her nostrils were filled with the sweet odor of the oil, and she returned the flask to its compartment quickly.

She felt just now that she would never think of her lover without pain, that this part of her past would forever go unhealed.

But lifting her eyes to the window where the sun was approaching its noon height, she remembered the Nazarene. The impression of his spirit seemed to promise hope for all things. And she wondered if his touch could extend even to the void Judah had left in her heart.

Suddenly, Mary was desperate to ready herself for the Master's visit. She lifted a hand to her face and then smoothed her hair. What must she look like right now? She had given little attention to her appearance since coming here. And the need to be as beautiful as possible gripped her like a fever.

Carefully Mary tipped the box back at an angle and looked at her reflection in the lid's brass mirror. Her lips were pale, her face white and shapeless! Where was her berrystain, her charcoal and her shadow? Her hands were a disaster, but here was the stain for her nails!

This was the first time she had thought of cosmetics since being with Suzanna. Nervously she pulled out the small drawer at the base of the box, and found, much to her delight, that they were all here—the paints, the brushes, the colored creams.

Her feminine heart thrilled as she fondled them one by one, and she set about the routine, her pulse pounding anxiously. "Oh, it will take hours!" she groaned, looking once more into the mirror. "He will be here this evening! I must begin this instant!"

She set the box upon the dressing table, taking out and lining up the appropriate contents before her until the vanity was fairly filled with them. Then she picked up Suzanna's hand mirror and surveyed her hair carefully. "It must be washed," she realized.

Leaving the cosmetics, she ran to the chamber door, where she hailed a passing servant. Forgetting her intentions to offer help in household preparations, she called out, "Water!" And then with more patience, "Please, if I might have some hot water. . . ."

CHAPTER SEVEN

S imon the Pharisee spared no expense in making his courtyard as festive as possible for the coming celebrity. One would have thought it was a holiday, so grand was the appearance of things.

Indeed, the host was known for his generosity, and the fact that he did not necessarily embrace the Nazarene's teachings, whatever they were, would not pinch his pocket when it came to providing a dinner party in his honor.

The most influential and highly reputed of the local citizens would be present tonight. Simon had ordered the servants to arrange the low tables and couches in a semicircle rather than in traditional facing rows, so that all eyes could be upon the honored guest, who would sit with him and a few key associates at the head of the room. He was preparing for the anticipated conversation, which would focus on the Rabbi's doctrine and teachings. For indeed this was the central purpose of tonight's affair, to give the community's religious leaders a chance to inquire of the Nazarene's theology.

Simon knew there would be many questions about the miracles that seemed to be an inevitable part of the man's ministry. Most recently, after the healing of the notorious "devil-woman," news had come from a nearby town that Jesus had actually raised a boy from the dead! It was reported that a certain widow of Nain had been taking her only son to be buried, when the Rabbi stopped the funeral procession, interrupted the mourners, and told the woman not to weep.

He had then approached the bier, upon which the corpse lay stiff and cold, and had spoken to the body: "Young man, I say to you, arise!"

Instantly, the boy had sat erect, had begun to speak, and was restored to his mother.

Because the widow was well known in the region, a tremendous crowd had been present at the funeral and there could be no question regarding the authenticity of the miracle. So great fear had taken hold of the populace, and the sensation was being touted as far away as Judea. Folks were now insisting that Jesus was "a great prophet," a "sign from God."

News carried well throughout Palestine, and therefore the miracles had always been well broadcast—from the first appearance of the Nazarene at the Jordan to his most recent achievements. But as to his teachings—they were harder to transmit.

That the Rabbi was a great preacher and master

of doctrinal discourse was undeniable. He had been creating a stir with his pronouncements since his spectacular demonstration of zeal in the Jerusalem Temple a year earlier. At the Passover, he had entered the Court of the Gentiles, and, using a whip, had driven out all the moneychangers and their wares. Rumor had it that he had claimed on that day to be the Son of God, saying, "Take these things out! Do not make my Father's house a marketplace!"

Of course, at that blasphemy the Jerusalem leaders had been greatly offended, and his reputation from that moment had been a perpetual consternation to the religious hierarchy. While John the Baptist continued to support the Nazarene, and an epidemic of Messianic mania was sweeping the land, Jesus repeatedly brought himself into conflict with the teachers of Judaism, claiming utterly fantastic things for himself: the ability to forgive sins, the right to reinterpret the Mosaic Laws, and even to wantonly violate them.

It was these matters which Simon and his friends would pursue tonight.

The Pharisee stood in his courtyard overseeing the servants' remaining projects and he glanced at the open sky above. It was, as usual, fair weather. The light of the retreating sun told him evening was not far away.

His pulse raced. Yes—the linen was brilliant white, the dishes and utensils gleaming. He saw that the couches were arrayed with colorful bolsters, and a fine carpet spread from the entryway to the head table. Great cisterns of wine stood conveniently near the dining area, and finger bowls of garnish and spice lined the tables. Every place had a goblet, every setting a napkin, and the odors of roast bullock and herbs, sauces, and cakes, poured from the back room where the cooking was done.

Tapestries lined the gallery rail, and ample baskets of fruit and flowers hung from the courtyard beams. Servants would soon be lighting numerous candles about the house and inner grounds, and the stringed instruments, which now lay silent upon the small corner stage, would be alive with sound after the minstrels arrived.

"Ah!" he sighed. It would be a fine night, and he would revel in the talk. As he scanned the place once more, his eyes stopped at the door to Suzanna's gallery room. The harlot was in there, he knew. Had he done right to let her stay here?

Well, surely there would be no problem. She would keep to herself, as would all the women of the house. And no one would question him, who as much as any man in Magdala was known for his love of Israel and devotion to the Law.

CHAPTER EIGHT

As the sun was setting and the sky growing dim, the court of Simon took on life. Guests arrived one after another, filling the patio with conversation and excitement.

To the unaccustomed eye they would have made a peculiar grouping. There was color here, to be sure. But the wealthy laymen, with their silken striped robes and turbans and ring-laden fingers, mixed oddly with the black-robed and austere Pharisees. As for these religious leaders, only their broad shawls with the wide borders and fringes added any zest to their costumes, and even these symbolized piety.

Regardless of vocation or dress, however, all present had a few things in common: they were devoted Jews, loyal to the nation and its theocratic system. They were curious to hear how the "prophet" of Nazareth related to Judaism, and they eagerly awaited his arrival.

Jesus would not draw special notice to himself by being either the first or the last to arrive. But when he did appear, followed by several of his disciples, all eyes were fixed on him, some guests standing on tiptoe or leaning around each other for a glimpse.

Nor did he presume as to which place had been set for him. But when Simon led him to the head table, he accepted graciously, untroubled that he and his followers, seated at the nearest table, were the least finely dressed of all present.

It was customary that dinner conversation be light and casual. If a host and his guests had business to discuss, it was best left until after the dishes had been cleared and everyone sampled sweets or partook of after-dinner wine.

But this was not a typical dinner party. While the guests wondered who would begin and how the questions would be raised, Jesus surprised them all by opening the discussion forthrightly.

Early in the meal, he set his cup aside and turned inquisitive eyes to his audience. "Who do men say that I am?" he asked.

Silence overtook the gathering. Had he posed the question to someone in particular? No, it appeared that the ripe morsel dangled for anyone who had courage to partake.

Jesus' disciples stirred uneasily, wondering what trouble the Master might be creating for himself with such a query.

But at last it was the host himself who replied. Clearing his throat, he boldly offered, "Why, good sir, there are many theories. Some say you are just a great teacher, or a mighty healer." The crowd seemed pleased with this response. "Some suppose you are a great prophet, even Elijah or Jeremiah reincarnated," he added, a mischievous twinkle in his eye. And at this a chuckle rippled through the court. But then Simon grew quiet and said, half-apologetically, "It is even rumored that you are the Messiah himself." With a shrug, he turned to his companions, and the laughter increased. As the Nazarene waited, however, a nervous undercurrent swelled through the hilarity, and the people wondered what he would reply.

Again he was to confound them. "But, you, Simon . . . you call me 'good sir,' and no one is good but God."

At first the host grinned politely, but when the Master studied him, soberness replaced his amusement, and a half-suspicious laugh rose to his lips. As he peered about at his friends they sympathized with his quandary and stared at the floor or smiled awkwardly.

Surely the Nazarene toyed with them. Surely he did not mean to imply that he was . . . God!

"We have heard of your reception in your own home village, Jesus!" someone challenged. "We hear that after you spoke there in the synagogue they chased you out of town. Apparently they do not consider you a prophet, much less divine."

The dinner guests approved this rebuttal and some applauded. But Simon sensed that the evening could too quickly become a sparring match.

"Nonetheless," he defended his star visitor, "we cannot deny the miracles. It is said that even the demons obey this man." At this Simon's eyes jerked nervously toward the gallery, and Mary's door. He had not intended to remind the crowd of his daughter's houseguest—*his* houseguest. So he quickly went on, hoping no mention would be made of her. "Now, my honored friends, if we let the Nazarene speak, our inquiries will be satisfied, I am sure."

"That is well enough, Simon," yet another chimed in. "Then I should like to question the Master directly on a matter of great concern to myself and all gathered here."

Simon deferred to this gentleman, a wealthy dye merchant who traded between Magdala and the coast. "Of course, Jonah," the host replied. "It is not often you are in town, and we are fortunate you could be here tonight."

"Very good," the merchant nodded, stretching his slight stature to full length upon the divan and rubbing his short, pointed beard. "Then, Rabbi Jesus, if you please, we have heard of your talk with the paralytic in Capernaum."

Everyone knew he referred to the case of the invalid lowered into a crowded house through the roof, whose friends could not find entrance at the door. Not only had the Master seen fit to heal him, but he had offered something much greater. "It is said," Jonah continued, "that before you restored the man, you told him his sins were forgiven!"

"Blasphemy!" someone muttered, accusing the

Nazarene of a capital offense, and many agreed, shaking their heads in outrage and indignation.

The merchant went on. "Now we know that no one can forgive sins but God alone. It would appear you press the issue at every turn. If you are not claiming to be God, who are you?"

But Jesus did not make a defense, neither admitting nor denying the crime. And the dinner party began to call up other matters, all related to the greater question.

A very regal-looking Pharisee, his height emphasized by his tall black headdress and even longer white beard, scrutinized the Master with a piercing gaze. "It is reported, Rabbi, that you bend and twist the laws of our father Moses to suit your own ends. You do work on the Sabbath, we hear, and then excuse it by some flimsy rationalization, saying that the Sabbath was made for man and not man for the Sabbath! Is this not utter blasphemy?"

"Yes," someone else added. "You were found healing on the Sabbath—which is a work—and you excused it as 'doing good' rather than 'evil.' But not only this, you did such a menial thing as picking grain on that holy day!"

"Indeed, Amos," a comrade confirmed. "And once again, Jesus, when challenged for these offenses, you alluded to some kind of personal divinity, saying, 'The Son of Man is Lord of the Sabbath!' "

Emotions were rising in Simon's courtyard, and the host feared loss of decorum at his well-planned event. He turned anxiously to his nearest servant and whispered something about more food. The man hurried off toward the kitchen and soon fresh plates of bread, cheese, and spiced fruits were circulating from hand to hand. Then Simon stood up, rubbing his chin and smiling nervously.

"Friends and brothers," he called, "you show, as always, that you are well informed on issues of concern to our laws and nation. But what we have presented today is mere hearsay." And turning to Jesus, Simon said, "Rabbi, your miracles are indeed great, and we cannot deny that you receive your power from a supernatural source; but we have not been privileged, as have some, to hear your teachings firsthand. When you have discoursed in our province, few of us have been able to sit at your feet for hours, as have many of the . . . common folk." The Pharisee referred as kindly as possible to the poor and itinerant who spent their time following the Master and hearing him speak. "Perhaps you could tell us now of your doctrine."

Jesus looked patiently at his host and nodded. "Indeed, Simon. What in particular interests you?"

"Well, Lord," Simon sighed, "this 'kingdom' you are so famous for preaching . . . what is it?"

Now the crowd chafed, for it was in reference to this topic that the Nazarene had made some of his most inflammatory remarks.

" 'Lord,' you say?" Jesus spoke compassionately. "Simon, not everyone who calls me, 'Lord,' shall enter my kingdom."

The host took a sharp breath and drew back. But Jesus went on:

"You take comfort in your piety, Simon," he said, "but in fact, unless a man's righteousness exceeds

that of the Pharisees, he shall never enter the kingdom of heaven."

Simon's face grew pale, and he said nothing for
a moment. When he did find courage to speak, he
could only stammer, "Rabbi, we are the lawkeepers
of Israel. How can any man be more righteous than
to keep the Law?"

"Such a man should *indeed* be righteous, Simon.
Do you know such a man? Do you keep the Law
perfectly?"

The Pharisee cringed. "Well, to the best of my
ability. . . ."

But even as he said this, his pulse raced, for he
and all gathered knew the Law allowed no failure.

"Of course, Master," another interjected, "no man
keeps the Law perfectly. But," he gave a nervous
laugh, "how else shall we please God, but to try?"

"He who does the work of my Father pleases
him," Jesus replied.

"Yes." Jonah heaved a frustrated sigh. "This is
what we are saying. The work of God is. . . ."

". . . to believe on him whom he has sent," the
teacher interrupted.

A hush fell over the crowd as they studied Jesus
in bewilderment. What was he saying? Did he refer
to himself? He had again called God his "Father."
Righteousness consisted in believing on the
Nazarene? Bodies squirmed uneasily, robes were
drawn about angry and uncertain shoulders.

And yet the Rabbi continued:

"Woe to you," he said, surveying each face, "when
men speak well of you. For men have praised false
prophets! Woe to you who are well fed, for you do

not feel your own emptiness, or to you who are well dressed, when it conceals the nakedness of your souls."

With this statement, Jesus' eyes traveled from the courtyard to the gallery rail, where Simon's houseguest now stood. As each visitor followed his gaze, the host was terrified. How long she had been there, no one knew. None had recognized her presence or knew when she had crept out of her room to view the Nazarene and hear him speak.

And now it seemed he referred to her when he said, "But happy is the one who recognizes his poverty. For his is the kingdom of heaven."

Mary gripped the railing with one hand, her heart speeding. In her other hand was the alabaster flask, and her knees were weak with anticipation. How she had dreamed of this moment! Just now, Jesus' words had melted her and charged her. Never had she felt such a burning in her soul . . . never, since the day she had first seen the Stranger on the Magdalene street.

And suddenly, as she looked on the one who had saved her life and renewed her spirit, she remembered. Yes! How could she have failed to recognize him? This was the same man who had exposed her heart that long-ago day!

On shaky feet she came forward, all eyes upon her.

Mary had spent a lifetime parading before the masculine gaze, but never had she been so self-conscious and never had any walk seemed so long.

She could feel disapproval ascend from the court floor as she approached the gallery stairs and made her way to the banquet hall. A low murmur filled the room. "What is she doing?" whispers asked. "Surely she doesn't mean to . . . ?" "A disgrace. . . ." "Will Simon allow . . . ?" But no one stretched forth a righteous hand to stop her. And certainly none of the men admitted to the appeal of her beauty, the inevitable attraction one glimpse of the woman aroused.

Instead, all watched incredulously as she came directly toward the Master.

Indeed, she found that if she kept her eyes on the Nazarene, the way was not so long, and the urgency to reach him replaced the dread of the taboo she was breaking.

She was very close now. Just a few more steps, around this couch, past this guest and that table, and she would be beside him.

His attention was hers, and her soul thrilled. Surely no man had ever moved her as he did.

As she drew behind the divan upon which he reclined, her heart rose to her throat, and her body tingled with anticipation of touch. She had knelt beside a hundred men. She had anointed a hundred men. For only one had she done so in love, and even that had not compared to this.

As she bowed to the floor, resting upon her heels, her heart was a mystery. What was this she felt as she lifted the flask and reached for the stopper with shaky fingers? If this was love, had she ever loved before?

She turned a wistful glance once more toward him and found him still gazing upon her. His eyes . . . there had never been such eyes. He was but a man, surely. Yet what was it he called forth in her?

She remembered having wondered long ago what it would be like to "offer" herself to him. But now, as then, such a proposition seemed more than unworthy. More than inadequate. Unthinkable.

Suddenly, she turned from his gaze and trembled. A well of tears broke within her and soon her vision was blurred. She reached for the edge of her garment and wiped her eyes. Her fingers grappled with the ruby stopper, and the flask nearly slipped from her hands.

But at last the odor of balm filled the niche between herself and the Nazarene, and Mary set about the task of love.

Once more tears distorted her vision, but she managed to pour a small amount of the precious ointment into the hollow of one hand.

Inevitably, memories of performing this service at the inn flooded her mind, and it suddenly seemed that the vial contained her past, her sins.

As she reached out to touch the Rabbi, she hesitated. It was all unclean, her offering. Dare she soothe him with such a gift?

She turned her glistening palm upward and studied the silky sheen. Fearfully, she looked at the Master, but there was no condemnation in his eyes. His expression seemed to urge her on.

She would not stop with the ointment. She would raise herself up and let her tears fall, as well, upon his feet. Quickly the hands did their business, loosing his sandals and spreading the penetrating oil over the arch and ball, the heel and toes of first one foot and then the other.

Her crying grew from quiet weeping to the release of throaty sobs. The room was filled with the sound, but she did not stifle it. Nor did she stop with this. What she had done for no other man in her life she would do for her Lord. Lowering her veil and reaching for the great fall of dark, fragrant hair that draped her shoulders and tumbled about her torso, she lifted a handful and began to wipe his feet, easing the balm into the road-hardened skin and weeping yet the more.

Her head was very close to him as she performed this service, and her cheek caressed the smooth flatness along the top of one foot. It seemed natural to kiss him, and she did. Her lips lingered over the veined flesh where his sandal had raised seams of calluses along the arch and where the straps had worn grooves into the creases of his toes.

Repeatedly she kissed him, first upon one foot and then the other, and her tears flowed unhindered until dark streaks from her mascara mixed with the massaging fluid.

She took note of this, but could not contain herself, though hours of painstaking artistry were being washed away. Blotting her cheeks with her hem, she found to her dismay that the linen garment was soiled with rouge and ochre. And when she felt a gentle touch upon her shoulder, she turned sad eyes toward the Nazarene.

With a look of acceptance, he reached out a hand to stroke her flushed cheek, and with his thumb he smudged away the residue which salty tears and paints had left upon her face.

The crowd, which had observed the entire episode with surprised silence until now, murmured disdainfully. And Simon, who sat directly beside the Master, watching with great agitation, bristled at the Nazarene's familiar gesture and squirmed uneasily. He was willing to concede that likely the Rabbi did not recognize this glamorous creature as the ravaged demoniac he had healed just days before; but he thought, how could he possibly be a prophet? A prophet would have known who and what this female was who touched him. Indeed, it would take no spiritual depth to determine from her dress and behavior that she was a fallen woman!

Suddenly, however, Jesus addressed the host, as if reading his mind.

"Simon," he declared, leaning forward, "I have something to say to you."

"Rabbi, speak."

"A certain money-lender had two debtors. One owed five hundred denarii and the other fifty. And as neither could pay, he kindly forgave them both. Now," Jesus asked, studying the Pharisee carefully, "which, would you say, will love him more?"

Simon thought a moment, then shrugged his shoulders, looking uncomfortably at his companions. "Why . . . I suppose the one who was forgiven more."

"You have judged rightly," the Teacher assured him; and then he drew back, waiting for the moral to take hold.

When Simon only eyed the Master and then Mary with a perplexed stare, Jesus continued. "Do you see this woman? I came into your home. You gave no water for my feet. But she, with her tears, has washed my feet and with her very hair has wiped them. You gave me no kiss of welcome; but she, from the time I came in, has not ceased kissing my feet."

Mary, who had been looking on Simon, her accuser, turned wonderingly now to Jesus. Since he had come in, she had done this? In reality, yes; for her heart had planned and dreamed of the opportunity, and though she had interrupted the feast to perform the task, it had been in her heart for days.

But the Nazarene was not finished. Still addressing the Pharisee, he continued: "You did not even do the customary thing and anoint my head with oil, but she has taken that which is very precious and rare and has anointed my *feet* with ointment."

Then Jesus gazed again upon Mary, announcing to the host, "Therefore I say to you, her sins, though many, have been forgiven, for she loved much." And studying Simon once more, he concluded, "But he to whom little is forgiven loves but little."

Simon had no reply. He only turned shamed eyes toward his lap and contemplated the message.

Yet Jesus was still not finished. Bending forth, he reached for Mary, who pondered the words incredulously, and drew her close. His ruddy face was soft with feeling and his blue eyes filled her soul. "Your sins have been forgiven," he repeated.

A flood of release welled up in her and once again the tears came. But this time they were of joy as well as gratitude, and she did not hold them back.

The murmur in the court was unrestrained now. "Who is this, who even forgives sins?" The men muttered, shaking their heads, some in mocking laughter and some in fear.

But the Master's gaze and Mary's heart were locked upon each other, and the rumble of the crowd was irrelevant. Bending down, Jesus lifted her up. "Your faith has saved you," he said. "Go in peace."

PART V
The Love
of a Woman

I will rise now, and go about the city
in the streets, and in the broad ways
I will seek him whom my soul loveth . . .
(Song of Solomon 3:2).

CHAPTER ONE

The wind off the Sea of Galilee was cool tonight. Not since Mary had walked along the beach each evening with her mother, as they watched Papa set out on his nightly fishing ventures, had she been exposed to the invigorating sound of lapping waves and the feel of nature's pulse.

She was seated in a circle of firelit faces, huddled beside a low-flaming pile of crackling driftwood. She privately surveyed the small congregation and moved a little closer to the only person she knew.

Suzanna's golden hair, where it peeked from beneath her veil, caught the amber light in a glistening sheen—and Mary noticed the frequent glances of male eyes in her friend's direction. Despite their admiring, however, it was plain from the strained silence that the men were unused to the growing company of women trailing after their Lord. Like children at a festival, they kept to one side of the gathering and the women to the other, perhaps wishing to intermingle but feeling bashful about it.

Much more than shyness, though, contributed to this delineation. Jewish culture had instilled this segregation into its people; synagogues kept the women behind a wall, as did councils and governments.

And then there was the protective pride of these particular men toward their calling and mission. If it had been difficult for the Galileans to admit the tax collector, Matthew, into their select fraternity, it was even more unthinkable to consider women of equal stature.

And so the rugged fishermen, Peter, James, and John, the schoolmaster Philip, and his companion Nathanael, as well as the other seven of Jesus' men chose to separate themselves from the matter. It was just another of the Rabbi's enigmatic statements, they reasoned. And though it would raise the eyebrows of onlookers, stirring yet more controversy regarding his ministry, the Master had never discouraged a female disciple.

It was inevitable that Mary should leave Simon's house to go with Jesus.

The night of the feast, when he had departed with his men, she had quickly run to the gallery room and put some of the clothes Suzanna had given her along with a few essentials into a bag. She had then slipped quietly out and pursued him at a distance. Not knowing if he would have her, she was nonetheless drawn like iron to a magnet, and crept through the familiar Magdalene shadows on a new life errand as clean as the old had been defiled. Should he turn her away, she was determined never to be far from him. She had given no thought to survival without sustenance and shelter, for the Nazarene was her sole focus.

When the Lord and his disciples had camped outside town that first night, she had stayed in the low bushes close by; she would continue behind them, she decided, to go wherever they might head, when morning came.

But Jesus had seen her. Before early dawn he had risen, and when all his men were still sleeping he had approached her. Bending over, he had touched her hand and wakened her. "See, Mary. There are other women with us," he said, pointing to the little gathering of females who even now collected firewood for the morning meal. "Do not be afraid. Follow me."

With this he had turned back toward camp and began rousing his men. "Friends," he called while Mary was yet approaching, "we have another disciple." He directed their attention her way, and through the foggy predawn light they strained to see who she was.

"Another woman," someone grumbled, and then the big man who had first answered Suzanna's summons, the night Mary was healed, sat up with a start. "It is the harlot who was at the Pharisee's house last evening!"

"She is your sister, Peter," Jesus had replied. And the husky sailor had said no more.

But Peter's sensibilities would not be silenced for long. When the sunlight found yet one more female coming down the beach, he growled some curse beneath his breath.

The same sight that dismayed him, however, filled Mary with joy. "Suzanna!" she cried, leaping up from the group and running to meet her friend. But she had suddenly stopped short, staring in amazement at Suzanna's gait. The gold-haired beauty was not hobbling. Her characteristic limp had disappeared, and she walked with grace and ease.

"Mary!" she responded, running now like a child who had been confined for years. "Do you see? Look at me! I too am healed!"

When Suzanna drew near, the two women embraced, laughing and crying. "But how . . . ?" Mary stammered.

"I observed the feast from a corner of the gallery all evening," Suzanna explained. "Jesus never indicated that he knew I was there, but when dinner was ended and he rose to go, I followed him to the door. It was then that I realized I was walking properly! He had neither touched nor spoken to me —but I was healed!"

Mary looked at the Nazarene who sat now some distance away. "Is there nothing too difficult for him?" she marveled.

"Nothing, I am certain!" laughed Suzanna. "I once heard of the Master's healing a dying boy who was in Capernaum. Jesus was in *Cana* at the time!"

Mary's eyes grew wide, and she studied the Rabbi. "Time and space as well as sickness and demons bow to him," she whispered. But now she recovered herself and focused on her friend.

"Suzanna, are you joining us? What does your father say?"

"We talked all night, Papa and I," she replied, her blue eyes reflecting zeal and excitement. "How could he question the Master again, seeing that I was healed? He said he would not withhold me from my heart's desire and would have come with me himself, were he younger. Oh, Mary," she said, breathless, "I know his heart has been touched, as surely as my leg has been restored!"

Mary embraced her again and asked, "If you were on the gallery, then you know what Jesus said to me?"

"Of course. I lacked the courage to step forth as you did, but I heard everything. And now, like you, I must follow him!"

The two young women clasped hands in a manner reminiscent of childhood and laughed jubilantly. "Come, my Lily!" Mary insisted, tugging on her arm. "You must meet the others."

With daybreak, a great crowd from the city had begun to collect on the beach where Jesus had stayed. And so the interlude of quiet which he had enjoyed since leaving Simon's house was replaced with the pressing demands of his public.

The crowd had not dwindled, but had increased, as Jesus had toured the province. And as Mary observed the faces about the campfire this evening, she saw weariness imprinted on each one. The Master especially showed fatigue as he sat staring silently into the flames, his shoulders stooped from the day's travel and the requirements of his ministry.

How she longed to understand everything about him! Upon his brow were signs of premature age, and her heart ached to soothe him with her touch.

"Jesus, who are you?" she wondered. "What thoughts are yours tonight? I wish I knew just how to love you. But I fear to tell you so, for I do not know who you are."

CHAPTER TWO

Mary was in love with Jesus. While the nature of this love was unlike any emotion she had before experienced, she no longer questioned it.

She did not know what to do with it, nor how long it would last. She had loved but two other men in her life: Papa and Judah. One had betrayed her and the other deserted her. Jesus alone had been able to save her. And she lived now to serve him in any way she could, for as long as he would have her.

Jesus was currently on an extended tour. City by city, village by village, he was going through Galilee and Decapolis, across the sea.

Some of the women who followed with the disciples were wealthy, and continually provided food, material goods, and comforts for the itinerant Rabbi and his men. One of them, a certain Joanna, was actually the wife of Herod's steward. When she had been cured of severe chronic seizures, she left all to follow the Nazarene. Her purse had often serviced the company with fine meals when they entered well-stocked towns. Salome was another, the wife of wealthy Capernaum fishing magnate, Zebedee, and the mother of two disciples, James and John. Because she was a wonderful seamstress, she often provided fine fabrics and needlework for her Lord and his companions.

There were others, less well moneyed, who nonetheless possessed talents and abilities which contributed to the group's welfare. Maria, wife of Clopas of Nazareth, was said to be the sister of Jesus' own mother. Because her children were grown and she was a dowered widow, she was able to follow after her nephew, whom she had always believed to be a very special child. And it was said that she frequently sent news home to her sister regarding Jesus' activities.

In time, Mary began to get a picture of the Nazarene's family. It seemed that his mother, also called Mary, the wife of Joseph, was another widow. But she, being the younger of the two sisters, still had children at home, so could not follow after the Lord. And while she was a believer, her other sons and daughters were skeptical of their elder brother's claims, even calling him "mad" and "lunatic."

Mary the Magdalene often contemplated that situation. How it must have pained the mother's heart to see her firstborn rejected by his own kin! How sad that she must stay behind while other women were able to forsake home ties to follow the Master.

And many women there were. On this tour at least ten were in the ranks, and while the number varied as they came and went along the way, there were never fewer; of these all had a story to tell, of healing and restoration. Some had been rescued from physical maladies, some from emotional and spiritual wounds. And all had something to offer in return.

But what of Mary? What had she to give? She certainly had no money and she had never developed a talent beyond her profession at the inn and her adeptness with cosmetics. She remembered being a good housekeeper when she was with her mother, and she did enjoy tidying up and organizing the camps.

But she wished to do more.

The cool evenings of autumn were replaced by hot days this season, and this afternoon the sun was especially persistent. No cloud from the sea had risen to cover it since early morning. As Mary gathered up utensils from the midday meal, she glimpsed the Master catching what rest he could beneath a roadside palm. Since leaving Magdala, the Lord had been traveling toward Capernaum, and all the way a great crowd had dogged his steps. When the Rabbi rested, the throng rested; and when he rose to move on, they did likewise. Mary could see from the Master's weary expression that the demands of his career were brutal. The heat had raised a glistening sweat upon his face, though he sat in a swaying patch of shade. And as he glanced toward the people waiting along the shore, he took a deep sigh.

Mary's heart ached for him, and she longed to do something to bring him comfort. Among the "essentials" she had brought from Simon's house was the alabaster flask, which in her haste she had thrust into the bag with her other belongings. Dare she use it once more?

Secretly she found her satchel and rummaged until she felt the cool surface of the bottle. Drawing it out, she set it on the ground and then dug deeper, seeking the hand mirror and the modicum of cosmetics she had thought to bring. Quickly she ran a comb through her hair and did what she could to add color to her face. How she wished her cedar chest were here! But as it was, she was more painted than any of the other women in the company, and she knew she must settle for restraint.

Picking up the ointment vial, she left her satchel and tiptoed up beside the Master. "Sir, you are weary," she said. "See here I have balm for your brow. Let me anoint you." Her voice was shaky, and she trembled as she knelt next to him. She feared to see his expression, not knowing whether he would accept or reject her. And so, without waiting for a reply, she held out the vial, poured a small amount onto her fingertips, and drew close behind him.

With small circular motions, she eased the fluid into his temples and across the span of his forehead. He did not resist her, but allowed her to work the ointment through his hair, down onto his neck and then into his shoulder muscles. As she did this, the tension of recent days seemed to ease out of him, and he let his head droop forward, resting his chin upon his updrawn knees.

While Mary ministered in this way, she found herself longing to reveal to the Rabbi her heart. Yes, to speak a woman's love. And then she wondered what would happen if he returned that love, if he said he loved her, too.

Suddenly her pulse throbbed unevenly. Her hand slipped on his shoulder and her breath was shallow. In that instant she knew she could not live with such knowledge. It would overwhelm and terrify her.

But she did not long dwell on this, for someone was speaking. Looking about, she found several disciples observing her activity with dubious eyes. Some of the women whispered among themselves, and men shook their heads. Suzanna looked on without judgment, but a blush rose to Mary's cheeks. She fumbled for her veil, which she had let slip from her head, and drew it over her hair, staring at the ground. It had not occurred to her that her act of love would meet with disapproval. Once again, she had failed to consider the bounds of propriety her world had taken on, and she feared she had disgraced her Master.

"This was a waste of valuable ointment," came an objecting voice. Mary identified the speaker as Judas, who had always been most intolerant of her. His black eyes snapped and he demanded, "What is in the container?"

"Spikenard," she replied weakly.

"Ha! Just as I thought!" he growled. "Such ointment could have been sold for a great deal of money!"

Judas was the business manager of the group. He was in charge of the company's funds, limited though they were. And he had a keen eye for value and profit. But while the onlookers disapproved of Mary, they were not so certain this line of attack was appropriate. Judas sensed this as soon as he had spoken, and quickly added, "What I mean is that the ointment could have been sold and the money given to the poor!" He drew their attention to the masses along the shore. "There are many hungry people following us!"

Mary studied the little flask and felt even more miserable. Was it indeed improper to lavish such a small thing on the Nazarene? If so, she had been doubly wrong in reaching out to him. Tears threatened and she summoned all her strength to force them back.

But now the Lord was speaking and her soul rose up. "Judas, the poor are always with us. I will not be here forever." And then, drawing Mary to him, he said, "What the woman has done she has done because her heart is right."

CHAPTER THREE

The Master was eager to reach Capernaum. Because of his frequent stops upon this tour to speak with the throngs and reach out his healing hands, the company often took several days to go a half-day's journey.

But this morning the small white city could be detected shining beneath the autumn sun about two miles distant. On a rise sat the famed synagogue, built with the help of a wealthy Roman centurion who had fallen in love with his assigned province and its culture. The Master's feet picked up pace as he saw it. In a while he would be resting beside Peter's hearth, a favorite refuge in the fishermen's quarter of Bethsaida.

Mary had learned a little about the disciples' attachment for Capernaum. John and James had grown up in the wealthy district, and their mother, Salome, was a well-loved woman here. Her generosity, more than her status as a leading Pharisee's wife, had earned the respect of rich and poor alike. And then there was Philip, the schoolmaster, who had often been criticized for encouraging studies beyond Jewish literature. The Greek classics were well known to him and he had been the first to introduce Capernaum's young scholars to the wide world of thought.

But perhaps Matthew was the most affected by the sight of the city gates, as the company passed through. For he had spent several years seated here at the customs bench, collecting Roman taxes from his fellow Jews. Even now it was difficult for him to be greeted by former companions and fellow employees at the post. Mary noticed the awkward shuffle of his feet and the nervous smile he flashed on them.

It occurred to her what a peculiar grouping the Master's followers must seem to those looking on. All types were represented: here was the wealthy son of a Pharisee, there a burly fisherman; here was a brilliant scholar, there an elderly widow; here a shrewd businessman, there a beloved seamstress. And at the far extreme were the social outcasts: Matthew, a publican, and Mary Magdalene, a former harlot demoniac.

No wonder heads shook as the company entered town. No wonder lips curled in whispers and sneers. And no wonder Jesus would one day warn his enemies: "Verily, I say to you, the tax collectors and the prostitutes are going before you into the kingdom of God."

Word of his approach had preceded Jesus to Capernaum, and the long-deserved rest he had hoped to find at Peter's house would be shortlived. In fact, when they reached the door a crowd had already begun to assemble about the building. Deborah, Peter's pretty, red-haired wife, greeted the disciples and ushered them into the vestibule. Her eyes were wide with urgency and she rubbed her hands together in nervous anxiety.

"Lord," she whispered, looking behind her into the court, "we have visitors. Men from the council in Jerusalem. They have come to question you."

The Master peered into the yard, and then turned patiently to Deborah. "Thank you," he answered.

"But, sir," she said, holding onto his sleeve, "they are saying terrible things!"

"What things?" he asked, stepping back to hear her.

"Why, they say you have a demon! That you cast out demons by the prince of demons! By Beelzebub!" The woman trembled at her own words.

By the prince of demons! The accusation pierced Mary's heart. No! The Master had restored her to sanity! How could such a thing be done by Satan! But the very thought terrified her. The gift of life was too nearly in its infancy to take on such a challenge—and especially by leaders of Judaism.

"Tell me it is not so!" she longed to cry. "Assure me such a thing cannot be!"

The anxious Deborah could not have known what effect the news would have on Mary. She had never met the newcomer, and so was unaware of her personal history. And now Peter's wife was speaking again. "Before you go in, Master, I must tell you one more thing," she breathed out heavily. "Your kinfolk from Nazareth will be coming today. They have heard of these accusations and are coming to take you home!" It was only at this news that Jesus became troubled. But he showed it in his eyes alone, and placing a comforting hand on Deborah's shoulder, he took a deep sigh. "All will be well," he said, and then turning to the court, he went in.

Mary, like Deborah, feared for her Lord, but her mind was set on how he would answer his accusers. Not only was his welfare tied up in the incident, but her own hung precariously on the response he would give.

"How can he be so cool?" she wondered as he entered the arena, drawing off his cloak and sitting before the disapproving gaze of his enemies. "My heart pounds like a hammer," she thought, "and he walks into this like a teacher into a schoolroom."

But now he was speaking and her ears strained to catch each syllable.

"How can Satan cast out Satan?" he inquired. "If a kingdom be divided against itself, that kingdom cannot stand. And if a house be divided against itself, that house is unable to stand. So," he deduced, "if Satan has risen up against himself and been divided, he cannot stand, but comes to an end. No one can go into a strong man's house and plunder his things, unless he first binds the strong man, and then can he plunder his house."

Once again, the Master's wisdom sent healing to

Mary's soul. Of course, he was right! How could they all have been so blind? Satan cast out Satan? The notion was illogical—ludicrous! She must learn to rest in the certainty of her deliverance.

But while she savored her great relief, Jesus waited to see if the visitors would debate with him. They, however, were speechless. So he went on:

"Verily, I say to you, all the sins of the sons of men can have forgiveness, and whatever blasphemies they may have blasphemed, and everyone who shall speak a word against the Son of Man, it will be forgiven him. But he who blasphemes against the Holy Spirit will not be forgiven forever, but is guilty of an eternal sin."

The Pharisees had made a long journey for nothing, except to be left sitting here, faces whitened not only by defeat, but now by fear. Was he saying they were damned for all time? That their insistence that he performed miracles by an evil spirit would bar them from eternal life? They stared stonelike, each with his own thoughts, as Jesus called Deborah to let the people in.

Mary's head spun. It seemed the Master's ministry was always like this. To leap from one moment of confrontation to another hour of crowd-pleasing with hardly a second of reprieve! But how else could it be? For the world was full of sickness, she was learning. Sickness of body, soul, and mind. The well did not need a physician, Jesus had often said, but the sick. And all were sick: harlots, paralytics, and Pharisees alike.

The crowd was immense. By the time the court, the gallery, and the side rooms were filled, no one could even eat. Deborah's task, then, as hostess, would be simple—though she must have feared for her home. Mary sat on the court floor with the other disciples, nearest Jesus, and gazed above at the crowded mezzanine. So this had been the scene when the palsied man was lowered through Peter's roof on a pallet, to be healed and forgiven by the Lord. The beating the roof had taken was still clear. The husband of the house had not been back since that day to repair the tiles and mortar torn up for that purpose. Mary looked across the room at Deborah, who had seen her scrutinize the place, and when the fisherman's wife shrugged with a sigh, both women laughed in feminine empathy.

As the day wore on and the sun pounded into the court, Jesus announced that he would be lunching by the sea. The crowd, relieved to hear this, began to gather their things while he told them one more parable. But as he spoke, a buzz traveled from the entryway, and Maria, who had picked up the message, turned wide eyes to Jesus. "Son," she caught the Lord's attention, "they say your mother and brothers are standing outside seeking to speak to you."

Mary turned about, thinking to catch a glimpse of them, and Jesus looked over the heads of the seated crowd. He knew his family could not make it through the press, but seemed to hope they would hear him when he responded, "Who is my mother, and who are my brothers?" Then studying those who sat about him, he stretched out his hand toward his closest followers, "Behold my mother and my brothers!" He declared, "My mother and my brothers are these, who are hearing the Word of God and doing it. For whoever does the will of my Father who is in heaven, he is my brother," he said, looking at Philip, "and sister," studying Suzanna, "and mother," he added, looking at Joanna.

The house was as quiet as a synagogue at that moment, and Mary's heart was filled with wonder. But she considered, "Am I only your sister, as well? Can I ever be more than that to you, my Lord? Or is it a sin to desire more?"

CHAPTER FOUR

During Jesus' stay at Capernaum, the weather had turned from the bright, sunny days of autumn to the more temperamental ones of approaching winter. After the incident with the Pharisees, Jesus had proceeded to spend time teaching by the sea, and the same day had set sail with his fishermen friends across the Galilee waters.

That evening he had performed one of his greatest miracles, it was reported. When a seasonal storm had arisen, threatening the crew with destruction, the Master had shown he possessed power not only over sickness and Satan, but over nature itself. Rebuking the winds and raging water, he had brought peace to the sea and sky, stilling the storming elements with his word.

Mary sat beside the hearth this afternoon musing on that tale and upon the other happenings which had transpired since they arrived here. Jesus had been called across town today, and so Peter's house was quiet and the women of the company were resting. Mary's mind, however, was too full to allow repose.

A recent incident, central to her own history, concerned a demoniac of Gadara, across the sea. The tormented being had spent years among the tombs in the hills above his city. It was said that his cries, provoked by a multitude of possessing spirits, could be heard for miles as he ran naked through the mountains, cutting himself with stones. Mary and Suzanna could remember stories of him from childhood, brought by sailors who had been to his region. It was said no one could pass near his area for fear of him. "My name is Legion, for we are many!" he had cried out when Jesus approached. But now he was telling the good news of God's power to all Decapolis, for a life of hideous travail was ended and he was freed by the Master's touch.

Thinking on this, Mary relived her own miracle of healing and her heart stirred afresh with love for her Lord. She glanced about the quiet chamber, the indoor living quarters of Peter's home. All around the room women rested on pallets. The intrusion of daylight, limited by an overcast sky, was further prohibited by reed blinds on narrow court windows. The only other illumination came from the flickering glow of the hearth fire. As she studied the scene, she remembered her first encounter with the women's chamber at the inn. How far removed was this situation from that, she thought. How different were these ladies from those! "And how *I* have changed," she marveled.

Across the room today was a newcomer. Jesus' mother, at her sister's urging, had decided to stay in Capernaum a few days before returning to Nazareth. Her sons had given up hope of convincing Jesus to forsake his ministry—his "madness," as they called it. And at their mother's insistence they had gone home without her. She would join them shortly, she had promised, and she now slept quietly in a corner of the parlor.

Mary studied the woman's peaceful countenance and wondered if she, too, believed Jesus was mad. Somehow, from the look of her, she could not imagine such a thing. Surely this lady, who knew the Lord better than anyone ever had, would believe in him.

A little pang of jealousy pricked Mary. How enviable, to have been so close to the Master. She longed to experience what this woman had known, a bond with the Rabbi which spoke of intimacy and family.

But for Mary such bonds had always been harbingers of pain. The death of her mother and the betrayal of her father had shattered family and trust. And her one intimacy, shallow as it was, had only ended in abandonment.

"Bar David!" Mary sneered to herself. "Judah Bar David—son of princes—when were you ever as strong as your name?"

Her attempt at callousness, however, was ineffective. It seemed the scar left by that man's departure would forever remind her of her past, her own inadequacy.

Only the notion that Jesus could replace him gave hope that she might someday realize true love. But with the very imagining came such fear, her heart stopped, and she could not dwell on it long.

Mary's mind drifted between the flames of the stone-bordered fire—between Judah and Jesus, the past and the present. Had she not soon been roused, she might have fallen asleep like the others. But a cry of voices was heard in the street outside, and Mary rose to see what it signified.

"What is it?" Suzanna asked as she passed toward the door.

"Someone is calling out to the Master," Mary replied.

Several women rose and followed her, and as they did so they could make out the words. It seemed Jesus was approaching the house, and within the great crowd which followed were two men pleading, "Have pity on us!"

Mary poked her head outside the street door, and when they called again, her breath came in a jolt. "Have pity on us, Son of David! Jesus Bar David, have mercy!"

"Bar David?" she repeated.

But the Master was now entering, and the throng pursued him, even into the courtyard. The two who cried out were assisted by friends in their walk, for they were blind. And still they persisted in the strange reference, "Jesus, Son of David, have mercy!"

The Lord stopped near the court fountain and motioned them forward. Gazing on them he inquired, "Do you believe that I can do this?"

"Yes, Lord!" they declared, their sightless eyes almost brightening with that assertion.

Then Jesus reached forth both hands, placing his fingers on each man's eyes. "According to your faith be it done to you," he commanded.

And their eyes were opened.

CHAPTER FIVE

That night was a restless one for Mary. She could not let go of the blind men's haunting words. She had not imagined them. The reference had been repeated several times.

But why would they say such a thing? If Jesus were a descendant of David, how would these fellows know?

Mary remembered when Judah's steward had brought word of his master's kingly lineage. "If you care for him . . . you must turn him away!" he had insisted. Such an act had been impossible for her. But it had ultimately been unnecessary, for with her sickness and with the same cry, "Son of David, help me!" she had *driven* him away.

The memory of Isaac's scornful eyes had never dimmed. Truly she had not been good enough for Judah. Was it any wonder that he should leave her at her lowest state?

But then she remembered his abandonment of Rachel and fresh hatred for him and for all men flooded through her. "I am so confused," she whispered to the blackness. Shaking herself, she sat up on her low bed and listened to the even breathing of the women nearby. The sound emphasized her loneliness, and she left the chamber, seeking a private spot in the court.

"It must mean something," she thought. "It cannot be coincidence, that I should fall in love with two Bar Davids." But the only omen she could imagine was that Jesus would also desert her, that the love and salvation he had shown would somehow betray her in the end.

As she pondered this, she felt a light touch upon her shoulder.

"Were you having trouble resting?" a feminine voice inquired. Turning about, Mary saw that the moonlight through the open roof lit up the smooth face of the Master's mother.

"Yes," she replied, hardly concealing her surprise at seeing her there.

"I too have such trouble from time to time," the gentle lady nodded. "May I join you?"

"Certainly." Mary smiled, making room on the cold stone bench. A warm glow rose to her cheeks and she laughed softly.

"What is it?" the newcomer asked.

"Oh, I was just recalling another lady who used to come to me on sleepless nights. She was my best friend at . . . the inn."

"The inn?"

"Yes . . . I was . . . employed by an innkeeper." She hoped the woman would not inquire about her work. "It seems I have often needed company on long nights. My mother used to comfort me when I heard strange sounds in the streets."

The listener sympathized. "I understand your city has its rougher elements, as do many seaports. Was it difficult to grow up there?"

Mary sensed that the Nazarene woman was not casting aspersions on her hometown. It was a simple matter of fact that Magdala was notorious for its night life. "It was sometimes difficult," she replied. "But not so difficult as being a woman there." This last she said beneath her breath, and the lady almost asked her to repeat herself, but thought better of it.

"Why couldn't *you* sleep?" Mary asked.

The mother's face took on a faraway look. "I suppose you gathered that my other children do not believe in my oldest son?"

"Yes." Mary nodded. "That must be hard for you."

"It is," she agreed, and the faraway quality attached itself to her voice. She seemed to ponder a time long ago and said, "They would not doubt if they had been there before he was born."

Mary listened respectfully, feeling that the woman was about to share something precious.

"My sons and daughters deny their heritage when they deny their elder brother. I have told them this, but they do not believe."

"Their heritage?"

"Yes. The promise given David."

There was that name again. It seemed destined to hound Mary mercilessly. "What do you mean?" she whispered.

"We are poor Nazarenes, you know. There are very few wealthy folk in Nazareth." The lady smiled. "But we have a proud lineage." With this she raised her chin nobly, her silver-streaked hair catching moonglow. And she explained, "My husband and my father, rest their souls, were Bar Davids, though they never flaunted it. Both took their fathers' names for their own, but they were always proud of their Bethlehem roots. In fact, Jesus was born in that city of David—did you know?"

Mary shook her head, wondering at the woman's willingness to share her tale with a relative stranger.

"We were called to Bethlehem during Augustus' census—to the town of my husband's forefather. And almost on our arrival, your Master was born."

The mother's expression was warm with remembrance.

"But," Mary hesitated, "are there not many Bar Davids? Someone . . . told me that once."

"Oh, indeed. Scattered all about. Some are more attached to the fact than others. But for me, it bears great importance. For my son will one day sit on David's throne."

Mary started, drawing back and studying the lady. She was becoming accustomed to the amazing works and claims of her Master, but this pronouncement seemed the most incredible of all to a daughter of Israel.

"You will find this hard to believe, I know," the gentle woman said, smiling, "but before Jesus was born, God told me what kind of man I was bringing into the world. I have shared these things with few people and . . . I do not know why I tell you. Except that it seems, somehow, important that I should."

Mary gazed at the door, remembering the events of the afternoon. "The two blind men called Jesus 'Son of David' . . ." she whispered.

"Yes. How do you suppose they knew?" the mother asked. "I assure you that no human being told them. Surely not my children or I. 'Bar Davids are commonplace,' my sons say. No, child, only God told those poor men about their healer. Just as he told me, years ago."

A tear slid down Mary's face. "Your sons speak the truth when they say Bar Davids are commonplace. I cared much for a Bar David once."

The older lady was silent a moment. "I perceive that you were badly hurt by that one."

"Yes. . . ."

The woman placed a loving hand on Mary's knee and bent close. "There are many sons of mothers and kings who do not stay loyal to their heritage, but my eldest boy is David's heir in truth, and the liberator of his people."

CHAPTER SIX

Many months had passed since Mary first grappled with the dilemma of her feelings for Jesus, and her longings to be closer to him than a sister. In all this time she had never found courage to speak her heart.

Her involvement with the Master and his company had continued to open her eyes to his power and majesty, and she no longer doubted that he truly would one day sit upon David's throne. Indeed, it was increasingly believed among his disciples that Jesus was the one promised of old, the Messiah, who would deliver Israel from oppression and establish a kingdom greater than Rome.

Mary's decision to follow Jesus had fulfilled her girlhood dreams of travel and adventure. She now found herself, for the second time since leaving Magdala, staying in the magnificent city of

Jerusalem, a place she had known only in fantasy.

In fact, today she was with her Lord and his disciples in the Temple Porch. She stayed close to Suzanna, who had visited this holy place numerous times with her father. This season was the Feast of Tabernacles, the most important and well known of the Jewish holidays, commemorating their dependence on God in the wilderness, as well as celebrating autumn harvest. It was early morning, hardly dawn—but suddenly the grayness was split golden with brilliance. As the eastern sun peeked up behind Mt. Olivet, its rays bounced off the gilded surfaces of the great edifice, and the entire rise of the holy mount on which the Temple sat reflected a radiance.

"Lily!" Mary whispered, clutching her arm. "Are the sunrises always like this in Jerusalem?"

Her friend shook her head and leaned close. "I don't know," she said smiling. "I have not been here for every sunrise. In fact, I have never been here so early in the morning."

The two women looked in amazement at the immense throng that had already gathered to hear the Master speak. Apparently many had even slept here the night before, hoping to be closest when he arrived.

The attitude toward the Rabbi was not all one-sided, however. There were those present who wished to see Jesus taken before the authorities, for his claims were becoming divisive not only between the Jewish leaders and the people, but among the people themselves.

Just yesterday, the last and "Great Day" of the

feast, the Lord had stood on this very spot, proclaiming, "If anyone is thirsty, let him come unto me and drink! He who puts his trust in me, out of the depths of his being shall flow 'rivers of living water.'"

Such a tumult those words had provoked! Jesus was quoting the Scriptures and applying them to himself in an unprecedented way.

Mary shuffled uneasily now as she looked on those nearby and wondered who among them might be the Master's enemies. It had been obvious yesterday that many had wanted to seize him, and she feared for his safety.

She gazed on him lovingly, and then her eyes traveled to the cedar and marble portico overhead and to the magnificent columns and arches of the mighty compound. *How life has changed!* she thought. She felt unworthy even to stand on this holy ground, and yet Jesus had given her dignity.

The Lord had selected as his podium a place on the steps leading to the Court of the Gentiles, in order that he might be seen of all. Mary was grateful that he always chose the common areas of the Temple in which to address the crowds. Had he passed beyond the next court, no female would have been able to hear him, for only men were allowed to enter the precincts closer to the sanctuary.

His choice of this open forum, however, would subject him today to an unusual test by his enemies. Their planned examination involved a woman, and had Jesus been stationed elsewhere, they might not have been able to bring her before him.

Just as the teacher began to speak, a disturbance was heard on the edge of the crowd. Soon the throng was parting as a commission of scribes and Pharisees made their way boldly toward the steps, dragging a weeping female with them. She was brutally thrust forward, and she stood there shaking and clutching a man's robe about her otherwise naked body. Her hair was disheveled, her cheeks wet with tears, as she stared, shamefaced and fearful, at the pavement.

"Master," one of the commissioners sneered, "this woman was taken in *adultery* . . . in the very act!" He gestured hatefully at the accused, who was the focus of a thousand glaring and curious eyes. And then, with a buttery smooth voice, he offered: "Now in the Law, Moses commanded us that such should be stoned. What do *you* say?"

Mary shuddered as the death of Rachel flashed across her memory, and her heart rose in terror at what she might be about to witness. She considered the events that must have preceded this moment. Apparently the men had dragged this poor creature from the very bed of sin, without even giving her time to clothe herself. They had thrust upon her one of their own garments as they seized her. The Magdalene wondered where the paramour was. If, as the prosecutor had witnessed, they had taken the woman "in the very act," the accomplice must have been present when they found her. Was he possibly one of these accusers?

How typical, she thought, to bring the woman for trial, while setting her lover free! Perhaps Suzanna considered this point as well, for she turned silently to Mary with an expression which bespoke the injustice of it all.

"Oh, Mary," she whispered. "What will the Master say?"

"Perhaps he will suggest they stone the *adulterer,* if he can be found!" Mary replied, teeth clenched.

But Jesus seemed bent on saying nothing at all. Looking at the commissioners and their helpless charge, he stooped down and began to write with his finger upon the broad stone steps. A fine harvest dust, stirred up by the crowds the day before, had settled on the stage during the night and had not yet been cleared away by trampling feet this morning. Only those nearby could discern what was written. But the commissioners were closest, and it was to them especially that he directed his inscription.

First he drew what appeared to be a simple tablet, like those that Moses carried down from Sinai. And along one side he etched the numerals one through ten. No Jew could fail to see what this symbolized. Jesus was alluding to the most quintessential part of Moses' Law, to which the accuser had just appealed—the Ten Commandments.

This sparked a round of questions, and they kept asking him, "What are you doing?" "It seems you avoid the issue."

But finally Jesus stood up and confronted them. "He that is without sin among you, let him cast the first stone at her."

And stooping down once more, he continued writing upon the ground, this time putting a small mark beside each numeral, as if to emphasize it and to force introspection upon the onlookers. As he checked off the list, etching the lines into the tablet, the commissioners grew uneasy. Could any one of them claim to have kept all those commandments perfectly?

The eldest was the first to leave. A wizened man with a hoary beard and penetrating eyes, he was looking very meek as he turned his back and, with lowered head, made his way past the crowd. His comrades peered after him in amazement and murmured among themselves. But as Jesus continued slowly to designate each category of God's Law, others were convicted of conscience and began to walk away.

At last, only the primary accuser was left, the one who had demanded an accounting of Jesus. And only one law remained to be marked. Apparently this man had felt free of condemnation to this point, and looked condescendingly toward his departed fellows. But now he saw Jesus point to the tenth commandment: "Thou shalt not covet."

Suddenly, the prosecutor's face grew pale. Surely he had never stolen, killed, blasphemed, or wantonly broken any of God's other laws. Surely he had kept the Sabbath, despised idolatry, honored his father and mother. He was neither a liar nor an adulterer—but could he truly say he had never desired anything which was not properly his? Had he never craved to steal, never hated another, never defied God inwardly, never wished the Law were more lenient, never devoted time to selfish pursuits, never hardened his heart toward authority, concealed the truth, or looked on another man's wife? Covetousness was such a broad term that it had a way of sweeping aside hypocrisy and exposing the spirit of an individual and the nature of the Law itself. Had he never lusted—never sinned? Never been guilty as this woman?

He did not look at the Master or at the accused as he departed. He did not look at anyone, and his feet made no sound as he went.

The Lord was left alone with the adulteress, surrounded by an awestruck crowd. And only now did he stand up, straightening himself and surveying the scene. "Woman," he addressed the bewildered and frightened female, "where are those who accused you? Does no one condemn you?"

The defendant clutched her cumbersome garment, her eyes wide with amazement. "No one, sir," she stammered, knowing that the Rabbi had just saved her life.

"Neither do I condemn you," Jesus said. "Go your way, and sin no more."

CHAPTER SEVEN

A knifelike wind whistled through the gorge where the famed John the Baptist had preached four years before. The wintry waters of Jordan tore through the rocky fissure of the precipitous Ghor with deafening force. And the same young woman who had, only two months before, stood marveling at the colonnades and porches of the Temple, huddled inside a wilderness cave, peering up at an ominous sky.

Mary, along with Jesus and his disciples, had stayed in Jerusalem through one more festival, Hanukkah; but as tension had grown regarding the Lord's safety, they had all withdrawn to Perea, across the river. For several days now they had camped in the rocky hollows along the bank, living on food sent by friends in the city, and on catches from the icy waters.

Life was not comfortable. Only three women had chosen to accompany the Master into the wilderness. Jesus had not allowed his mother to come, but Suzanna and Mary were young and strong enough to endure the harsh environment, and Maria would not hear of being left behind. The others had gone back to Galilee where they would wait until the Lord returned to Capernaum.

Suzanna shuffled about the back of the small mountainside room which quartered the little sorority, arranging a few sticks on the fire which the three kept burning day and night. And as she straightened up, wiping her hands on her skirt, she studied her friend. "Has he returned yet?" she asked.

"No," Mary replied. "I keep watching, but he does not come. He has been gone for hours."

"My nephew is not a man to worry about," Maria offered. "He is only praying alone again. He always returns with dusk." From the low rock upon which she sat, the older woman leaned closer toward the fire. Mary detected that a long monologue was about to ensue. In her months with the Master, she had grown accustomed to Maria's reminiscences, but just now she did not have attention to spare.

"I remember," began the woman with a faraway gaze, "when Jesus was about twelve years old and we took him to Jerusalem for one of the feasts. He was always such an independent sort," she laughed, shaking her head, "but this time he especially upset us—all of us. We had quite a large company, family and everyone. When we prepared to return home—and in fact were well on our way, a good day's journey into it—we suddenly realized that he was not with us. My sister and her husband had thought he was with friends in the group, and were genuinely panicked when they could not find him.

Well," she said slapping her knee, "they returned to Jerusalem, and do you know, they sought the lad *three* days before finding him! Finally they searched the Temple, and what do you think?" She shrugged, palms raised.

"They discovered him standing in the midst of a bunch of scribes and doctors of the Law. These wise old birds were all listening intently to this young twig discourse upon the Torah! Well," she said taking a deep breath and rolling her eyes, "you can imagine his parents! Of course they were relieved to find him, but angry at his seeming disregard for their concerns. But when they questioned him, he said one of the most peculiar things. . . ." Her voice broke off and she ruminated. "At least at the time it seemed peculiar. We are accustomed now to hearing such things from his lips. . . ."

Mary sighed and kept her focus on the shore. It was Suzanna who hastened the story to its conclusion. "What did he say? It must have been quite remarkable."

Mary smiled inwardly. Even as a child, Simon's daughter had been adept with older folk.

" 'Well,' he said, 'why were you troubled? Why did you seek me? Didn't you know that I must be about my *Father's* business?' Ha!" Maria laughed, a twinkle in her old eyes. "Can you imagine? Of course, these days we know what he speaks of, being God's own Son. . . ." Her voice trailed off and she was lost in the import of it all. Suzanna, who stood close by, leaned down and patted her upon the knee, grateful for her story and the sharing of it. And then Maria studied the one who still watched the stormy shore for a sign of Jesus. "No, my dear," she addressed Mary again, "my nephew is not a man to worry over.... Sometimes I fear you fret too much after him," she offered, eying her perceptively.

Mary winced and turned a nervous smile to the scrutinizer and to Suzanna. Surely they could tell, she thought. Her love for Jesus must be emblazoned across her breast. She had tried, over the months, to contain it, to keep it to herself. But although she never declared them, her feelings spilled forth in everything she did and said.

Maria's story was revealing, but the more recent incident in the Temple with the woman taken in adultery had impressed the Magdalene beyond words. What could have been a reenactment of Rachel's execution had turned out to be the greatest example of the difference between Jesus and Judah. And ever since, she had hoped for the chance to speak with her Lord in private.

The men of the party were braving the elements today, gathered about a little bonfire on the beach. As Mary surveyed them, it occurred to her again what a cross-section of male Jewish society they represented. And yet there were none with whom she felt comfortable. Not that they had all treated her badly. With time, some had accepted her as a near equal, and had displayed kindness on numerous occasions. No—she knew the alienation she felt was not so much a product of their behavior as of her own previous experiences. For life had colored her view of all men—

All but one.

A thick fog blanketed the shore, limiting her vision to a brief stretch of terrain. But she was certain she saw movement some distance from the gathering. Yes, it was the white robe of a man—and now the figure took on personality. Jesus had returned from his meditation.

He passed by his men with a hasty salutation and sought the solitude of a nearby cave, apparently still wishing time to himself.

Mary's pulse sped. She knew Jesus wanted to be alone, but this seemed such an opportune moment to approach him. She felt she must act now, or she might never act at all.

She said nothing to the other women as she left the cave and hurried, unseen, toward the Master's private retreat. As she did so she remembered snatches of a story her mother had told, of a lady named Ruth and her beloved Boaz. She remembered how Ruth had crept into the sleeping hall of the fieldworkers to find the man, planning to let him know, symbolically, that she wished to be his wife. It was considered highly improper for a female to enter those quarters, to say nothing of the intimate manner in which she would reveal her desire. Locating the slumbering Boaz, she had lain down at his feet, drawing his cloak over her and waiting to be discovered in the morning. The design had worked. Far from despising her boldness, he had lost his heart to the clever female who had broken tradition.

Mother, who had loved the tale, also revered custom and propriety. She had impressed upon Mary that this was an unusual circumstance, and that God had blessed it because he had seen the "limitations" of the Moabitess, who would not have had the advantages of a Jewess. But the Magdalene identified with Ruth just now. She must grasp this moment to lay her claim. Although she would not make such a dramatic appeal, she knew she was risking censure by her behavior. Yet her heart would not be satisfied to keep its secret forever.

Fog concealed the cave to which the Master had withdrawn. When Mary found the opening, she knew her entrance would not be visible to those below.

She placed a hand on the stony upper lip of the cave's mouth and set a hesitant foot before the portal. It was very dark inside, but she could see the Lord reclining upon the floor.

"Master," she whispered, afraid of her own voice.

A moment passed. Perhaps he was asleep. "Master," she called more definitely.

"Mary?" he answered.

"Yes, Lord, it is I," she replied, tingling as she always did when he used her name.

"What is it?" he asked.

Her heart skipped, and she found words hard to come by. "May I speak with you?" she managed.

"Of course," he said, acceptance in his tone.

She perceived that he sat up, and as she entered the cave she allowed her eyes to adjust to the darkness before drawing near.

"They tell me you were found speaking to a Samaritan woman one day beside a well . . . alone," she reminded him. "I know that your friends were upset by that. I do not wish to cause you trouble."

"Sit with me, Mary," he offered, a smile in his voice. And she could see his outstretched hand.

Her eyes were well adjusted now, and she found that the foggy light outside was adequate so that she could see his face. As she knelt beside him, his kind gaze took her back to the first day she had seen him upon the Magdalene street corner—the Stranger who had exposed her soul with a glance.

Suddenly she trembled, and the speech she had rehearsed so often, the words she would say if ever she had the chance, fled her.

The Lord was patiently silent, sensing her awkwardness.

"Master," she whispered at last, "I have wished to talk with you for so long—for months, really."

Jesus said nothing, allowing her to pursue this at her own pace.

"Oh, Lord, you know my past, my life. There is nothing hidden from you, I am certain . . . ," she began. The words were halting at first, but picked up speed as she warmed to his attentive spirit. "I have tried to understand myself and what brought me to the condition in which you found me. I had not known or remembered who I was for many years. How much was my responsibility and how much was forced upon me, I cannot sort out, and yet I felt the guilt and stain of my experiences nonetheless. I guess—" she paused, "I guess it does not matter after all, who made what choices. I am beginning to see, after being with you, that no one is really whole until. . . ."

The Lord studied her quietly.

"... until you touch him."

A large tear spilled down her cheek, and she reached up to wipe it away.

"Do not be ashamed to cry, Mary," Jesus said. "Your tears were kind to me when you washed my feet."

"Oh, Master," she groaned, "I must speak my heart or it will surely break within me!"

"Speak," he prompted.

"I have changed, Lord! You have changed me. I, who have hated men, now love for the first time. Oh, I thought I cared for a man once, but," she shook her head, "that feeling was untrue. And now I know what it means to love."

Mary's face was flushed and her eyes intently locked on his. When he took her hand, holding it without shame, she trembled violently.

"You love me?" he asked.

"Truly, Master!"

"And I love you," he replied.

Mary studied him numbly, and then her pulse thundered. "No!" she cried, wrenching her hand away and striking the ground at her side. "No. I do not mean that kind of love! You offer the love of a brother. Don't you see—I do not speak of brothers and sisters or mothers and sons!" Her spirit embraced all the zeal of the past months, and she declared, "I do not wish to be your sister!"

As the words echoed out, dying toward the back of the cave and leaving silence, she could scarcely believe her own daring.

Suddenly she could not bear to remain and stood to flee.

"Mary!" Jesus insisted, holding her by the arm.

"Stay a moment. I have something to say."

The woman stepped back into the shadows and listened with lowered eyes.

"I know the love of which you speak," Jesus assured her. "And I do not mock you. The love between men and women is a creation of my Father, and a most powerful human force."

Mary discerned the sincerity in his voice, and drew courage from its tenderness.

"Your Father?" she asked, thinking of Maria's story. "You speak of God."

"Yes," he said nodding.

"Truly, I know you come from above," she whispered. "I know your majesty. But, my Lord, you are a *man* as well!"

Jesus gazed into her pleading eyes. "You are right," he agreed. "And I am subject to all the emotions of a man. But it is not for me to enjoy this kind of love." With that he rose and walked to the cave entrance, where he looked toward the river. The fog had somewhat dissipated and he could see his disciples below. "The Son of Man has not even a place to lay his head," he said. "No home, no family: I have only the friends my Father has given me."

Mary's heart ached at the sound of his voice, so full of heaviness. She had often sensed the solitariness of his life, but in this moment he seemed the most tragic, the most lonely of figures. And her own selfish needs paled by comparison.

Now, however, the Lord turned to her again. "*You* have been my friend," he asserted, "as much as any of the *men* who follow me. But surely you must understand that I have a destiny to fulfill, and that my way cannot follow after the comfort to be found with a woman."

Mary's eyes welled with fresh tears, and she sighed. "What 'destiny,' Lord? Your tone does not bode well when you speak the word."

Jesus faced the river once more and gazed at the rushing waters. "I shall never forget your kindness to me at Simon's house," he said. "I know that was a hard thing for you, but your way was very gentle and your touch a healing thing."

The Magdalene was warmed by his sentiment and she smiled through her sorrow.

"Indeed, you anointed me with kindness," he whispered. And then, turning, he drew near, taking her hands in his and studying the wrists which had once worn Satan's brands. His face bore a strange expression, something of pain and a little fear. She thought perhaps he trembled, and she wondered at the meaning of this alteration. "But were you to anoint me again," he explained with measured syllables, "it would be in preparation for my burial."

Surely she misunderstood. "Your burial?" she stammered.

"It is not my destiny only to heal and preach deliverance," he declared. "It is my destiny to lay down my life. Not until I have done this, will all be accomplished."

Mary could not bear these words. She shut her ears, refusing to let them penetrate. "Do not speak so!" she cried. "I cannot imagine life without you!"

Weeping, she clung to him, burying her head on his sturdy shoulder. He did not resist, but let her claim him. And then he went on, his voice throaty with the sense of her pain. "What you have now shall never be taken away, Mary. You are like the tower of Migdal, the great lighthouse of your town. The beacon of your heart cannot be dimmed, for it has life eternal, and when you have conquered your greatest fear, love will be everywhere for you."

The woman pulled back and lifted her eyes. "My greatest fear?" she repeated.

"Your spirit has been freed, but there is yet one thing remaining before you can know full joy," he explained.

"Full joy is to be with you!" she objected. "And you speak of leaving me."

"I will never leave you, Mary. Though I go away, I shall always be near as your heart."

The Magdalene shook her head. "You speak in riddles, Master. What joy can exist if you are gone?"

"The joy of doing those things which please me, of doing my will."

Mary sighed helplessly, turning her face to the floor. "And what must I do to please you, Lord? I would do anything."

"Forgive your father," he said.

The woman surveyed him mutely. Her father! What had he to do with any of this? Yet, in the silence of the cave, and in the presence of her Lord, the answer really was not so elusive.

"You have never mentioned my father before," she whispered. "How do you know of him?"

"He is the one who hurt you most in your life. To forgive him is to free yourself entirely of the past—to free your heart to love all people."

Mary faltered weakly. "I came here to speak of you and me," she insisted, shrinking from his gaze.

"I do speak of us," Jesus explained. "The good of your spirit lies in what you do to fulfill my will." And then, lifting her tear-stained face in his hands, he said, "This way lies happiness, Mary. If you love me, keep my commandments."

The Magdalene lowered her eyes and stepped back with a sigh. "I do not know that I can accomplish what you ask. I fear it is beyond me," she admitted.

"It is beyond human ability," Jesus agreed. "But in this you must think of me as *more* than a man. For through me you can do all things."

Mary was silent a long while. All her emotions rose up to fight against his demands. But her heart at last submitted and she said, "More than anything I long to please you, Master. Be my strength."

At this Jesus lay a soothing hand upon her shoulder and assured her with his expression that he would be just that.

She knew she should not stay longer, and quietly moved toward the cave door. As she departed, however, the thought of a future without his physical presence flashed cruelly before her, and she suddenly turned back, clutching him to her and weeping miserably. She recalled the first time she had touched him, and the fount of emotion which the memory always evoked spilled forth unhindered.

"Oh, Jesus," she pleaded. "It is hard to let you go."

The Lord's eyes were mellow, and with a tender voice he replied, "I will be your strength for even this."

PART VI
The
Liberation

And if Christ be not raised ... we are
of all men most miserable.
If ye then be risen with Christ, seek
those things which are above
(1 Corinthians 15:17, 19; Colossians 3:1).

CHAPTER ONE

A little more than a year later, the same woman would seek out the same man within another cave and in another kind of darkness. Though it was spring and not winter; though signs of new life shone brilliantly in the earth—the King of all life was gone. Surely the universe was held by an icy claw and spun to the devil's tune, for the Lord was reclined now, not in rest, but in the sleep of eternity. Now his sanctuary was not a cave of solitude—but a grave, and a house of sorrow.

Jesus was dead.

Since the afternoon Mary had witnessed the execution—since Friday, when the whole of creation had groaned under the murderous hand of Roman guards and priestly prosecutors—she had followed the other women through the process of tradition. While most of the Lord's apostles had been in hiding, she had watched as the Master was lowered from the cross, and as two previously secret disciples, Nicodemus and Joseph the Arimathean, boldly took the body to be wrapped for burial. She had followed when they carried the corpse to the tomb, and she had observed how Jesus was laid out on the hard stone slab. Then she had waited through Sabbath, not disturbing the others' rest, but all the while wishing to go to the grave site, to be as near the Lord as possible.

The women planned to go to the tomb at sunrise to complete the anointing of the body, which had not been finished before the "day of rest" came. Except for a hasty trip to the market at Sabbath-end to purchase spices for burial, neither the Magdalene nor any of the other women had set foot outside.

Mary tried to sit quietly by Suzanna, to say comforting words to the Lord's sleepless mother, to bear patiently Maria's analysis of it all, to endure calmly the sounds of sorrow. But she was not capable of sitting. She had intended to wait until morning, when she would accompany the women to the grave site. But she could not tolerate the delay.

In the depths of night, between the close of the holy day and dawn of Sunday, she took her own little collection of prepared spices, along with the precious alabaster flask of ointment, and crept silently from the house where the disciples were stationed.

The unfamiliar streets of Jerusalem were even more foreign in the dark. It seemed the specter of death peeked from every window, for her mind was full of the phantom. But somehow she found her way to the garden where the Lord's tomb was secluded.

She entered the little oasis as in a trance. Though her body functioned, her pulse measuring the seconds—her breath coming evenly and her senses making order out of space and time—her spirit was in another dimension. It was the hour of heaviest blackness, the soul's midnight, as she had always thought of it. And this was the midnight of her soul, just as surely as the first time the demons had come.

In fact, this dark hour was worse than the first, for now that she had tasted life, she had learned to hope and believe for all things. Yet she was bereft of the one who had released her from torment, deprived of that which had set her free.

Did not Satan laugh? If he had conquered the Master, would it not be only a matter of time before he eradicated all the Master's work? Was Mary not once again prey to the locusts?

Sitting in the bleak house this evening, she had recalled a story which Jesus had told, of an unclean spirit who left a man and later returned, finding his abode empty, swept, and furnished. Fetching seven other demons even more wicked than himself, he brought them with him and they all entered the house and dwelt there. "And the last state of that man became worse than the first," Jesus had warned.

When Mary first heard this tale, it did not trouble her. But that had been when the Lord still walked with her, when she could hear him speak and feel the reassuring warmth of his presence. Tonight, just remembering the story had terrified her, filling her with such anxiety she feared her heart would burst.

Perhaps there had been some original demon in her childhood, she thought, who came and went at pleasure, and who had at last brought seven others with him. Perhaps even those were not gone forever, but would return to feast upon her soul, now that the Master was dead!

How could she know? Even if they never returned, would she not live out the days of her life in fear that they could, at any moment, descend upon her?

The days of her life, indeed! What life was there for Mary now? Were she to enter the future with no spiritual fear whatever, she still had the fear of destitution. When all this had passed, her friends would go their separate ways, to homes and families, to vocations and life as usual. But what would the Magdalene do?

For each of them there would be the ordeal of facing a scoffing world, of admitting their mistaken search for the Messiah. But her friends would overcome all that. How would Mary overcome? She was trained for nothing but men's pleasure. She knew nothing beyond cosmetics and ointments, perfumes and winning wiles. And survival had always meant the prostitution of her self.

She remembered having planned, as a child, to do housecleaning for the mothers of Magdala. With Papa's assistance so unreliable, she had dreamed of providing in this way for herself and the twins. But even that door would be closed now. No decent family would hire a woman with a "past." Suzanna could go home to her father, in the respectable quarter of town. For Mary there was no quarter—except the inn.

A chill ran through her at the thought. "Ezra!" She shuddered. "Oh, please, God, no! I could never go back to Ezra!"

Suddenly tears dimmed her eyes and she stumbled against a stone in the path. The moon, which had done little to aid her journey on the city's shadow-strewn streets, was more helpful now; but her own sorrow obscured the way. Ahead, however, lay the clearing that opened on the tomb, and she managed to follow the steep, rocky trail with eager feet.

Strange, she thought, to take comfort in a graveyard. She remembered the Lord's words at the Jordan, when he had said with a constricted voice, "Were you to anoint me again, it would be in preparation for my burial." And at that memory, sorrow welled fresh within her. *How had he known?* she wondered, fondling the little flask of ointment with which she would caress his cold flesh.

"Oh, Jesus! How could you leave me?" But the closest thing to life she had ever known lay buried here, and the mere fact that the body which had housed him was interred in this place gave her a measure of solace.

Ah, here it was now. The tomb.

But where were the Temple guards who had been set to watch it? Were the Jewish leaders no longer concerned that the disciples might steal the body, that some hoax of resurrection might be foisted off on the gullible public? And who would roll back the enormous stone door for her, that she might anoint her Lord?

But what was this? The sepulcher was open: indeed, the moonlight showed a gaping maw where the seal had been!

A surge of energy rushed through her being. "Jesus!" she cried. "What have they done?" Racing to the entrance, she leaned inside. Empty: the Lord's body was gone!

Mary fought dizziness. "Peter ... I must tell Peter!" she reasoned, stumbling from the doorway, her face drained of color. Could Jesus' enemies not let him rest, even in death?

"They have taken my Lord ... stolen my Lord ..." her pulse repeated. "Peter, Peter—must tell Peter. ..."

Her cloak caught on a brittle snag as she pursued the path from the garden, and the alabaster vial slipped from her hands, but she did not retrieve it. As she raced back to Jerusalem, a puddle of silky oil oozed from beneath the ruby stopper, spilling a silver moonsheen into the graveyard soil.

CHAPTER TWO

N o matter that they did not believe her right away. Mary was used to men's lack of regard. They would believe her soon enough, and she only wished they might prove her wrong.

She wished she had not seen what she had seen, and that the tomb had not been empty, but had still cradled the Lord's body. Such a cruelty, to rob mourners of the tangible memory of their beloved! What demented minds would think of such a thing?

She watched helplessly as Peter and John threw on their cloaks and raced from the silent house. Their eyes had been incredulous, even mocking, when she roused them with her news. She thought perhaps she should race to the garden with them. But their anxiety was due to lack of knowledge, their hasty run because they must see for themselves if such a thing were true. When they made the discovery, they would be lifeless as she. They would no longer have strength to run, or hearts to be moved.

Nothing mattered. Did it really matter that his body was now gone? With no soul to enliven it, no spirit to warm it, the body was but a husk.

And yet, it had given her a ground in the present, something to turn to when loneliness obsessed her. Had she spent her remaining years at his grave, the tomb shutting out all else, to attend his crumbling body, she would have had a focus.

Now even that was gone.

It was not because anything mattered that she turned to follow the two men to the garden. It was because she had nowhere else to go, and because her heart had stayed behind, at the sepulcher.

Peter and John had reached the place well ahead of her, and had already assessed the situation. By the time she arrived, standing at the leafy edge of the clearing, she found them departing.

She knew the feelings etched across Peter's brow. As for John, his face bore a peculiar quality. If sorrow and anger had recently marked him, something else now overlaid those emotions. He said nothing as he passed her on the garden path; but his eyes, compared to Peter's stormy expression, were stamped with a secret excitement—and even joy.

Mary did not question him, but rebelled inwardly at his seeming disregard for the horror of things. And when they had gone their way she was left to face the empty tomb alone.

She drew near the stony chamber and stood outside for some time. She was weeping now, the utter dejection of her state sweeping over her with vivid clarity. But some move must be made, and she was compelled to look one last time on the place where Jesus had lain.

Stooping down, she leaned under the low portal and peered into the dusky sepulcher. The sun was just ascending and it threw her shadow onto the already dreary interior. But some kind of whiteness caught her eye, to the right of the place where the body had been. And now another to the left. Her senses were scrambled by grief and by darkness. At first she could not identify what she saw, but as her eyes adjusted, it became clear; two men in white garments were seated within the tomb—on the very spot where Jesus had lain!

Instantly, she identified them with a confusing kaleidoscope of explanations. They were jokesters intruding upon a holy site; they were the grave-robbers themselves; or, most terrifying, they were apparitions, spirits within a spirit's house!

Which impression came first, and which accompanying emotion, was irrelevant. Before she could draw breath to question or challenge, they spoke to her.

"Woman, why are you weeping?"

Why? Couldn't they see why—they who occupied the place which belonged to Jesus alone?

"Because they took away my Lord," she cried, "and I do not know where they laid him!"

The two figures gave no response, but took their eyes from her to the doorway, and presently she heard a soft footfall behind her. Turning around, she saw yet another man in white, standing in the clearing.

"Woman, why are you weeping? Whom are you seeking?" he asked.

Tears of mourning still dimmed her eyes, and the sunlight behind the figure cast him in silhouette. She could not make out his face, and her emotions prevented any recognition.

"Are you the keeper of this place?" she asked. But there was no reply. And then the loneliness of her soul spoke forth. "Sir, if you bore him away, tell me where you laid him and I will take him."

Then casting her gaze to the sepulcher, she buried her face in her hands and wept yet more.

The gardener, as she supposed him, stepped close but did not touch her. And at last he spoke one word.

"Mary."

She would know that sound anywhere. No one spoke her name like Jesus! With those two syllables he had, once upon a time, returned her identity. He had raised her from despair and set her on the road to liberation. In all the months she had followed him, her name upon his lips had never failed to reassure her.

"Dear Master!" she cried, wheeling about. Her hands reached forth to touch him, her arms to embrace the lover of her soul.

But Jesus stepped back. The one who had never rejected her attentions, who had always allowed her approach, drew away now. "Do not hold me," he said, his voice firm but compassionate, "for I have not yet ascended to my Father."

The meaning of this, she could not analyze. She had not yet contemplated the meaning of anything. The fact that her Lord stood alive before her had only impressed her most primitive sensations, and she longed for just one thing: to clutch him to her. But he was saying, "No."

"But go to my brethren," he continued, "and tell them, 'I am ascending to my Father, and to my God and your God.'"

The angle of the sun now allowed her to see his face. The eyes were warm as ever toward her, the expression gentle and affirming.

"Master . . . ," she whispered.

But he was gone. As quickly as he had come, he was gone.

She studied the ground where his feet had touched, and her heart cried out against the emptiness.

She knew, however, what she had seen. Death no longer held him! Jesus had conquered the greatest enemy of all.

"Go tell the brethren," she repeated his request. "Must tell Peter—tell John."

Joy gave her wings. The thrill of life energized her whole being and she sped up the path without looking back.

Nor did she look down as she ran, or she might have remembered the alabaster flask. It was empty now, the contents absorbed into the earth. And it was lost in the undergrowth, where the green of spring would overtake it.

Epilogue

Stand fast therefore in the liberty wherewith Christ hath made us free (Gal. 5:1).

The morning fog had not yet burned away from the Galilee shore. Though they were not far from the city gate, the three figures who walked up the beach would have been lost to sight by anyone watching them.

The leader was the tallest and walked with defined femininity. The two younger ones were strikingly similar in appearance, except that one was a boy, well past Bar Mitzvah, and the other a girl, of marriageable age.

The two youngsters lingered behind as they walked, perhaps lacking the eldest's conviction for their venture.

"Toby," the leader called over her shoulder, "there is a group of sailors ahead—see? Near the water. Go ask them if they can direct us."

The young man hesitated. "It will do no good, Mary," he objected. "Since dawn we have been asking every stranger we've passed. None know of a Michael Bar Andreas or his hut."

But Tamara, the boy's twin, nudged him. "Don't argue, Toby. She is determined."

Toby peered down the shore until his eyes made out the dim figures. Then with a sigh, he headed toward them.

Mary and her young sister followed more slowly behind, and when they were near enough to observe the encounter, they waited.

"We are looking for a certain little house—a hut, they say," Toby called out. "It's supposed to be along the shore somewhere, not far north of Magdala. Are you familiar with such a place?"

One of the sailors looked up from the net he was mending. "A fisherman's hut?" he asked.

"Yes, at least he used to be a fisherman," Toby replied.

"There are many such places along this stretch," another offered. "Homes of poor folk who can't afford to live in town."

"Yes, he would be one of those," Toby reasoned. "And he would probably be quite solitary. Perhaps drinking more than he should." The description was painful for the young man to speak, but the first sailor only laughed coldly.

"You wouldn't be looking for old Bar Andreas, would you?"

Mary's heart surged at the reference, and she would have stepped forward to answer, except that she suddenly felt sure she recognized some of the men from her old profession at the inn.

"Yes, we are!" Toby spoke for her.

"Then look for a little hovel up that way," he said pointing at a distant sandbar, "where the greenery begins toward the hills. You'll know it by the strips of black mourning he always keeps hanging by the door."

Strips? Mary wondered. She remembered the single ribbon which had never been removed from the doorpost after Mama's death. But why would he have added more?

"Thank you," Toby nodded. "We will find it easily now."

Turning to his sisters, he waited for Mary to lead the way. She passed the men, hoping they would not remember her, and as she did so she raised her veil over her head—not for Mama, but for the Lord.

Ever since the disciples had returned to Galilee, Mary had known she must find Papa. Suzanna's father, Simon, had kindly taken her in, allowing her to do housecleaning in exchange for her keep. But with each passing day, she had felt the imperative of fulfilling Jesus' command. And when she had awakened this morning she had known it could not be put off any longer.

"If you find him, he will be welcome here, as long as he needs a place to stay," Simon assured her. But his eyes had betrayed doubt that his old neighbor was yet alive.

Nevertheless, Mary had set out on the quest with the hope of faith, and as soon as she had done so, she felt the strength of Jesus lifting her up.

Yes—his power was real! All his followers now knew that Jesus lived. The disciple John had been the first to sense the truth that morning at the tomb, and Mary had been the first to see the Lord. But Jesus had continued to appear to others over the next days, and now no one doubted.

As he had promised, he had then ascended to his Father, to his God and theirs. But his presence was not gone from them. Because of his death, their sins were pardoned; because of his resurrection, the power of life eternal was theirs.

"All is 'accomplished,' as you said," Mary mused while she headed toward the distant sandbar.

No powers unleashed against her could prevail. She need no longer fear the hounds of Satan. As for her daily bread, she knew she would find more employment in her hometown, now that she had Suzanna's father as a reference.

The sun was beginning to peek through the fog. Mary lifted her face to it. The dream of one day having her own home was almost too good to think on. But just now she allowed herself to savor the thought. In fact, it suddenly seemed that if Jesus had rescued her and provided a bright future, he could also *restore* her lost years—make up for the desolation of her past.

At this her feet picked up speed. It could not be far, she reasoned. Around this little bend, ahead into those bushes. Yes—that appeared to be a roof of some kind. And now, drawing closer, she could see a makeshift building of driftwood and reed-woven mud.

"Oh, Papa . . . ," she whispered, when she first spied the tattered black ribbons fluttering beside the doorpost. There had been three added to the first, one for each child he had lost.

The twins drew near and looked on silently. "What does it mean?" Toby asked.

Mary wiped a tear from her eye. "It means that our papa has always been the saddest of us all."

A curl of gray smoke could be seen winding up from a hole in the thatched roof. Mary did not knock, but slowly pushed open the flimsy door and peered inside. Her pulse skipped as fear touched her for the first time this morning.

The room was sparsely furnished. Only a low stool and a few utensils sat by the small fire at the center. And on the far end of the hovel, she saw the form of a man bedded down upon a very narrow cot.

He had always been the most handsome of fellows to her little girl eyes. Now she barely recognized him. She waited a moment to see if he would stir, but he was asleep and made no move.

Setting a tentative foot inside the door, she at last drew near his bed. She stood very still, afraid to touch him, but stooped down carefully and said, "Papa?"

Still there was no response as she studied the weathered face, the nearly bald head. It had been more than twelve years since she had seen her father, but she never dreamed he would look so old. Laying a gentle hand upon his shoulder, she shook him a little and repeated, "Papa."

The hollow eyes now opened and Michael Bar Andreas stared into the face of his eldest child.

For a fleeting second it appeared there might be recognition in his gaze. But he quickly turned away, clutching his cloak to his chin.

"Papa, it is I—Mary," she whispered.

The old man groaned pathetically.

"We are all here, Papa. The twins wait outside."

"I have no twins—no Mary," he muttered. "All gone to scavenge. No twins, no Mary. . . ."

"Yes, Papa," she insisted. "Sit up and look at me." She drew the frail shoulders toward her and held him close.

"They scavenge for their food. Will be back soon," he mumbled. "I have no children."

Somehow, she got him to his feet and called for Toby. With great difficulty they walked him to the door and into the sunshine.

The fog was completely gone now, and Michael shielded his eyes against the glare of day. As he did so, he took in Mary's face again, and this time he knew her.

A strong twitch worked at the side of his mouth, and tears glistened along his lashes. Suddenly he turned to run, but she followed after him. "Yes, Papa!" Mary responded. "It is I, and I am well."

"No—" he stammered, shrinking from her hold. His voice was husky and broken as he cried, "My Mary is dead!" And then, striking his fist upon one temple, he raised it heavenward, as if to say he had killed her with his own hand.

"I am well," Mary repeated. "And I love you."

The old man, stooped by years of grief and guilt, studied her incredulously. He had no strength to argue or to reason. As the children wrapped their cloaks around him, he surveyed them in bewilderment, and questioned nothing.

"We're going home," Mary said, placing an arm about his shoulder.

Now that the fog was gone, Magdala did not seem so far away. The white stone buildings glistened like a virgin's gown beneath the sun. And the great tower of Migdal captured the light in a gleam.

As Mary and her little family headed toward the gate, the wings of a seabird in mid-arc caught her eye. And she remembered the Master's words.

"Your spirit has been freed, and when you have conquered your greatest fear, love will be everywhere for you."